Daring to Dream: A New Destiny

Liz Hamilton

This is a work of fiction. Names, characters, businesses, places, events, locales, and incidents are either the products of the author's imagination or used in a fictitious manner. Any resemblance to actual persons, living or dead, or actual events is purely coincidental.

CONTENT WARNING: The main characters in this book endure an intense attack from their abductors. The female and male protagonist along with their other friends involved will seek counseling to work through their traumatic experience. If this may be triggering for you, please put your mental health first and proceed with caution or skip this story entirely .

eBook Edition ISBN-13: 979-8-9916755-5-0

Paperback Edition ISBN-13: 979-8-9916755-6-7

Cover design by GetCovers.

Dedication

Dedicated to...

I dedicate this to my wonderful husband who has been my biggest supporter in my writing and self-publishing journey.

Contents

Also By

Prologue

Alex (Fall 1988)

Alex Fleming fought back tears as he climbed into his car and drove away. This night ought to be one he would remember forever. It was a night to remember, but not how Alex wanted. He had never cried over a girl before, but Rhonda was scary! The two of them had been hanging out for a couple of weeks, and Alex enjoyed her personality.

Alex shook his head at himself and murmured, "Hannah and Michael tried to warn me." Alex and Michael Davis were roommates, and the two of them rented an apartment. Hannah was the lovely girl who had caught Michael's eye. Rhonda was Hannah's roommate, but Rhonda had gone absolutely crazy!

Alex asked Rhonda to go to the freshman back-to-school dance with him. He and Michael began hanging out with Hannah and Rhonda after settling into college. Rhonda's sense of humor came across as quirky, but something about it hooked Alex. He recalled the time when the four of them played several games of ping-pong. Alex, himself, loved making other people laugh. It often got him in trouble in school. He cracked several jokes, and Rhonda cackled in response. A moment later, Rhonda missed a serve over the net. Immediately, she whacked herself in the head with the paddle. Alex found it hilarious.

He made a boneheaded move and repeated the gesture. The movement created a wild connection between him and Rhonda. Now, Alex wondered if he was attracted to her because of the edge she seemed to carry. Despite Rhonda's behavior, did Alex come across as crazy as well? It was hard not to fear the same thing about himself.

As he drove his car, he thought about the great time they were having at the dance, along with Rhonda's immediate emotional change. Suddenly, Rhonda's nostrils flared. She began shouting at Alex.

"I don't understand you!" Rhonda shouted. "All I wanted was for you to get me some punch like a gentleman! What is wrong with you??"

"I'm sorry," Alex said, looking around in embarrassment. "When I asked you a little while ago, you didn't want any. It didn't occur to me you changed your mind, but I will get you some now." He stepped back.

Rhonda growled. "Just forget it. You're such a jerk!!" she said, as she slapped his face, and then she pushed him.

Several chaperones walked in their direction. With a shocked expression, Alex looked around at everyone staring at him and he swallowed rapidly because of the many eyes staring at him. He escaped out the door. Alex had never been so humiliated in his life. His heart was in shock after Rhonda slapped him, and he wanted nothing more than to get out of there. His cheeks were hot from shame. Tears sprang to his eyes from the sting of Rhonda's hand, but now the tears returned as he thought about how devastated he felt when she assaulted him in front of everyone.

Alex reached to turn on his radio, and he hoped it would get his mind off of the events of the evening. His mom lived thirty minutes away from the university where he attended school. After the debacle with Rhonda, Alex drove home to visit his mom. He also knew that

Hannah was coming over to the apartment with Michael. Alex liked Hannah. She quickly became one of his best friends. However, he didn't want to be there when they made out in Michael's room, and any other things they may want to do.

***

Sunday morning, Alex drove himself and his mom to the church where they were members. His mom had been wonderful all weekend. Alex shared very little with her, but he said that he was dating a girl and that they broke up. His mom made homemade pancakes for him on Saturday after he woke up. Alex appreciated her comforting ways with him.

Alex took his relationship with his mom seriously. He had older siblings, but they moved out of the house before he could even remember. Alex was three when his dad left them. He had no memory of it. Now that he had grown, it was his priority to make sure that he cared for his mom, and she had everything she needed. Alex was determined to help his mom in every way possible. Watching her scrape by and barely pay the bills gave him determination to step in however he could to support her. Alex's goal after college was to get a solid job. He planned to be an accountant. His paycheck would be large enough so that he could share some of it with his mother.

Alex's mom, Tammy Fleming, touched his knee, drawing him out of his daydream. "I will see you in the sanctuary."

"Sure, Mom," Alex said, as he leaned across and kissed her cheek.

Once both of them climbed out of the car, they walked in separate directions once they entered the building.

Alex walked toward the college Sunday school classroom when he noticed one of his favorite people, his youth pastor. Brian Woods spotted Alex, and he grinned. "Well, look who's back!"

"Hey Pastor Brian," Alex said.

Pastor Brian frowned immediately, and he said, "What's wrong with you?"

"Why do you ask that?" Alex asked.

"Alex, I know you well. When you're not making jokes from the minute that I see you, I can tell there's a problem. I understand when something is going on in your head." Pastor Brian clasped Alex's shoulder. "Do you want to talk about it?"

Pastor Brian was the father he didn't have. Alex admired him greatly. Even though Alex graduated, he hoped to maintain a close relationship with Pastor Brian.

Alex sighed. "I think so. Do you have time?"

"I will always have time for you. Let's go to my office." Pastor Brian guided Alex down three more hallways and into his office. Once they sat down, Alex leaned forward with his head in his hands. Pastor Brian said, "It must be terrible if you can't even look at me."

Alex sighed again, and he relayed what happened between him and Rhonda on Friday. Pastor Brian didn't interrupt, but he frowned a few times. He nodded his head to show he was listening.

Once Alex got all of his feelings off his chest, a heavy burden was lifted just from talking about it.

Pastor Brian said, "Alex, you are not at fault with any of what you shared. That young lady has her own struggles, and you happened to be in her pathway at that moment. It sounds like her roommate, Hannah, has also taken the brunt of her anger."

Alex shook his head in disbelief. "I've met no one like her. One minute she is happy and the next minute, she becomes a totally different person." Alex raised his hands. "I am done trying to date her, that's for sure." Then Alex glanced up. "I appreciate you listening."

"That's why I'm here." Pastor Brian said. "My suggestion to you is to take this moment in your life and allow yourself to learn from it. You didn't control how this girl treated you. But you can let what happened shape you into a better person by thinking about how you want others around you to be treated."

Alex adored talking to Pastor Brian. His wisdom in manners like these was what Alex missed from having a father in his home. Pastor Brian had always been the role model Alex needed to offer him advice. Alex watched his youth pastor in how he related to his own wife and kids. He dreamed of following in Pastor Brian's footsteps.

Suzanne

Suzanne Marks waved as her parents drove away. It was an unexpected visit, but Suzanne was so lonely that she didn't mind. As she returned to her dorm room, she thought about their time together over the weekend.

Suzanne was an only child. Her parents doted on her every single day of her life. Many days passed, and she wished for a brother or sister so her parents could pay attention to them instead of her. She adored her parents and was thankful to be a part of such a wonderful family. But it seemed as if they smothered her with too much love. All her life, Suzanne wished to become more independent so she could prove herself to them. Many kids her age struggled with getting attention from their parents, especially if their parents were divorced. That was something Suzanne never had to worry about. Suzanne knew herself as too sheltered from the real world. She didn't have many close friends growing up, and Suzanne felt frustrated about appearing as someone who is naïve to her peers. The few friends she grew up with often made fun of her sheltered viewpoint in life. Suzanne withdrew into herself resulting from the pain and hurt from their remarks.

Suzanne went on one date with a guy from college the first weekend she arrived, but it was rather boring. There wasn't much to talk about, and both of them sat in awkward silence. She made the mistake of talking to her mother about it and received a phone call from them that night. Her mother said she was checking to make sure Suzanne made it back to her room safely. Suzanne recalled the ridiculous conversation with her mom as she tried to argue that she was eighteen now. Her mother dismissed the comment, changing the subject, which she often did.

Aggravation filled Suzanne's thoughts, but she felt thankful for her parents' weekly visit on Saturdays. It seemed a bit much, but it also eased Suzanne's loneliness. Her mixed emotions were a constant these days with her family.

Suzanne unlocked her door to see her roommate Jessica was not there. Suzanne took a shower. She climbed onto her window seat-type bed with her textbook and binder. She realized that to prove she could be independent, she needed to do well in her classes. The thought of excelling was slowly becoming an obsession. However, she was lonely at school. Jessica was the only other person with whom she had made friends. Even though her parents drove her crazy by coming to visit her often, she welcomed their visits by seeking the human contact that was lacking at college. Doubts ran through her mind, and she wondered if she made the right decision to come to this university.

An hour passed. Suzanne placed her work back on her desk when her phone rang.

"Hello,"

"Hi, sweetie," her mom said.

"Hi Mom," Suzanne said, and she had to restrain herself from rolling her eyes. It had only been a couple of hours since her parents left.

"I just wanted to check on you and ask about your afternoon," her mom said.

Suzanne rolled her eyes this time. "Mom, you just saw me two hours ago. There's not much to tell."

"I know," her mom said. "I just wanted to call in one more time before the busy week starts again."

Suzanne's mom was a second-grade teacher, and her dad worked as an attorney in the town where she was from. "All I did was complete homework and study for a test later this week."

"Well, good luck," her mom said. "We love you and we will call in a few days."

Suzanne told her mother goodbye. She sank down on her bed in exasperation. Suzanne talked to her parents every single weekend, and sometimes in between. She often wondered what to talk about with them. Her mother memorized Suzanne's schedule, and sometimes she made surprise phone calls to her daughter throughout the week.

The door opened, pulling Suzanne out of her thoughts, and her roommate walked in the door.

"Where have you been?" Suzanne smiled at Jessica.

"Remember that guy, Tommy?" Jessica asked.

"Yes." Suzanne learned about Tommy. Every girl in the school knew him because he dated a different girl every weekend. Suzanne had no desire to accept one of his many invitations to go out with him. Not when she discovered he wouldn't ever be serious.

Jessica rolled her eyes dreamily and said, "We drove to get an ice cream together. He's so hot and I hope he asks me again!"

Suzanne looked at her roommate, debating whether to warn her not to trust that Tommy would be serious with her. However, seeing her roommate's expression, she decided not to say anything.

"Are you ready to go to dinner?" Suzanne asked. Despite her lack of friends in the past, Suzanne and Jessica formed a genuine bond. Therefore, the two of them ate most of their meals together.

Jessica nodded her head, and the two of them walked out of their room toward the dining hall.

Suzanne sighed. At least her parents loved Jessica. When they visited, her mother often invited Jessica to eat with them. One time, her mother bought something for Jessica when they all visited the local mall.

Stephen

He sat in the parking lot of a restaurant when he noticed her. The young woman stepped out of the driver's seat of a car, and his jaw dropped. She was the most beautiful woman he had ever seen. There was another girl with her, but he didn't even spare her much of a glance. The blond hair on the other girl was striking, but her beauty was lacking compared to the lovely dame with long chestnut hair. Both of them had enormous bangs, the current hairstyle. It framed the brown-haired girl's face like an angel. She adorned her wrists with multiple bracelets, or bangles, which jingled as she talked with her hands. When he watched her face light up in a smile as she laughed with her friend, he determined to befriend her. Eventually, he hoped she would grow to care for him.

The two of them left the restaurant, and he followed behind them. His heart skipped when he observed them park in front of the dorm in the small college in the town where he lived. The beautiful girl seemed to float as she walked, and her chestnut hair hung down her back, crowning her face like a halo.

He had a deadbeat job working in a fast-food restaurant because his mother would do nothing to help him financially. He made little, but it helped put food in his belly. Food was something he lacked in all of his years growing up.

He stayed in the background. It was something he was used to doing all of his life. He never knew his dad, and he seemed to only get in his mom's way. She spent most of her life working and dating loser men who used her. Her job as a server didn't bring in much. His mom dated men, hoping to find someone to support her. When those relationships failed, she drank multiple bottles of cheap wine. Even though the money should have provided more food for their pantry, she continued buying it to drown out her misery of being left by Stephen's jerk of a father.

He parked. Then he walked into the front door of the dorm. He walked to a desk where a resident assistant sat with a textbook in front of her. He walked up and pasted a friendly smile on his face. "A young woman just came in, and I would like to learn her name."

"I can't give out information on residents unless you are a family member." The girl didn't even look up, and he burned in anger at her dismissal.

"The thing is that I found something of hers on the ground. I would like to return it to her. Is it possible for me to at least get her name so that I can return it to her?"

The girl finally looked up at him with a guarded expression. "If you saw her drop it, how do you not know her name?" Then she continued, "You can leave it with me and I will give it to her."

"How will you know who she is?" he asked. Then he leaned forward with a friendly expression. "I kind of have a crush on her, too."

"Okay, describe her to me," the girl grabbed a pencil.

He shared what she looked like, along with the other girl who was with her.

"You're talking about Suzanne Marks," the girl blurted out. Then she clapped her hand over her mouth as she realized she blurted out her name.

He grinned at her while stepping back. "Thanks for her name. I will find her tomorrow and return the lost item."

The following day, he walked into his workplace and told the manager that he quit. His boss had choice words with him for leaving him short-staffed, but he didn't care. That afternoon, he parked behind the registrar's office at the university.

When he walked into the building, he observed a woman sitting behind a receptionist's desk. "Where is the registrar's office?"

The woman glanced up with an insincere smile on her face. "It is down the hallway to the left."

With clenched fists, he walked to the offices that the receptionist had pointed out. He didn't like being treated rudely. After he walked inside, he made a show of asking questions about enrolling as a student at the school. The secretary told him to take a seat, and someone would come out to speak with him. Instead he chose to stand as he glanced around. Rows of filing cabinets lined the wall behind the secretary's desk. He made a show to pace back and forth, but his gaze zeroed in on the cabinet labeled *Student Enrollments*.

A man walked out and shook hands with him. He ushered him back to his office, where the man asked a bunch of questions. With paperwork in hand, he promised to fill them out and bring them back the next day.

He watched and waited while most of them left the registrar's office for the evening. He slipped in the unlocked door of the building, knowing how he blended into the background. A custodian ran a mop over the floor and he glanced up with narrowed eyes.

"I'm a student employee, working in this office. My classes ran late this afternoon and I am behind on my filing. I promise to keep everything neat and clean," he said.

The man's eyes cleared. As he cleared his throat, he nodded. "That's fine," the man said.

He nodded his thanks and stepped toward the registrar's office. Then, he pulled his knife from his pocket and he jiggled the doorknob. Thankful for a sliver of light from the blinds in the window, he cracked them open more. He slipped around the counter to the filing cabinet. He quietly opened it. He thumbed through until he found her name. The man pulled out a manila folder with her name on the tab. He opened it and rifled through all of her paperwork, including her application with her family's name and where she was from. The last page in the file was her schedule. Bingo! Just what he needed. He pulled out a small notepad and jotted down the classes she was taking. Once he brought back his own application, he would request as many of those classes as he could.

Chapter 1

October, 1988

Suzanne glanced at her alarm clock, and she jumped out of bed. "Why didn't it go off?" she asked herself as she rushed into the bathroom. Suzanne set her alarm every morning for six o'clock, but she remembered turning it off over the weekend. She chastised herself for forgetting to turn it back on.

Suzanne slung open the bathroom door as her roommate, Jessica, roused from her bed.

"Good morning," Jessica commented with an enormous yawn.

"Morning," Suzanne replied in haste as she pulled out acid-washed jeans and a neon pink t-shirt from her closet.

"Everything okay?" Jessica asked. Her first class started an hour after Suzanne's on Mondays.

Suzanne's voice sounded muffled as she pulled on her shirt. "I forgot to reset my alarm for the week and I overslept. I have class in fifteen minutes."

Jessica was a math major, and she planned to become an accountant. However, they both had the same professor for a prerequisite course in algebra, just at different times. "Old man King is a stickler if you're tardy."

"Don't I know it!" Suzanne swept her dark chestnut hair into a ponytail. She quickly fluffed her bangs. It took a few seconds for Suzanne to spray hairspray over her head. Once she tied her shoes and grabbed her denim jacket, Suzanne shoved her math textbook into her backpack. The jacket was the same acid wash style as her jeans. Suzanne gave a terse "goodbye" and the dorm room door slammed behind her, its sounds echoing on the walls. She didn't stay to hear Jessica tell her goodbye.

***

Relieved her second class was finally over, Suzanne exited the classroom. She walked down the long hallway in Boughton Hall toward the exit, which would lead her to the dining hall. Suzanne was starving. Because she ran late that morning, she forgot to eat breakfast.

Suzanne quickened her pace, not paying attention to her steps. As she turned the corner around the building, her eyes widened when she noticed someone walking toward her. He stared at a paper in his hand and he didn't see her. It was too late for her to say anything because he plowed straight into her. "Oof," she said as the book and notebook in her hand flew onto the sidewalk. It seemed like she hit a brick wall.

"I'm so sorry," a deep voice spoke, but Suzanne was speechless as she gazed up at a guy. He was well over six feet, with dark hair and hazel eyes. "Are you alright?" the guy asked.

Suzanne shook her head, embarrassed for staring. She said, "Yes, I'm fine. Sorry! I wasn't paying attention to where I was going." She didn't comment about failing to place her textbook and notebook in her backpack. Had she done that, they wouldn't have gone flying when she ran into him.

"Let me help you," the guy said as he reached down and picked up the textbook and notebook. Pages had also flown out from the pocket inside the notebook.

Suzanne reached to grab a few of the loose pages. They reached at the same time and bumped heads. "Ouch" "Oh, man," they both said.

Suzanne, mortified at her clumsiness, shoved the book, notebook, and papers into her backpack before zipping it. She attempted to dart away before she could do anything else to embarrass herself.

However, the guy reached out his hand and said, "I'm Alex Fleming."

Suzanne stared for a moment before she clasped his hand. "I'm Suzanne." Then she realized she forgot to tell him her last name. "Suzanne Marks."

When their hands touched, heat charged through Suzanne, straight to her core. Flustered, she pulled her hand back and attempted to step away. Suzanne dated in her years of high school, mostly guys from the church where her family attended. Her parents had selective requirements for who she dated. However, she never felt a zing just like now.

"It's nice to meet you, Suzanne," Alex smiled.

Oh my word, his smile is gorgeous, she thought to herself. Suzanne said, "Nice meeting you, too. I need to go now."

Suzanne shook her head at herself. After the boring date at the beginning of the semester, Suzanne focused on her studies. She spent many evenings at the library, including Fridays. The determination to excel ruled over every other part of her life. Not knowing anyone other than her roommate helped to increase her study time. *Now is not the time to be interested in a guy no matter how gorgeous he is,* she thought to herself.

***

Alex stood in the same spot for several minutes, admiring Suzanne's beauty. *Man, she's hot!* Her dark chestnut hair curled in a high pony-tail. Her porcelain skin and demure facial features gave her a doll-like quality. Alex had seen no one that pretty before. When they clasped hands, an electric charge coursed through him and he couldn't help but wonder how it would feel to kiss her lips. As she walked away from him, he perused her lovely curves and the graceful way that she walked. Alex didn't want to come across as a creep by following her. At that moment, he was determined to get to know her. Her soft and wispy voice made him want to talk to her again just so that he could hear her speak.

Alex frowned slightly at himself. After the debacle with Rhonda, he wasn't sure he could trust himself with another girl. As sweet as Suzanne seemed to be, Alex cautioned himself to find out more about the girl before he tried to go out with her. He also needed to keep his focus on his plan for graduation and working to help his mom.

He glanced at his wristwatch and headed toward dining hall for a quick lunch. Alex had a one o'clock class, but he forgot to eat breakfast that morning. Hopefully, Hannah and Michael would also be in there, along with their other friends.

***

The next day, Alex left the science building when he noticed Suzanne leaving the building beside him. He didn't know her well enough to call her name, but his desire to learn more about her caused him to increase his stride. Once he caught up with her, Alex tried to look nonchalant when she glanced over at him. He asked Hannah about Suzanne at dinner the night before because he watched Suzanne and Hannah walking into the student center together. Hannah told them they had several classes together, and she gave a glowing review of Suzanne. Alex considered Hannah to be an excellent judge of character because of being caught up in Rhonda's anger earlier in the fall when the two of them were roommates. Alex shook his head as he remembered Rhonda's abduction and her intention to kill Hannah at the beginning of October.

Recognition filled Suzanne's expression, and a crimson color crept up her cheeks. Alex would not let her get away without speaking to her.

"Suzanne, right?" Alex smiled with an open expression.

Suzanne glanced down before she moved her gaze back to his. "Yes."

"It's crazy to see each other twice in two days," Alex widened his smile, hoping it would start a conversation.

A soft laugh came out of Suzanne and she said, "It appears to be that way."

Alex almost couldn't breathe as he stared at her lovely face when she smiled. "Are you going somewhere in particular?"

"I'm heading to lunch," Suzanne answered.

Perfect. Alex thought. "Can I walk with you?"

Suzanne looked away again, and the blush from earlier reappeared on her cheeks. "Okay."

Alex matched her stride as they walked side by side toward the student center. Absent-mindedly, he glanced behind him and saw another guy following behind. However, he dismissed it, focusing on starting a conversation with Suzanne.

They approached the door to the student center. Alex opened it and held it open for Suzanne.

"Thank you," she whispered.

"Sure. So, I usually sit with my roommate and some other friends. Would you like to join us?" Alex braced for disappointment in case she turned him down.

Suzanne glanced at him and said, "I'd like that."

"Great!" Alex grinned, and he hoped this to just the start of getting acquainted with this lovely lady.

Once they moved through the line, choosing their lunch items, Alex led the way toward a table near the windows.

Alex made the introductions. Suzanne smiled at the welcoming smiles from Hannah, whom she already knew, Michelle, and Jackie. Alex also introduced Michael as his roommate, along with Danny, the guy who lived beside their apartment.

***

When Alex led her to his table, Suzanne saw two other great-looking guys and two girls that she remembered seeing at the dance. Suzanne knew Hannah from several of her classes. That memory brought back the crazy girl slapping Alex, and she gasped. Suzanne couldn't believe she hadn't recognized him from that night.

Suzanne looked around for Jessica, but she didn't see her in the dining hall at the moment. Most days, the two of them sat together. Slight guilt filled her. Suzanne would make sure that Jessica would join them in the future.

"Everything okay?" Alex asked, seeing her glancing around.

Suzanne smiled. "I was just looking for my roommate. We usually sit together at lunch."

"She's welcome to join us," Alex said.

"Thank you," Suzanne said, relieved to hear the invitation.

The time eating with Alex's friends was by far her best moment at college thus far. Suzanne hadn't met many other students other than her roommate, and it was rather lonely. She didn't really know Hannah outside of their classes. Suzanne felt like dancing when Hannah, Michelle, and Jackie invited her to join them for supper that night, and she nodded. "Can my roommate join us, too?"

"Sure," the three of them replied at the same time.

"Thank you for inviting me to sit with your friends," Suzanne said as she and Alex walked out together. Lunch ended and he fell into step beside Suzanne as they walked out.

"You're welcome." Alex's expression appeared pensive, causing Suzanne to wonder if she did something wrong. As she worried, he said, "Would you like to go out with me sometime?"

"On a date?" Suzanne asked.

"Yes." Alex said, and she stopped.

A few seconds later, Suzanne said, "Yes, I would like that."

Relief filled Alex's gaze, and he balled up his fist like he wanted to pump it in triumph. Instead, he simply said, "How about Friday night?"

"Okay," Suzanne said.

"Great! Let me get your room number so that I can call you and we can talk about the details," Alex said.

Suzanne found paper in her backpack, and she wrote her room number. Her hand tingled when Alex reached for the paper.

"Thanks." Alex smiled at her as he folded it and placed it in the pocket of his jeans.

They both continued to stand there as if neither of them wanted to leave.

Finally, Suzanne said, "I need to get to my next class."

Alex touched her arm. "Will you join me at dinner tonight?"

"Hannah, Michelle, and Jackie also asked me, so I'm going to ask if my roommate wants to come with me."

"Great," Alex said. His fingers traveled down her arm, and Alex raised her hand to his lips. Suzanne's eyes fluttered as he placed a soft kiss on her fingers. "See you later."

"Okay," Suzanne whispered, quivering all over. Alex's lips on her hand were soft, and she wanted nothing more than to lean up and touch them with her lips. Goosebumps raised all over her arm.

***

That evening, Jessica joined Suzanne at dinner. The conversation remained light and natural. It was as if she had known these girls her whole life. Jessica fit in from the first moment. The five girls bonded quickly during the meal. Suzanne's heart soared from the fact that she was finally making friends. She and Hannah were both majoring in elementary education, with many classes together. Suzanne was happy to get better acquainted with her. Jackie and Danny wanted to be physical education teachers, so she had a connection with them as well. Jessica and Michelle knew each other from having classes together, so that made things even better. Alex and Jessica realized they had several classes together as well.

Suzanne's lips curved with a smile as she pondered the meal. Suddenly the phone rang. Without thinking, she grabbed it and said, "Hello."

"Hello, Suzanne." Alex's deep voice boomed across the line.

"Hi," she answered, as tingles covered her body in response to Alex's voice.

"How was the rest of your evening?"

"Kind of boring," Suzanne replied. "I read two chapters, and studied for a quiz on Thursday."

"Same here. I walked to the library to get some research done for a paper." Alex's voice deepened, increasing the butterflies in Suzanne's stomach. "There's a great restaurant in the next town where I would like to take you on Friday. Do you like seafood?"

"Yes, I love it."

"Great. I will pick you up at six."

"I'm looking forward to it," Suzanne said.

"Me too, but can we talk for a while longer? I want to learn more about you before Friday."

The two of them talked about their hometowns and families. Alex told her about growing up with his mom. Suzanne shared about living in the same town as both sets of grandparents. When they hung up, Suzanne's smile widened. Her brow pursed when she wondered if Alex had a dad in his life. Her heart tugged at the idea that he didn't.

Jessica walked into the room from the library. Seeing Suzanne's dreamy smile, she asked, "What on earth is going on with you?"

"I'm going on a date with Alex on Friday."

"The totally hot dude who sat beside you at dinner tonight?" Jessica's face became more animated.

"Yes," Suzanne said, giggling in a silly way.

"Good for you," Jessica said with a wide grin. Suzanne chuckled when Jessica bounced up and down on her bed.

The two of them talked for a few more minutes before preparing for bed. Both of them had similar family backgrounds. It was one reason Suzanne connected with Jessica. Her roommate was also an only child. Their conversation centered on the frustration of their parents' constant attention.

"Do you feel you're under a microscope all the time?" Jessica asked.

"Totally," Suzanne said. "It's triple with my grandparents involved in my life, too."

The two girls laid on the opposite sides of their beds with their heads together. Jessica continued talking about her family and her wish for siblings. Suzanne's chest expanded and her shoulders relaxed. She had never had an opportunity to open up with another girl like this.

***

Michael passed by Alex's room when he finished talking to Suzanne. He still had a goofy grin on his face. The two of them shared the apartment. It was actually an older home which had been renovated into two apartments. Their neighbors were also guys, Danny and James. Alex loved the original hardwood floors and linoleum in the kitchen. When Michael passed, the creak could be heard on the floors.

"What's with the smile?" Michael asked, grinning at him. Alex sat up straighter on his bed.

Alex sighed. "I've met a gorgeous girl. You met Suzanne. She ate with us at lunch and dinner today." Alex's heart leapt over the way Suzanne gazed at him after dinner. Tempted to lean down and kiss her, Alex believed it was too soon. But he had never experienced a connection like he had with her. Alex knew she sensed it as well. He hoped it would deepen on their date.

Michael nodded, "Suzanne, right? Yes, she's beautiful." He leaned on the frame beside Alex's door in a casual pose.

Alex knew Michael was head over heels for Hannah, so he didn't take offense at Michael's compliment. A twinge of envy filled his gut over Michael's relationship with Hannah. "I asked her out for Friday, and she said yes."

"I'm happy for you, man," Michael said. "You deserve something good after all that happened with Rhonda."

"Thanks. There was a spark between us, but I'm not sure if it will turn into anything serious," Alex said, plowing his hands through his hair.

It was him and his mom during his years of growing up. The only male role model in his life was Pastor Brian, so Alex didn't plan on getting married. If he did, Alex would want to follow in his youth pastor's footsteps with a wife and family. *Pastor Brian was lucky,* Alex thought, *but that kind of happiness isn't in the cards for me.* But with the heartbreak he observed with his mom, Alex didn't think that kind of lasting happiness would ever happen for him. *Look at what happened with Rhonda, he thought.* As he remembered the debacle with Rhonda, Alex wondered if going on a date with Suzanne was a mistake. His plan during college was to focus on getting his degree. Then he would spend his adult years being loyal to his mom and helping to care for her needs.

Alex's reverie was interrupted as Michael spoke up. "I felt the same way about Hannah. Look at us now. After the terror I went through when Rhonda abducted her, I realized what an idiot I was to end things."

Alex nodded. "That was scary, man. I'm so happy for you both." Alex paused before he continued, "I don't believe that a deep relationship is actually in the cards for me." Alex paused before he said, "Am I crazy, like Rhonda? Is that why I was drawn to her?"

Michael shook his head, fervently. "Absolutely not, man! Rhonda deceived everyone. Why on earth would you think that?"

"I don't know," Alex said. "Maybe I shouldn't try to date anyone else for a while."

Michael stepped forward and placed a hand on Alex's shoulder. "Not every girl is like Rhonda. In fact, I doubt any other girl is like Rhonda," Michael chuckled at his joke. Alex couldn't help but laugh along with him.

Michael and Alex both opened up about their childhoods through the months of living together. Michael knew about his dad leaving when he was three. Alex also shared his desire to make sure his mom was taken care of.

Michael's voice softened as he spoke. "I love how much you care for your mom. But there's no reason you can't have your own love along with caring for her. Don't rule it out, especially if you and Suzanne truly have the connection you've shared. Well, I've got some studying to do."

"Me too," Alex said.

***

She was going on a date!

Her admirer leaned against his car and watched Suzanne and Alex stroll toward her dorm after dinner. He quickly walked a respectable distance from him and heard Alex ask her on a date. She was his dream come true! As he observed Suzanne, he knew it was love at first sight. His biggest desire was to win her heart. His eyes narrowed as they zeroed in on Alex. At one point, Alex glanced in his direction. Stephen rushed back to his car. He started it quickly and sped off. As much as he would like for Alex to go away, it was too early for intimidation.

The first step was complete. He had successfully enrolled to be closer to her. Stephen had been following her for several weeks now. A few weeks back, he observed her go on a date with another guy, and his gut burned from the idea. He itched to have her soft fingers clasped in his. The date flopped. Suzanne looked bored when she stepped out of his car. Stephen sighed with relief.

Suzanne was his forever love! Within his heart, he knew that eventually, she would realize she also loved him. He would do all he could to prove it to her.

Stephen wished he could sift his hands through her silky, long hair as he followed her into the student building that afternoon.

Until fate brought them together, Stephen would continue to be her protector and watch over every move she made. She had no idea when he tailed her from class to class or from class to the student center. Stephen sat two tables away from Suzanne and her roommate.

One guy, Tommy, stopped by almost daily and flirted with both girls. His gut burned when Tommy's eyes remained on Suzanne each time.

One time, she dropped a paper and Stephen handed it back to her. Other than saying thank you, Suzanne didn't see him. Disappointment filled him because he wanted her to sense the connection he did. Stephen hoped that one day soon, she would appreciate all that he did for her.

Most of his time was spent by himself. After he quit his part-time job, Stephen had time on his hands. Now he spent his time following Suzanne around the campus. One instance she looked at him and Stephen thought their eyes had a brief connection. It proved that Suzanne was meant for him. Yesterday, he saw her bump into Alex, the guy who just asked her out. Stephen's gut burned at the way Alex smiled at her. He didn't like how Suzanne stared at him. Now, he would have to watch Suzanne and Alex go out on a date.

It showed Stephen that it was time to step up his game to get to know Suzanne. She must have liked it because the two of them began spending time together.

Chapter 2

Friday night arrived, and Suzanne dressed for her date with Alex. Her stomach had bricks in it. Suzanne skipped lunch because of nerves and spent the time in the library working on a research paper. It was difficult to concentrate, and her hands shook as she thought about their upcoming date. Suzanne felt excitement, but also nerves.

She glanced at her clock and noticed it was five thirty. Jessica had gone home to visit her parents for the weekend. Suzanne was happy to have the room to herself. Her nerves were totally on edge.

Suzanne pulled the rollers out of her long chestnut hair, but before she styled it, she pulled off the t-shirt she wore while getting ready. She pulled a navy sweater over her head, and she pushed down her sweatpants to don the tan tweed skirt that had stripes of navy running through it. Once she had her clothes on, she ran a brush through the curls down her shoulders and back. Then she styled her bangs in the typical eighties fashion. After giving them a final fluff, she spritzed hairspray all over. Suzanne pulled out her gold hoop earrings and a matching necklace. Once she pulled on pantyhose, she stepped into knee-high boots and studied her appearance. As she applied perfume, her phone rang.

"Hello."

"Hi," Alex said warmly. "I'm in the lobby whenever you are ready."

Breathless, Suzanne said, "I will be right there." She double checked her appearance while placing the matching purse on her right shoulder before she opened the door and walked out to meet Alex.

Suzanne stopped in front of him and smiled. "Hi."

Alex's gazed at Suzanne with a smile. "You look beautiful."

"Thank you." Suzanne's eyes softened. "You look nice, too."

Alex glanced down at his chino slacks and button-down shirt. "Thank you." He held out his hand. "Are you ready?"

"Yes," Suzanne said, and she placed her hand in his. She appreciated being able to avert her gaze because she knew her blush was evident. Alex looked devastating tonight! The shirt and slacks he wore fit him perfectly as he towered over her. Suzanne took deep breaths to slow her heart rate. Her blush deepened when Alex glanced over at her.

Alex led Suzanne out to his car, and he opened the passenger door to help her inside. Once she placed her purse on her lap, he shut her door and walked around to the driver's side.

An electric current charged the atmosphere of his car. Suzanne inhaled Alex's spicy aftershave, and she wanted to lay her head against his shoulder from her intense attraction toward him.

"Seafood is still okay, right?" Alex asked as he draped one hand over the steering wheel while the other hand gripped the gearshift in the middle of their two seats.

"Yes, I love seafood," Suzanne smiled at him.

"How was your day?" Alex asked.

"It was fine. I didn't have time to stop for lunch because I spent a while in the library working on a research paper." Suzanne listened to how breathy she sounded. However, her stomach twinged as she thought about her new obsession with grades.

"I knew you weren't in the dining hall. My lunch was in a hurry, so I wouldn't be late for my afternoon class. We had an exam, and I wanted to get there early to study for a few minutes." Alex said.

Suzanne inhaled a deep breath, and she rubbed her sweaty hands over her skirt. The scratchiness irritated her hands, but at least they were slightly drier. She wondered if Alex would hold her hand. Would he be grossed out with her clammy hands? As Suzanne blew out a breath, a hair came loose and fell over her face. She moved it out of the way. Glancing over at Alex, relief washed over Suzanne that he didn't notice.

"Tell me about your research paper," Alex said, breaking the silence. Suzanne wondered if this would be her first and last date with him. He might be bored with her.

"Oh. Our professor has us researching philosophies of teaching from the past. It is super boring. Trying to use the microfiche machines to track down proper research is also tedious." Suzanne said, glancing at Alex.

When Alex looked over at her, their gazes held for a split second. Finally, he said, "Yeah, I hate using those machines."

Thirty minutes later, Alex pulled into the parking lot of the seafood restaurant and parked.

"Wait for me to come around." Alex walked around and opened Suzanne's door. He held out his hand. After a heartbeat, Suzanne took it to step out of the car.

Suzanne gazed at him, feeling the flush on her face returning.

***

When Alex spied Suzanne in the dorm, his words left him. The short skirt stopped just above her knees, giving him a lovely view of her long legs. The turtleneck sweater hugged her curves, and Alex wanted nothing more than to pull her to him to kiss her passionately. He wanted to run his hands through her soft curls that floated down her back as he kissed her lips.

Alex walked her to his car and opened the passenger door for Suzanne to step into the car. As he did, Alex noticed a black car in the distance. It was one street over from the dorm. A guy stood, arms crossed, in front of it. Alex frowned, wondering who it was and what he was doing. After shutting Suzanne's door, Alex soon forgot about it as he walked around and started the car.

Suzanne's perfume permeated the air in his car. He wanted to bury his face in her neck to savor the aroma. Alex wanted to reach for Suzanne's hand, but he didn't want to appear too forward. The way she kept glancing at him in the car gave him the idea that she was nervous. Alex didn't want to increase her anxiety. He frowned slightly as he considered it. *What if this date was a mistake?* He didn't think she had the temperament like Rhonda, but Alex's heart was still bruised from that encounter. He smiled at himself when Suzanne brushed a hair out of her face. Her demeanor differed from Rhonda. In fact, she was the total opposite.

After walking to open her door, Alex held out his hand. His heart skipped when Suzanne just sat there, staring at him. *Definitely too soon,* he thought to himself.

Suzanne sighed, surprising Alex. "My hands are really sweaty. You may not want to touch them."

Alex chuckled. He touched her forearm.

Suzanne's eyes widened at the dampness of his palm on her arm.

"Does that soothe your fears?" Alex said, holding Suzanne's gaze.

Suzanne smiled softly. "I guess so. My fear is that you will be disgusted by them."

Alex leaned close. "Not at all." He held out his hand again. This time, Suzanne took it.

"Thank you," she whispered.

Alex kept her hand clasped in his as they walked to the entrance of the restaurant. He hated letting go to hold the door open for her, but he placed his hand on the small of her back to usher her inside.

Alex took her hand again as the hostess led them to their table. He couldn't help but observe the admiring looks from other men as they walked by. Alex tightened his hold on Suzanne, pulling her closer to his side.

Alex held out her chair for Suzanne before sitting across from her. Once he sat down, he leaned toward Suzanne and said, "Did I tell you that you look beautiful tonight?"

"Yes," Suzanne said, blushing again. "Thank you."

As they studied the menu, Alex smoothly reached for her hand again.

Suzanne watched as he entwined their fingers together. The server came and took their drink orders. As they waited for their beverages, Alex leaned across the table and smiled. "Tell me more about where you are from."

Suzanne smiled back, and she talked more about the town where she grew up. She mentioned her dad was a lawyer and her mom a teacher. One set of grandparents lived nearby, but the other set lived about two hours from there. A brief silence filled the air.

"It sounds like you have a great family," Alex said, experiencing a twinge of envy.

"What about you?" Suzanne asked. "You've told me about your mom. Do you have any other family?"

"I have an older brother and sister, but they were in high school when I was born. They moved out, and it was just my mom and me." Alex paused. Suzanne remained silent, and he appreciated how she allowed him to think before he continued.

Suzanne paused. "What about your dad? Was he in your life?"

Alex's face tightened. "My dad left when I was three."

Suzanne's eyes widened. "Oh, I'm so sorry!" She glanced at the table in embarrassment. "I didn't mean to pry."

"It's okay. I don't really talk about it much," Alex said. He squeezed Suzanne's hand, also gazing at the table. "My plan is to have a decent job after college so that I can help support my mom. It's my dream to pay off her house and any other debt so that she can live much easier."

"That's so thoughtful. Instead of focusing on yourself, you are thinking of providing for your mom. I truly admire that." Suzanne said.

The two of them placed their order and enjoyed more conversation together. At one point, Alex placed another kiss on Suzanne's hand, watching goosebumps raise on her arms. It seemed like they had known each other for a long time, and yet the electricity between them felt completely new. Alex felt an addiction toward her.

Two hours later, Alex drove her back. He held her hand, which he had been doing all evening. When Alex pulled up in front of the dorm, he insisted Suzanne wait for him to come around and open her door.

Suzanne stepped out with Alex standing close to her. Her breathing became shallow as he stared into her eyes. As if in slow motion, one of his hands caressed her right cheek. Suzanne stood motionless, and Alex found himself lost in her eyes. It took little effort for Alex to tug her closer with his other hand. The hand on her cheek trailed down to her chin. He tipped her chin up and Suzanne's eyes closed as if she expected he was going to kiss her. She didn't move a muscle as he closed the distance between them. When his lips touched hers, everything around Alex vanished. Suzanne leaned into his kiss as his lips continued brushing back and forth on hers. She gasped when he grabbed her waist and tilted their heads to deepen the kiss. One of his hands grasped her hip while the other hand feathered through the hair cascading down her back. Alex pulled back briefly before kissing her again.

Once Alex finally pulled away, it took a few seconds for Suzanne to open her eyes. Her hands were grasping his upper arms. Alex smiled at her and caressed her hair, relishing the softness. Alex pushed it back from her face. "I had a wonderful time, Suzanne."

"Me too." Suzanne whispered.

"Would you like to go out again tomorrow night? We could go to a movie."

Suzanne appeared reluctant to leave him as she smiled. "Yes, I would like that."

Alex kissed her softly a final time before he stepped back and shut the passenger door. He trailed a finger down her cheek and said, "Good night."

"Good night." Suzanne whispered, and she turned and walked inside.

As Alex got back into his car, he noticed the same black sedan across the street. It was the same car from the beginning of the date. Frowning, he noticed the guy watching the dorm. Alex shook his head, finding it slightly peculiar. *Probably likes a girl and is too chicken to ask her out.* As Alex drove to his apartment, his thoughts returned to Suzanne and their night together. The smile on his face widened their connectedness. It seemed as if she sensed the same emotions.

***

Suzanne seemed to be walking on air as she walked into the dorm's lobby. She knew she had a stupid smile on her face, but she didn't care at the moment. Alex's kiss was like none other than she'd ever experienced on the few dates she had ever been on. Suzanne felt cherished by how he grasped her and caressed her hair. Lightheadedness overcame her just remembering his lips and how they felt on hers. Suzanne flushed at the wish that Alex would kiss her again soon.

Hannah, Jackie, and Michelle sat in the lobby, and their eyes lit up at seeing Suzanne. "How are you?" Jackie asked. Michelle studied her face, and she finally said, "You've been on a date. Am I right?"

Suzanne couldn't stop her deepening blush as she said, "Yes, Alex and I went out for the first time." She wanted to roll her eyes at how her voice sounded at the moment, but Suzanne knew it would only draw more attention.

Hannah squealed, and she did a small dance before hugging Suzanne. "I just knew the two of you would hit it off!"

"It must have been an enjoyable time, from what I can tell," Michelle was sarcastic as she grinned at Suzanne.

"Yes," Suzanne said. She shared where she and Alex went on their date, relishing a growing connection with these two girls. Suzanne even shared about the kiss, something she would not have ever done with any of her friends in her hometown. The kisses she shared with boys there were not worthy of conversation, anyway. Suzanne did not spend her high school years confiding in other girls. Suzanne always wondered what was wrong with her and why other girls didn't seek companionship with her. Because of the isolation, Suzanne did not spend time with tasks other high school girls took part in. She completely lacked understanding of driving through their town, hanging out at parties, or even the practice of toilet-papering a house.

Suzanne never felt close enough to anyone other than her mom, and she would definitely not tell her about kissing any guy! Suzanne frowned slightly. Her mother would definitely call in the morning. Suzanne decided not to mention the date.

Jackie wagged her eyebrows up and down, bringing Suzanne back to the present. "That sounds like a hot date."

Suzanne laughed. More than anything, she wanted to get better acquainted with Michelle and Jackie, along with Hannah. Surprise filled her that Hannah wasn't out with Michael on a date.

"Where is Michael?" she asked. "Why aren't you making out with him?" Suzanne laughed again when Hannah blushed.

"The three of us decided to shop and spend some quality time together," Hannah said, gesturing to Jackie and Michelle. "Our hot date night is tomorrow night." She grinned at Suzanne. "Michael didn't know if Alex would bring you back to the apartment."

Suzanne slapped Hannah's shoulder. "It's way too soon for that!" However, her heart jumped at the idea. She told the three of them good night.

"We will see you tomorrow morning at breakfast," Michelle said. "You can tell us more about you and Alex."

Joy filled Suzanne's heart upon hearing the invitation. "Okay, I look forward to it." She was still smiling as she let herself into her dorm room and locked the door behind her. In one week, she had met a wonderful guy and made new friends. She would have much more to share with her mom when she called the next morning. *Just nothing about the date with Alex.* Suzanne thought.

***

Intoxicated was the word on Alex's mind as he walked to his apartment. He found himself captivated by Suzanne. Alex felt he was drowning in Suzanne's eyes as they shared about their lives growing up. Slight envy had filled him when she shared about her life. Her life sounded like a storybook, and Alex couldn't help the twinge of envy he listened.

Alex hadn't planned on kissing her on the first date, but when she stepped out of the car and looked at him, he hadn't been able to control himself. His mouth dried out as he pulled into the driveway of his apartment. Maybe he shouldn't have acted so quickly. Alex didn't want Suzanne getting the wrong idea of his intentions.

Unable to stop himself, his mind drifted back to the jarring kiss. The hands that itched to caress her hair all evening got their wish. As he deepened the kiss, his fingers couldn't stop from running through her silky curls. Alex's heart skipped a beat after he pulled away, and Suzanne hesitated to open her eyes. It made happy to know that she seemed as drawn to him as he was to her. Doubt sliced through him at being able to provide for Suzanne like her family. Alex shook his head at himself, concluding that this was just casual dating. It wasn't like they were getting serious soon.

Danny and James lounged in the living room with Michael, watching an action movie.

"How did the date go?" Michael asked with a smirk on his face.

Alex knew his face gave him away as he walked in. "Great," he said.

"Just great?" Danny asked. "That girl is a knockout. Surely, you can do better than that."

Alex couldn't help but chuckle. "Shut up," he said. "She's a lovely person on the inside as well. And I thoroughly enjoyed it."

Michael continued smirking at Alex. "Your face tells us more than that. Did you kiss her?"

Alex sensed the blush rising as his friends laughed. "For your information, we did. Are you happy now?"

All three of them laughed. Alex frowned, and his chest tightened. Maybe he shouldn't have kissed Suzanne.

"Where's Hannah tonight? Why aren't you with her?" Alex asked, changing the subject.

Michael smirked again. "Out with Jackie and Michelle. They decided to go shopping."

Alex dropped into the open chair. "What were you watching?"

Michael let the subject of his date drop when he answered, much to Alex's relief.

Alex finished the movie with them. Then he took a quick shower and prepared for bed. Doubts continued flitting through his mind about his date with Suzanne. However, it didn't stop him from picking up the phone and dialing Suzanne's number. Alex told himself that he was calling out of courtesy before going to bed.

"Hello," her soft voice carried over the line.

"I just wanted to tell you what a great time I had tonight." Alex's voice deepened as he remembered her soft lips on his.

Suzanne laughed softly and said, "Me too. Thank you for the wonderful dinner."

"You're welcome. I'm looking forward to tomorrow night. How about we get pizza before the movie?"

"That sounds great." Alex's heart turned over at hearing her enthusiastic reply. He hesitated to hang up, so he asked her more about her years of growing up. The conversation was natural, as she inquired more about his life as well.

Before he hung up, Alex felt he needed to be honest with Suzanne. "Look, Suzanne. I didn't mean to kiss you tonight, and I'm sorry if I came on too strong."

"Alex, that's okay," Suzanne said in a wispy voice. "To tell you the truth, I liked it."

"You did?" Alex's heart skipped at her words. "I don't normally kiss a girl on a first date, but I really liked it, too."

"Don't worry, Alex. I don't have any expectations because of it." Alex's eyes widened. He shook his head, wondering if Suzanne could hear his thoughts or if he actually spoke them aloud.

"Good night, Suzanne." He said the words before he could stick his foot in his mouth and say something he would regret.

"Good night, Alex."

***

He grasped the plastic cup containing the drink he had carried out with him from the dining hall. Stephen saw them drive off, and they didn't come back for four hours. Part of him wanted to follow them on their date, but he didn't. He had followed her to many other places, including her hometown and the mansion she lived in with her parents.

He wandered around and waited near the dorm for them to return. Anger filled him when he saw her sitting in the passenger side of the car. His fingers squeezed the sides of the cup he held as he saw the guy open her door and help her out of the car. Then the jerk leaned down and kissed her. He should be the one kissing her!

The way she looked into his eyes afterward made him worry she was falling in love with this guy.

He understood he needed to get to know her before it was too late. Liquid dripped onto his hand, and he glanced down to see he had completely crushed the cup. He crumpled it in his hand and walked to the trash can and tossed it inside before stalking away to his car.

A loving home had not been a part of his upbringing. Stephen never knew his dad. His mother flitted from one guy to the next, usually drunk or high. The idea of building a life with Suzanne filled him with a warmth he'd never experienced from his mom.

Alex glanced in his direction, and he narrowed his eyes. Stephen quickly climbed into his car, throwing the destroyed cup into the back. That Alex looked at him twice made him reconsider his plan to follow Suzanne so closely. He needed to find another way to get to know Suzanne. As Stephen started his car, his mind developed a plan. It would include a lovely meeting where, hopefully, Suzanne would be impressed by him. The ideas would help him win Suzanne's heart once and for all.

Chapter 3

As was her habit, Suzanne's mom called at ten the next morning. Suzanne was back from breakfast in time because she knew the routine by this point.

"Hi sweetie," her mom said. "How was your week?"

Suzanne couldn't contain the enthusiasm in her voice. "Mom, I made friends this week. I've been eating meals with them in the dining room."

"How wonderful!" her mom gushed. "I am so happy to hear that. We will have to come up there and meet them soon!"

Suzanne told her about Hannah, Jackie, and Michelle. She mentioned that she and Hannah shared classes because they were both majoring in elementary education. She hesitated before saying, "I also went on a date last night with an amazing guy." Suzanne wanted to slap herself for opening her mouth.

The tone of her mom's voice changed, and she asked, "Really? What's his name?"

Suzanne rolled her eyes, knowing her mom was going to warn her about trusting some random guy. "His name is Alex." She made a quick decision not to share anymore.

"Honey, I know you are in college, but please be careful," her mom's voice was filled with worry.

Suzanne rolled her eyes. "Mom, it's fine. We've only been on one date. He's a nice guy, and he even goes to church when he is home with his mom."

The line was quiet, and her mother finally spoke up. "I'm glad to hear he goes to church. We will need to meet him as well when we come to see you next time."

"Mom, it's only been one date. I'm not sure whether we will go out anymore, so wait on meeting him. Okay?"

"Your dad and I can't help but worry about you, sweetie. We want to make sure you are making good decisions."

"I'm fine, Mom. I can make good decisions now, remember?" Deep in her heart, she didn't think her parents really believed that she was actually old enough to figure out her own life. Her mom mumbled a response and Suzanne changed the subject. The conversation was lighter when her mom updated her on her grandparents and taking them for doctor's appointments.

A half an hour later, Suzanne felt numb because of how long her mom talked to her. She breathed a sigh of relief when they finally said their goodbyes. Suzanne sat for a moment, staring into space. She knew that her life was too sheltered because of her parents' smothering. Also, the doting of her grandparents didn't help. Suzanne knew that there was much about life she needed to learn. Suzanne stood up, thinking about her future. It was time to prove that she could stand on her own two feet and be independent. As she got out homework, Suzanne's brow pursed in deep thought. *Was the doting of her family why she struggled with friendships as a child?*

Her phone rang seconds later and Suzanne groaned, wondering what else her mother needed to say to her. "Hello." She replied tersely.

"Suzanne?" Alex's deep voice reverberated across the line.

"Hi, sorry about that. I thought it was my mom calling back. We just talked for thirty minutes and I'm exhausted."

Alex chuckled. "Sometimes my mom talks on and on, too. I wanted to check with you about tonight. There's a movie at seven, so do you want to eat around six? The pizza restaurant is right next to the movie theater."

"That sounds wonderful."

"Great! I will be there to pick you up at six."

Suzanne smiled and said, "I'm looking forward to it."

"Me too," Alex's voice was filled with warmth, and it spread through Suzanne straight to her core.

As she hung up, she wondered if he would kiss her again. Then she chastised herself for feeling this way after one date. "You need to get a grip," she murmured to herself.

She shook her head before she began cleaning her room. Then she took out a textbook and binder. Loose pages slid out onto the floor and she groaned as she picked them up and shoved them back inside of the notebook. Maybe she needed to get organized. Suzanne ignored that thought and sat down to complete her homework that was due on Monday. In her mind, maintaining good grades was the best way to build independence and separation from her parents. Right now, she had all A's. Suzanne worried that focusing on dating might help her lose focus. She told herself not to let Alex distract her from her goal.

***

Suzanne waited in the lobby when Alex walked inside. His eyes lit up when he spotted her.

"Hi," he smiled, and he grasped both of her hands. "You look beautiful."

Suzanne smiled softly. "Thank you. You look great, too."

They were both dressed in jeans. Suzanne had a flowy top on to match them with black flats. The flats were a perfect match to her top, a typical eighties fashion. Alex had on a button-down shirt with tennis shoes.

"Are you ready?" He held out his elbow, and she took it, thinking about how he had impeccable manners.

The conversation flowed as they drove to the pizza restaurant. Alex talked about spending the day at the library, and she talked about the project she was working on as well.

Alex smiled in her direction. "You and I are like-minded. We both want to focus on our studies. I told you my goal of graduating at the top of my class so that I can become an accountant."

"Yes," Suzanne said. "I remember that." Her brow pursed. "I need to learn how to be on my own. The best way to do that is to be the best student I can."

"You're doing a good job so far," Alex commented as he turned on his blinker to drive into the restaurant parking lot.

When he pulled into the parking lot, he said, "Stay there and I will come around."

A blush stole over Suzanne, but she sat there until he came around and opened the passenger door. She took the hand he was holding out for her, and that zing from the previous night rushed through her.

Alex laced their fingers together as they strolled into the restaurant. Suzanne learned he had a wonderful sense of humor. The stories he told had her laughing out loud to where other patrons glanced their direction. After dinner, they strolled hand in hand to the movie theater, where Alex bought drinks for both of them. Neither of them wanted food because they were full of pizza.

They sat in the middle of the back row in the theater, where Alex put his arm around the back of Suzanne's chair. After pulling her closer to him, he said, "I've been thinking about this all day."

"Seeing this movie?" she teased as she smiled at him.

"Something like that." His expression changed from teasing to intense. Alex pulled her tighter against him as he leaned to kiss her. His lips were soft on hers as he brushed his mouth against hers several times. Suzanne hesitated. Deep down, she feared the garlic bread eaten at supper made her breath stink.

When Alex finally pulled back, he studied her face. "Are you okay?"

"I really like your kisses," Suzanne blurted out. "But I hope the garlic I ate for dinner isn't grossing you out."

Alex laughed. "That's why you paused? I can promise you it doesn't because I have garlic breath, too. I ate garlic bread as well, remember?"

Suzanne frowned, deep in thought. "This is only our second date, but it feels like we've been going out for a while."

"I couldn't agree more," Alex whispered as he traced a finger down her cheek. Suzanne shivered from the touch. "I know I told you I didn't mean it last night, but I mean it now. I can't seem to stop myself from kissing you."

Suzanne knew her eyes were vulnerable when she looked up at him. The feeling scared her beyond reason. But the movie was starting, so Suzanne pushed her thoughts down. Alex pulled back slightly. He kept his arm around Suzann, and she leaned into him as they enjoyed the romantic comedy that he had chosen for the evening.

On the drive back to the dorm, Suzanne's thoughts were conflicted. She really liked Alex, but she was concerned that they were moving too fast. *Would it interfere with her plan to become her own person?*

"Suzanne, I want you to know that I'm not trying to use you or anything." Alex's voice startled her.

"I didn't think you were."

"I know we're getting to know one another, but there is such a connection when we are together. Please understand I don't usually kiss a girl on a first date. I actually have dated little to tell you the truth."

Suzanne sighed with relief. "Thank you for sharing that. I didn't want to come across as loose."

"I can promise you I don't think that about you at all." Alex pulled his car into a parking space outside of the dorm. "Would you like to walk for a little while? I would like to keep talking."

"Yes," Suzanne whispered. Alex came around to open her door. When Suzanne stepped out, he leaned in and kissed her softly. It was a short and tender kiss. When he pulled away, he entwined their fingers. Alex tugged her away from his car and onto the sidewalk where they began strolling.

"Why did you choose to go into education?" Alex asked, squeezing her hand.

"I love kids. My part-time job was babysitting. And I used to volunteer at my church every summer to help in kids' camp and other activities. One of my favorite times each month was helping in the children's church by leading a story or a craft activity."

Alex stopped at a bench and gestured for Suzanne to sit. He draped his arm behind her and leaned closer. "You have a gift for working with kids. I admire that. Whenever I volunteered at my church, I became impatient when I worked with kids. It's probably because I was rather rambunctious myself. My influence might have been teaching them to make fart noises into their arms or hands. I attended daycare when I was growing up, and I remember my teachers putting me into timeout most days that I was there."

Suzanne laughed as she searched his gaze. Her hand drifted up, and she touched his cheek. "I'm sure you were an adorable child."

Alex gazed at Suzanne. He whispered, "You are beautiful," as he leaned down and touched her lips with his.

Suzanne leaned into his kiss, opening her mouth immediately in search of his tongue. She breathed him in as Alex deepened the kiss. The kiss grew more passionate, and Suzanne found herself wrapped in Alex's embrace as he peppered her face with gentle kisses. Both of them were gasping for breath. Alex's hands were rubbing Suzanne's back, and his fingers were tangled in her hair. It appeared he was showing great restraint as he pulled back. "I don't know if I will stop if we keep going."

Suzanne's cheeks turned beet red. "I'm sorry. I didn't mean to appear too forward."

"Suzanne. That's not why I stopped. I don't think that at all, but I don't think you want my hands drifting under your shirt while we are out in the open." Alex kissed her forehead as he spoke. "I wanted this to be a casual relationship, but it feels so much more than that." Alex stared intently into her eyes.

"I was thinking the same thing about being casual. This is not me. I don't usually behave like this," Suzanne whispered. "I've never felt so connected to someone before."

"Me either. And I would like to continue seeing you to see where this may go. Are you open to that?"

Suzanne's eyes shone as she said, "Yes, I would like that."

"It's almost your curfew, so I should walk you back."

When Alex walked her back to the dorm, he pulled her close to kiss her goodnight. As she had the night before, Suzanne felt like she was floating as she walked to her room. She and Alex were getting to know each other. Suzanne had been physical with guys in high school, but she had not had sex more than twice. More than anything, she wanted to explore with Alex. If he tried to go further with her, she decided she wouldn't stop him.

***

Alex had never desired a girl as much as he wanted Suzanne. He thought he had similar feelings with Rhonda, but he could see it was only lust. What he felt with Suzanne was much stronger. The way she melted into his arms filled him with a possessive nature, and Alex wanted nothing more than to make passionate love to her. However, he wouldn't push her and would wait until she was ready. If she wasn't comfortable with the idea, Alex would respect her wishes.

In the movie, Suzanne looked up at him with a vulnerable expression. Alex promised himself not to hurt this gorgeous girl. He was learning she was just as beautiful on the inside. Alex loved the innocence that wrapped around her entire being. Alex admired her drive to excel in school so that she could prove her independence.

His best friend, Michael, had talked about these same feelings with Hannah. Alex laughed it off, thinking that Michael was a little over the moon for her. Now he understood. Doubts filled his mind as he thought about how he did not know how to treat a girl. Sure, he dated in high school. But he never was in a steady relationship with any of them. His only male role model was Pastor Brian. Would Alex be able to give Suzanne all that she needed? The fear of not measuring up was an underlying fear every day of his life. It was why Alex wanted to focus on his major and helping his mom. She was the one woman he could always count on.

The thought of Alex's mom made him pause in his thoughts. *Should he be focusing so much on Suzanne and a relationship with her? Wasn't his goal to take care of his mother?"*

Suzanne's background sounded completely different from his. Alex doubted their families could ever mesh. They just didn't have much common ground.

Conflicting thoughts continued tormenting Alex's mind as he took a shower and prepared for bed. He decided not to call Suzanne as he had the previous night. Alex decided to keep this as casual dating. He also told himself he wouldn't induce any more deep kissing because he didn't want any hard feelings if the relationship ended. *I will talk to Suzanne about it again tomorrow. She might even agree with me.*

***

Rage filled him as he watched Alex kiss Suzanne deeply. His hands tightened into fists and he wanted nothing more than to shove Alex off of her. What he couldn't understand was how Suzanne seemed to enjoy Alex's kisses. It was time for him to make a move and get to know her. Hopefully, he could dissuade her from Alex. He parked out of sight this evening, both at the beginning of the date and as they took a walk.

He already had most of his classes with Suzanne. He scheduled four out of the five classes with her. The fifth one, computer science, was full. Even though he tried to persuade the lady in the registrar's office to add him to the class roster, she adamantly refused. He could have forced his way into the class, but it would draw unwanted attention to him, and involve campus security along with the police. His beady eyes roved the secretary's face in hate, but he nodded his head, accepted his class schedule. He walked out, not wishing to cause a scene.

His eyes seared into Suzanne's back as she embraced Alex. If only she knew how much he loved her. He punched the steering wheel, growling and feeling pounding between his ears. At one point, he reached for the door handle. More than anything, he wanted to go up to Alex and knock his lights out. Suzanne must be confused, thinking she cared for Alex. It was time to let her see him. Most of his time was spent watching her, but he burned for her to truly know him.

He hit the wheel a second time before releasing the door handle. When Suzanne finally met him, it needed to be wonderful. If he acted in violence toward a guy she was dating, it might deter her from truly seeing him.

He chuckled to himself, thinking of what a moron Alex was for not even noticing him. When they bumped into each other the first time, he was behind Suzanne. As Suzanne began eating meals with him and his friends, the idiot never even looked up to see he was sitting at a table behind them. Last night, when Alex noticed him standing by his car, the dude didn't show any recognition.

Earlier that day, he was in her room. He slipped into the window, which was above the beds. Each bed was attached like a window seat underneath, and mattresses were placed in the middle of each window seat. Once inside her room, he quickly knew which bed was Suzanne's from the picture of her and her parents beside her bed. He picked up her pillow and held it to his nose, inhaling her scent.

Just being inside her room made him feel closer to her. She was in the one class he didn't have with her, so he knew the coast was clear. He watched to make sure her roommate had left for the afternoon.

Stephen walked to her closet and opened it, gazing at her clothing and shoes. He reached into a drawer at the bottom and found a nightshirt. He lifted it to his nose and inhaled. Stephen rifled through and found another one on the very bottom of the drawer, slipping it into the pocket of the large coat he was wearing. She probably wouldn't even miss it.

One day Suzanne would belong to him. For now, this would have to suffice. He stepped back onto Jessica's bed and climbed back out the open window. Sliding it shut, he crept back through the straw and grass. He hurried out of the dorm to the street behind it. There wasn't anyone around, so he walked to his car and slipped inside. He started it and drove away. As he did, he kept lifting Suzanne's shirt to his mouth and nose. He sniffed it and placed soft kisses all over it, wishing it were her skin.

Chapter 4

Alex and Suzanne spent many moments together the following week. The immediate friendships with Hannah, Jackie, and Michelle added to Suzanne's joy. The three roommates started inviting Suzanne and Jessica to join them for going out to eat and watching Michael, Danny, and Alex when they practiced with their intramural basketball teams. Her friendship with Jessica only bloomed as they took part in this group of friends. Suzanne's school schedule differed from Jessica's because of their intended degrees. They rarely had as much time together as Suzanne would have liked. The friendships with Hannah, Jackie, and Michelle filled in gaps of loneliness for Suzanne.

At one point, Suzanne questioned herself, asking herself if she continued to see Alex so she wouldn't lose these friendships. Suzanne allowed those doubts to fill her mind until she saw Alex standing in front of the student center. He waited for her, and the zing that ran through her assured her that she wasn't dating him just to make friends. That electric shock happened every time she saw him.

As she walked in to join him for breakfast, Alex looked in her direction. His entire face lit up with joy. "Hey gorgeous."

Suzanne leaned into him and accepted his kiss. "Hi," she said. She startled when he reached for her backpack. "What are you doing?"

"I'm helping you carry this. Wow, are there bricks in here?" Alex shouldered her backpack on his other shoulder.

Never in her life had a guy carried her books or backpack before. Suzanne stood motionless, not sure what to do.

Alex looked at her with a quizzical expression. "Everything okay?"

Suzanne shook her head to bring her back to the present, and she smiled at him. "Thank you. And if you mean textbooks which are just as heavy as bricks, then I agree with you it weighs like lead."

"I don't know that it's healthy for your back and shoulders." Alex said. With his muscular arms and firm shoulders, the weight didn't seem to bother Alex. "Ready for lunch?" he asked.

Suzanne smiled again and nodded. Once they got their food, Alex placed their bags on the floor beside their chairs.

"We have a great idea." Michelle said as she and Jackie joined them.

"I'm almost afraid to ask," Alex said.

Michelle stuck her tongue out at him. "You'll think it's good when you hear it, goofy."

"Then let me guess. You won the Publisher's sweepstakes and you're sharing your millions with your wonderful friends." Alex puffed out his cheeks like a blowfish when he finished saying it. Hannah and Michael joined them, and Hannah doubled over with laughter, even though she didn't know what the conversation was about. Suzanne couldn't help but join in.

"If you will be serious for two seconds," Michelle interrupted, "Hannah, Jackie, and I came up with something to do this Friday night."

"Oh, right," Hannah nodded. "It is a great idea."

Michelle smiled. "We found a sports bar where we can hang out and dance."

"We're not old enough to drink in a bar," Alex said.

"Yes, but this bar allows you to enter if you're eighteen years or older. You don't have to drink. They have amazing reviews for their food, and there are local bands who play there," Jackie said.

Alex grasped Suzanne's hand in his. The gesture made her heart skip with joy. "That sounds like fun."

"I told you," Michelle said. "So, do y'all want to join us?"

Alex turned toward Suzanne. "Is that something you would like to do?"

Suzanne squeezed his hand and she repeated his words. "That sounds like a lot of fun."

***

Hannah, Michelle, and Jackie invited Suzanne to go to the local mall the next evening to shop for their upcoming adventure on Friday. Jessica already had plans to study with some students from her class, so she wasn't able to join them. Suzanne took a night off of studying with the worry of whether she should.

Suzanne and Hannah shared similar mannerisms, and they hit it off as friends. Both of them were majoring in elementary education, and Hannah was sweet, like Suzanne. The shared connection cemented a solid friendship, and Suzanne silently experienced a gratefulness beyond what she could even fathom. Friends didn't come easily to her, and she was humbled to be included in this group. Suzanne sensed that the relationship with these girls differed from any she had experienced in her hometown. Suzanne wondered again if her lack of friendships was because of her parents. Did they coddle her so much that she didn't know how to start conversations with other people? Was being here on her own why she began being included with these girls?

Suzanne loved Michelle's quick wit, and she enjoyed Jackie as well.

Hannah and Suzanne wandered into the back of a department store to browse for dressier items. Michelle and Jackie had stopped off at the restroom and would join them shortly.

"I'm so happy to see Alex dating again," Hannah said. "He was devastated by Rhonda earlier this fall."

Suzanne's eyes softened as she flipped through several beautiful tops. "I really like him."

"I think he likes you, too," Hannah said as she spotted the royal blue sequined blouse in Suzanne's hand. "You need to buy that! It will look outstanding on you!"

"You think so?" Suzanne asked. She walked closer to a mirror and held it up to herself. Suzanne gazed at it. It was not really her style to wear clothing that sparkled like this. "I rarely wear anything this noticeable."

"I promise this will look great on you," Hannah said.

"You know what?" Suzanne said. "You're right." She took the blouse from Hannah and draped it over her arm. As she walked to the dressing room, Suzanne decided it was time to put her past and high school behind her. With her new friends, she wasn't afraid to step a little out of her comfort zone. Suzanne was becoming a new person who made her own decisions. Again, Suzanne questioned if her parents' doting was the reason why she didn't have any friends back home.

The two girls continued to chat as Jackie and Michelle joined them. Their time choosing clothes for each other was a wonderful time of companionship.

Two hours later, they stopped at a Mexican restaurant for supper. Suzanne relished the moments of laughter and fun. It was amazing how thankful a person could be for friendship after moments of loneliness and solace. Suzanne closed her eyes and raised her face upward, whispering a prayer of gratitude.

As they finished their entrees, a young man approached. Hannah, Jackie, Michelle, and Suzanne looked at each other before glancing back at the man. He was average, and there wasn't anything remarkable about his looks.

"You're Suzanne Marks, right?" the guy asked.

"Yes," Suzanne said, and Michelle spoke up as well. "She's not telling you any more information until you tell us who you are, and what you want." Michelle had a gift of speaking bluntly.

Something crossed the guy's face, almost like anger. He glared at Michelle. "My name is Stephen Matthews." Stephen turned his gaze back to Suzanne, and he said, "You're in four of my classes at school. The only one we don't have together is computer science."

"It's nice to meet you," Suzanne smiled. "I'm sorry I didn't recognize you. Hannah is in three classes as well." She gestured to her friend on the right.

Stephen gave her a passing glance, and he mumbled something before fixing his eyes back on Suzanne. His eyes appeared glassy. "I will speak up more when we are in class together. I just wanted to introduce myself. Maybe we can study together sometime."

Suzanne paused before she said, "Okay, that would be nice."

Stephen took a tentative step away as he said, "I will see you tomorrow in class. I just wanted to introduce myself."

"Bye Stephen," Suzanne smiled again, and Stephen's expression turned to adoration as he smiled back at her and waved.

"Well, that was weird," Jackie said.

"And he only looked at you, Suzanne. Kind of strange if you ask me," Michelle said.

Suzanne waved her hand in dismissal. "I'm sure he was just introducing himself. How harmful could he be if he's in the same classes as me? That means his focus is on elementary education. He can't be that bad if he wants to teach kids."

"I'm not sure," Hannah said. "It felt like it was planned. How did he know what your fifth class was if he wasn't in it with you? I thought Rhonda was fine, too. And you know what happened in that situation!"

Rhonda targeted Hannah because she was jealous of her friendships with Jackie and Michelle. Overcome with anger issues, Rhonda kidnapped Hannah, intending to kill her.

"I'm sure Stephen is harmless," Suzanne said. "Why on earth would he target me?"

The three girls dropped the subject, moving onto other topics.

***

Friday night arrived. Hannah, Jackie, and Michelle invited Suzanne to come to their room to get ready. Jessica had traveled home for the weekend. Suzanne brought her makeup kit and rollers. The three girls spent their moments of preparation by laughing and teasing one another. Suzanne blushed when the three of them teased her about Alex and their relationship. She leaned back on Hannah's bed as her chest expanded from the warmth in the room. Suzanne decided right then and there to be there for these girls in any way that they needed.

Two hours later, their phone rang, and Michael told Hannah that the guys waited in the lobby. As soon as they walked out, Hannah made a beeline for Michael. He stared at her before he pulled her into a tight embrace.

Alex stood slightly to the right of him, and his eyes turned smoky when he saw Suzanne. She had the sequined top on with a black leather skirt. The top shimmered and hung off of one shoulder, revealing the strap of the shell tank top Suzanne found on the shopping spree. Suzanne watched him scan her from head to toe. Her breath hitched as she wondered if she made the right choice by purchasing it.

"You are breathtaking!" Alex said, as he grasped both of her hands in his. He lifted both of her hands to his lips, and he kissed each finger softly.

Shivers wracked Suzanne's body, and her eyelids fluttered as if they wanted to close. "Thank you. You look amazing as well!" She smiled up at Alex.

She watched as he glanced around and saw that none of their friends paying any attention. Then he leaned forward and kissed her softly before they walked out to Danny's van. His family only lived an hour away, so Danny drove home that afternoon to borrow it so that they could all ride together.

The thirty-minute drive to the sports bar passed swiftly as they laughed and enjoyed time away from school.

Alex's arm rested on the back of the seat and around Suzanne. His hand softly stroked the curls in her long hair laying across her shoulder. Dizziness overcame Suzanne from the sensation of his fingers in her hair. Everything Alex did made her feel safe and adored.

She and Hannah talked about their class with the extensive project, and what they were going to do to complete it.

"Did you see that guy, Stephen, today?" Hannah asked.

"Yes, I didn't realize that he sits directly behind me. I said hello to him before sitting down."

"I still say that his coming up to you was strange. I don't know that I trust him," Hannah said.

They roused from their conversation when Danny turned up a song on the radio. They started singing and belting out the lyrics together.

***

Alex nearly lost his mind when he watched Suzanne walk toward him in the dorm lobby. She had on a sparkly top with a short black skirt. The top hung off of one shoulder, making him want to lean down and kiss the soft skin that was showing. Her legs seemed to go on for miles under the skirt, encased in dark pantyhose.

Unable to help himself, he leaned to kiss Suzanne softly in the lobby. Alex wanted to deepen the kiss, but he refrained because the group moved to walk out to Danny's van.

On the drive to the restaurant, Suzanne's perfume tickled his nose. Alex wanted to bury his face in her neck. All thoughts of taking things back a step and being casual flew from his brain as his arm pulled Suzanne closer against his side.

He half listened to what Michael told him, pretending to listen.

Earlier that day, Alex called ahead to reserve a table since they were a large group. The hostess seated them, and they perused the menu. As they did, Alex's arm pulled Suzanne's chair closer in order to continue touching her.

Alex leaned closer as they studied the menu. "What sounds good to you, baby?"

Suzanne inhaled, with a sharp look at him because it was the first time he used the word with her. She gazed into his eyes before shaking her head and smiling, "I think the wings sound good." Alex vowed to call her the name more often if she looked at him like that each time.

Alex smiled at her, and he leaned to kiss her gently. "I thought the same thing."

The group splurged together on a large platter of wings and fries. As soon as they placed their order, Michael pulled Hannah out onto the dance floor.

Alex pushed his chair back and stood, holding out his hand to Suzanne. She smiled at him as she allowed him to clasp their fingers together as he led her out to join their friends. The song was upbeat as they laughed and moved together as a group.

When the song changed to a slow beat, Alex pulled Suzanne into a tight embrace. "Mmm...this feels good."

He heard Suzanne sigh as she rested her head on his chest. His height allowed her to nestle against him, and Alex tightened his hold on her. At one point, she leaned back to gaze up at him. His eyes darkened with desire before he captured her lips in his for a slow and seductive kiss.

Suzanne moaned when he angled his head to deepen it. His tongue traced the seam of her lips and when she opened her mouth, his tongue tangled with hers. The moment was so charged with electricity that Suzanne seemed to be short of breath.

Alex pulled back slightly before continuing to pepper soft kisses on her mouth, cheek, and forehead. "Did I tell you that you look beautiful tonight?" His mouth slid across her skin as he whispered the words.

"Yes, you did," Suzanne gasped. Her eyes threatened to close from the intense emotions. Alex's heart skipped with joy.

He opened his mouth to say more when Michelle informed them that their food had arrived. The group feasted and enjoyed time together before heading back out to the dance floor.

As Alex and Suzanne moved into another slow dance, he said, "Michael wants to take Hannah back to our place. I don't really want to go back while they are there. Would you like to go somewhere for a coffee or a hot chocolate?"

"Yes, I would like that," Suzanne said.

"I want you to know that this is becoming more serious for me." Alex surprised himself at what he just told her. His plan of moving slowly was dissipating as he gazed into Suzanne's eyes.

Suzanne's eyes shimmered in question. "What do you mean?"

"I mean that I'm starting to really care about you. Suzanne, I want to establish this as a relationship. Is that alright with you?" Alex's eyes filled with intensity as he looked into her eyes.

Suzanne remained quiet for a few seconds before she nodded her head. "Yes. I'm beginning to care about you, too."

A breath whooshed out of Alex as he gathered her even closer to kiss her passionately. "Let's go out tomorrow night, just the two of us." Alex paused. "How would you feel about going back to my place tomorrow night? Is that something you are ready for?"

Suzanne studied him for a few seconds. Alex held his breath until she said, "Yes, I would like that."

The rest of the night was just as magical, as they enjoyed time as a group.

***

Saturday morning, Alex relaxed, and he allowed himself to be lazy for a while. He needed to go to the library to work on a research paper, but he stayed in bed. Another reason he lingered was being aware that Michael had just snuck Hannah out to take her back to the dorm. The difficulty of having a roommate was knowing what they had been doing all night. However, he hoped Suzanne might be ready for that step in their relationship soon. After last night, he certainly was.

Alex asked Suzanne with the fear of it being too soon. Even though she accepted his invitation, Alex asked himself if the action was premature in the status of their relationship. He knew he had deep feelings for Suzanne and he came close to telling her he loved her the night before. However, Alex refrained.

He thought about when they went out for a coffee afterward. He shared more about his years of growing up and she shared silly stories of her family, along with frustration at her parents' constant doting on her. Alex was surprised when Suzanne told him her parents wanted to drive to the school to meet him. He swallowed.

"Don't worry. I talked them out of it," Suzanne said. She shook her head. "I shouldn't have mentioned going out with you just yet. They both act crazy with my dating life."

Alex cleared his throat, and he fingered the collar at his neck. "They just worry about you. You're their only child. My mom worries, too, in her own way."

"They want to know every single detail that happens here at school." Suzanne rolled her eyes. "I convinced them to stop from driving here every weekend. They need to allow me to form my path."

Alex gazed at Suzanne with respect. She seemed naïve in certain areas, but he admired the fact that she recognized it as a weakness in herself.

When Alex drove her back to the dorm, they sat in the car and talked for a while longer. At one point, he leaned to kiss her. Their kiss was filled with the charged connection that had been between them from the first moment he laid eyes on her. As he tugged her closer with the console between them, Suzanne climbed over it and straddled his lap. Alex nearly lost his mind when she did that. Both of them roved their hands all over each other's bodies. When Alex touched the soft skin under Suzanne's top, she gasped in pleasure.

Suzanne leaned down to kiss his neck and the way her top was situated, it fell far enough that it gave him a glimpse of her cleavage. He groaned at her lips on his neck. His hands continued to travel north, and he watched Suzanne as he covered her breasts with his hands. Alex dipped a finger inside of her bra, and he moaned at the softness of her breast under his finger.

"Oh my," Suzanne whispered as he palmed her breast, fingering her tightened nipple.

"Shit, you're so beautiful," Alex murmured, and he pulled down the cups of her bra in order to fondle both of her breasts.

Suzanne's hand found its way up under Alex's shirt, and she caressed his muscled abs.

After a few more minutes of frenzied kisses and stolen touches, Alex pulled away. Suzanne gasped at him in surprise. "We need to stop."

"Why?" Suzanne continued peppering his face and neck with kisses without slowing down.

"Baby, I don't want our first time together to be in my car," Alex's words ended on another gasp as Suzanne ran her hands under the waistband of his pants.

She sat up and gazed at him with widened eyes. "Yes, I guess this is not a good idea; especially since someone might walk by the car at any second." As Suzanne looked around, she noticed the fogged windows and a blush stole over her at her assertiveness. "I'm sorry if I got carried away." She moved to climb off of Alex's lap, and he stopped her.

"All we're doing is postponing this. Believe me, I'm not at all upset." Alex reached up to kiss her forehead. "Please don't be embarrassed about this, baby." He let her go, and Suzanne climbed back into the passenger seat. Suzanne took a few minutes to straighten her top before she moved to step out. Alex, in his gentlemanly manner, made her wait for him to come around and open her door.

When Suzanne stepped out, he pulled her into a tight hug and held her for a few seconds. Alex moved back, but one arm remained tightly wrapped around her waist as he escorted her to the front door.

Suzanne turned to face him. "I had a wonderful time tonight. Thank you for all of it."

Alex kissed her before he replied. "Me too. I'm also looking forward to tomorrow night. I will call you in the morning, okay?"

"Okay." Suzanne smiled at him, causing him to frame her face with his hands.

"It's extremely hard to leave you right now. Good night, gorgeous!"

"Good night."

Alex almost groaned again as she turned to walk inside. He watched Suzanne's backside sway in her feminine manner. As his eyes traveled up her body, he saw her long hair softly swinging as it hung down her back. Alex wanted to run to her and pull her into his embrace again. His heart was still pounding at how aroused he was by the physical moment in his car. As he walked back to his car, he couldn't help but grin at the idea of making love to Suzanne. He hoped it would happen tomorrow night.

Chapter 5

Saturday morning, Suzanne's phone rang. Suzanne answered, sensing it was her mother. She answered while grabbing her textbook from her desk and shoving it into her backpack. Her goal was to spend time in the library completing research and other assignments before her date with Alex.

"Hi Suzanne, this is Stephen Matthews from class."

Suzanne was startled to hear his voice. "Hi. How did you get my number?"

"I spoke to your roommate, Jessica, and I mentioned our four classes together. I asked her for it so that I could call you about studying together. We have that test coming up on Friday, and I would love to have someone drill me," Stephen said.

"I guess we could do that. My plan is to go to the library to work on a research paper, so it will have to be this afternoon. I need to be back by five because I have plans tonight." Suzanne's hand shook in anticipation of going to Alex's apartment tonight. After their time spent talking last night, she was more certain about becoming more intimate together.

"How about two o'clock?" Stephen asked. "I could meet you at the library and we can meet in a study room."

"Yes, I think that will work." Suzanne said.

"Great, see you at two."

"Bye, Stephen."

Suzanne hung up, frowning. What made Jessica give Stephen her number? She recalled Hannah's opinions about Stephen. Did he randomly choose her to study with? Or was his attention something to worry about?

Suzanne shook off the worry. *Everything will be fine. Stephen just wants help in learning to study class material.* As Suzanne reassured herself, doubts continued to pop into her mind. Was Stephen someone to be trusted? With little experience in making friends, Suzanne didn't know how to judge another person's intentions. And Hannah endured a great deal during her abduction with Rhonda. Suzanne sighed inwardly. It would be much easier if she knew how to interact with other people. Suzanne tightened her jaw, allowing the resentment to overcome her thinking. The more she thought about it, the stronger her feeling became that her parents' doting prevented genuine friendships from forming.

After pushing those thoughts down, her mind drifted to Alex. He treated her so tenderly and Suzanne's emotions were totally new and exhilarating. At one point when they danced together, Suzanne felt like she was drowning as she gazed into his eyes. She reveled in the sensation of Alex's hands on her back as he held her close.

When the two of them got carried away in the car, she was extremely embarrassed. Empowerment overcame Suzanne, and she loved the groan that escaped from his lips. Alex's gentle words acted as a balm to her bruised ego as he talked about postponing their plans of becoming more physical. Suzanne's face turned red as she remembered how bold she had been, climbing on his lap and shoving her hands under his shirt.

Alex asked if she was open to becoming more serious in their relationship. Suzanne's heart skipped at the implication, but she nodded in affirmation. She had already been considering the idea of taking their relationship to the next level. Deep down, she understood it as the reason she became more physical toward Alex the night before.

***

Suzanne picked a sandwich for her lunch, grabbing an apple and some chips. Once she loaded her tray with food, Suzanne walked to join Jackie, Michelle, and Hannah at their table. Jessica also sat beside Suzanne, having walked to the dining hall together. Michael, Alex and Danny were practicing for their intramural basketball team. The girls were unable to join them today because of exams to study for and projects to work on.

"So, big plans with Alex tonight, right? You're staying over at his place," Hannah wagged her eyebrows up and down, causing Suzanne to giggle with her.

"Stop, please. Yes, we're going out again tonight. How did you know I was staying over there?" Suzanne tilted her head to the side and one of her eyebrows popped up.

"That's so cool that your eyebrow can do that!" Jackie exclaimed. Suzanne couldn't help but laugh at her words.

Hannah said, "Remember, I'm dating his roommate. I hear many things."

"Oh, right? You spent the night over there last night." Suzanne nodded her head in understanding.

Michelle snorted in an unladylike manner. "I'm not sure how much sleep they actually got."

This time, Hannah said, "Please stop," as her face lit up in a crimson blush.

All the girls laughed when they noticed it, and Suzanne relaxed as she joined in the joking.

Hannah quickly changed the subject, turning to Suzanne. "What are your plans for this afternoon?"

"Mmm…" Suzanne swallowed her food. "Remember that guy, Stephen, who introduced himself at dinner the other night? He called and wanted to study with me for our test this week."

"How did he get your number?" Michelle asked.

"He stopped me in the student center yesterday and asked for it," Jessica said. As she noticed the expressions on the girls' faces, she continued. "I guess I shouldn't have. Why are you worried?"

"You're not going, are you?" Hannah asked.

"Why not? It's just in the library."

Jessica repeated the question. "Why is that a problem? Suzanne, is there something I need to be aware of regarding this guy?"

"Suzanne, you're not going by yourself to study with that guy," Hannah said.

Suzanne waved her hand. "I think he's harmless. I'm sure it will be fine."

Hannah, Jackie, and Michelle glanced at one another in concern. Jessica had a similar expression on her face.

"It's natural for you to have anxiety, Hannah. You went through something terrible. But that will not happen to me." Suzanne thought the matter was finished as she gathered her trash to throw it away.

Jessica touched her shoulder on the walk back to the dorm. The other girls were behind them. "I'm in agreement with everyone that you shouldn't go. I'm really sorry.

"Will all of you stop? Nothing is going to happen to me," Suzanne raised her voice.

Hannah appeared beside her. "How about I come and join you? We can form a study group. I need extra practice for that test as well."

"Look, I'm aware of your concerns. But I think everything will be fine," Suzanne said. "I'm sure that Stephen won't mind."

A few moments later, Suzanne walked into her room, and she heard her phone ringing. Out of breath, she answered.

"Hi sweetie," her mom said. "Hey baby girl." Her dad's voice also piped in on the line.

"Hi Mom and Dad," Suzanne rolled her eyes.

"We're sorry we didn't get to call you this morning. There was a problem at Mamaw's house this morning. Your dad and I had to go over there early, and we took her to breakfast after it was taken care of."

Her anger dissipated. "Is something wrong? Is she alright?" Suzanne's voice was filled with distress.

"Her hot water heater stopped working, so your dad worked on it. I brought her back over to the house." Anne Marks spoke in a reassuring voice. "She's fine. She's eventually going to need a new one, but he has it working for now."

Suzanne's breath whooshed out in relief. "That's good. Are you calling someone to come fix it?"

"We hired someone to replace it and install a new one." Suzanne's dad piped into the conversation.

"Okay, that makes sense."

"Tell us about your week, honey. How's it been going?"

Suzanne talked about her new friendships with Jackie, Hannah, and Michelle. Her mom's voice filled with excitement to hear about them. She also mentioned the study group with Hannah and Stephen.

"I'm so glad you're making new friends." Her mother's voice sounded relieved. "We can't wait to meet them."

Suzanne refrained from sharing anything new about Alex because she understood her parents would ask a million questions about him. Her mother had already voiced her concerns last Saturday.

"We planned to come and visit you today, but the emergency with Mamaw happened. How about next Saturday?" her mom said. "We can meet your new friends and that boy you went out with."

"Mom," Suzanne's gut tightened, and she clenched her jaw again. "His name is Alex, not *that boy.*"

"Okay, we want to meet Alex," her mom said.

Suzanne paused. "That's not a good idea. You and Dad will interrogate him and it will probably scare him off. Besides, we aren't serious." Suzanne crossed her fingers behind her back, then she chastised herself for the childish move. She and Alex were growing in their relationship, but her parents didn't need to know every detail.

"Well, we want to see you. If Alex is available, hopefully we can meet him," her dad said. He hadn't spoken for a few moments. Suzanne hoped he had gotten off.

"Dad, please don't intimidate him," Suzanne said.

Her dad cleared his throat. "When have I ever been intimidating?"

"All the time," Suzanne said. "When anyone approached me in church, you wrapped our arm around my waist. I couldn't have a simple conversation with any boy in the youth group."

"I don't perceive how that is intimidating," her dad said. "I hope they realized how much I care about you."

Suzanne knew it was pointless to argue any more.

The three of them spoke for another thirty minutes before Suzanne told them she needed to get to the library for their study session. As soon as she hung up, the phone rang again. "What now?" She offered a terse hello.

A deep voice said, "Hey gorgeous. Everything okay?"

"Alex, hey," she answered. "I thought you were my parents calling me back. Sorry for sounding impatient."

"No problem. Are we still going out tonight?"

"Yes, I plan to be back at my room by four thirty to get ready." Suzanne smiled into the phone even though Alex couldn't see it.

"Okay...," Alex paused. "Are you still okay with coming over here tonight?"

Suzanne's heart began pounding at how his voice deepened as he asked the question. "I'm looking forward to that as well." Suzanne said.

"Great," Suzanne heard the smile in Alex's voice.

She asked. "Will Michael be there?"

"He's going to spend the night at his grandparents' house. They live thirty minutes from here. He said they invited him. Hannah's going to eat dinner at their house, and then she will drive back to the dorm."

Suzanne was grateful to hear Alex say that. She didn't want Michael there for their first time together. "Okay."

Alex's tone deepened. "I will be there at five. We can go out to eat and come back here to watch a movie."

"Okay," Suzanne whispered.

"I'm really looking forward to it, Suzanne."

"Me too," she whispered a second time.

"Bye, gorgeous."

"Goodbye."

***

Suzanne walked to Hannah's room and knocked on her door. Her friends advised her not to meet Stephen alone in the library. She thought they were being overprotective, but she promised that she wouldn't. Jessica also gave her an earful. Her roommate admonished her for not filling her in on meeting Stephen and how concerning it was.

"If I had been there, I would have told him to bug off!" Jessica yelled.

It took several minutes for Suzanne to reassure her. Thankfully, her parents' phone call interrupted the conversation.

"Hey," Hannah opened the door with her backpack on her shoulder. "Are you ready?"

"Yes," Suzanne said, "You don't have to come if you have other things to do. I'm sure I will be fine."

"I need the extra study time for this test," Hannah said. "But I need to be back by four."

"That's fine with me," Suzanne said.

It took ten minutes to walk to the library, which was on the other side of the campus. When they walked in, Suzanne realized the person standing in the lobby was Stephen.

"Hi Stephen," she said, "Hannah wanted to come and study with us since she's in our class."

Stephen's eyes narrowed and his mouth tensed. Anger radiated from him. A second later, he smiled, although the smile didn't reach his eyes. "That will be great."

"Great," Suzanne said. Hannah didn't say a word, but her eyes were studying Stephen before she smiled and tried to look unbothered.

They quickly found a study room in the back of the library. Suzanne didn't pay any attention as Stephen sat extremely close to her.

However, Hannah's eyes shot daggers at Suzanne. Upon noticing her pointed look, Suzanne shifted her chair slightly away from Stephen.

Two hours later, when they were walking back, Hannah asked, "Did Stephen act mad when we first got there and he saw I joined you?"

"I noticed it at first, but he seemed fine after that." Suzanne's voice was dismissive.

"I noticed how close he sat to you and when you talked, he looked at you in a worshipful manner," Hannah said. "I'm not sure why, but something doesn't seem right with him."

"You're worrying too much, but I promise to be careful."

"Please be careful," Hannah said. "I care too much about you to let anything happen to you."

Tears sprung to Suzanne's eyes, and she turned her head so Hannah wouldn't see them. Someone other than her parents actually cared about her to watch out for her! "I will. I promise." Suzanne frowned at how much it bugged her when her parents acted this way, but it didn't with girls her own age.

***

Jessica lounged on her bed as Suzanne got ready. She teased her about Alex and staying over with him. Even though tonight was more casual, she wanted to look good for their first time together. Suzanne did not realize she worried over nothing.

After dressing, Suzanne brushed her teeth and gave herself a last check in the mirror. Her hair rested softly across her shoulders and down her back. She believed her hair to be her best feature. Suzanne applied lipstick, earrings, and finally perfume. The moment she set the bottle back on the dresser, her phone rang. After answering and telling Alex she would be right out, Suzanne grabbed her purse.

"Have a great time," Jessica called. "I want details tomorrow." Her eyebrows wagged up and down, causing Suzanne to laugh.

When Suzanne arrived in the lobby, Alex stood by the window, gazing out. Suzanne's mouth curved softly as she watched him, overcome with how handsome and tall he was.

Alex turned, and his mouth dropped when he noticed her. His gaze was warm as he glanced over at her. Alex kissed her softly before he said, "Every time I see you, my breath is taken away. You're so beautiful."

"Thank you. You look wonderful, too."

"Are you ready?"

"Yes." Alex pulled her close to his side as they walked outside to his car.

Chapter 6

Alex took Suzanne to a steak place in town. He didn't know if he could keep his hands off of her during dinner because she looked so hot. And he wasn't sure if he wanted to.

His heartbeat increased as he thought about sharing his bed with her that night. Alex had driven to the store that afternoon, and he bought some things, including condoms. As he readied for their date, his brow pursed in thought. He had been with girls sexually before, but Alex predicted tonight to be the first meaningful time he would ever have. Alex didn't think he would feel that way after the mistake of having sex with Rhonda. He realized he was falling fast for Suzanne, and not just because she was beautiful. She was also gentle and sweet. He was also learning of her intelligence, and that was also a turn on.

Alex sat beside her in a booth, instead of across from her. Suzanne's eyes widened, but she scooted over to give him more room. Alex kept her hand in his the entire time during dinner. They smiled and laughed, enjoying being together. But the current between them was as strong as ever.

Alex even splurged on dessert. Suzanne claimed she was full, so they shared a chocolate brownie sundae. At one point, when she had a speck of chocolate on one corner of her mouth, Alex's eyes darkened. Unable to stop himself, he leaned forward and kissed it, using his tongue to lick it off. Suzanne's breath increased, and her eyelids closed slightly from his gesture.

When Alex paid for their dinner, he helped Suzanne out of the booth, keeping his arm wrapped around her waist. Suzanne paid no attention, but she was so lovely that she always turned the heads of other men wherever they went. Alex leaned in, staking his claim and kissing her, as possessiveness overwhelmed him. He wanted every man in there to know that Suzanne was his.

Alex stopped at the car and kissed her before opening the car door to help her inside. The drive seemed to last forever. Finally, Alex pulled up to his apartment. He walked around, and opened Suzanne's door. She slowly stepped out. The look in her eyes just about undid him. Alex groaned and pulled her close for another passionate kiss. When she pushed closer to him with hands caressing his back, his groan became louder.

It took all of his efforts to release her in order to unlock the door. Alex ushered her into the living room, and he used the lighter to ignite the candles he set out earlier.

Suzanne's voice brought him out of his head when she said, "I like your apartment."

"Thanks," he said. "Michael keeps everything clean. He can't stand a mess." Alex didn't know why he said such a random thing. He couldn't form coherent thoughts at the moment.

Suzanne chuckled as he stepped closer to her with intensity in his stare. Her chuckle died when he said, "I don't want to come across as someone who wants to maul you, but I don't think I can wait another second. Please tell me if that scares you, and we can stop right now." He placed his hands on her shoulders and gazed at her. "I will respect your decision if you decide you aren't ready."

Her breath caught in her throat. Alex's heart pounded. Finally, she whispered, "I don't want to wait either." Her eyes were filled with longing.

"Do you want to go into my room?" Alex studied her gorgeous eyes to make sure that she was truly ready for this step in their relationship.

When she smiled softly and held out her hand, Alex didn't hesitate as he took it. They walked into his room. Alex made a quick dash to the living room. He picked up the lighted candles, placing them on his dresser before closing his bedroom door.

***

Alex gently cradled Suzanne's face with both of his hands and he gazed lovingly at her. "This means something special to me. I want you to know that I don't take this time with you lightly."

Suzanne reached up to kiss him softly. "Me too."

Alex returned her kiss, and he angled her head to deepen the kiss. One hand ran through the length of her hair, brushing it behind her shoulder as he traced the seam of her lips with his tongue. When Suzanne opened for him, he didn't hesitate. He loved how she met him stroke for stroke, returning his passionate kiss.

His fingers were still tangled in her hair when Alex pulled back for a quick breath. His mouth found the soft skin of Suzanne's neck where her hair had been pushed back, giving him access. She smelled like an angel. Alex couldn't help it as his tongue traced the same trail his lips touched.

Suzanne gasped, and she angled her neck so that Alex could kiss down the column of her throat. His fingers found the hem of her top.

He lifted it slightly in order to slide a hand underneath it. Alex almost protested when she pulled away to lift it over her head.

Alex's eyes gazed at her cleavage as she stood there. "Shit, you're so beautiful." One hand lifted to cup one of Suzanne's bra cups and her lips parted, causing her to whoosh out a breath from his touch.

Suzanne's hands found the buttons of his shirt, and she quickly unbuttoned them before pushing it off of his shoulders and onto the floor. Alex kicked it out of the way as one of his hands reached around for the clasp of her bra. He unhooked it and threw her bra on the floor, along with their shirts. This time, Alex gasped as he took in her perfectly round breasts with perky, rosy nipples.

Suzanne's hands were running over his chest and down Alex's stomach as his hands cupped her breasts in his, reveling in the fullness of them. As his fingers stroked them, Alex pulled on her nipples and they became even tighter. "Uhmm," she moaned as he ran light circles around her breasts and back to her nipples. Alex leaned down and took her breast into his mouth.

"Ugghh," Suzanne moaned again as his tongue lapped around her nipple. Alex moved to do the same to her other breast as his hand made sure not to abandon the one he had just feasted on. His other hand ran down Suzanne's soft waist to the button on her jeans.

Alex paused, and he leaned back to look into Suzanne's eyes. "Yes?" he asked.

"Oh yes," she exclaimed, and her hands ran down his abs to the button on his jeans.

They helped each other with taking off the rest of their clothing, throwing them onto the pile on the floor. Alex surprised Suzanne by lifting her off of her feet, causing her to yelp. His lips were on hers again as he laid her on his bed. Alex let go as he pulled the covers back over his bed. Both of them were still in their underwear, but Alex made himself lean back so that he could gaze at Suzanne and how gorgeous she looked lying on his bed.

"So beautiful," he murmured as he leaned down on his elbow. Alex used his free hand to trace her neck, and he moved it down her body. Suzanne raised up slightly when he feathered his hand around her breasts and down her stomach to the waistband of her panties. Alex watched as her lips were parted in pleasure, and she stared at him with heavy lids. Alex didn't take his eyes off of hers as his fingers dipped into her panties. He watched Suzanne's mouth form an *o*, and her eyes closed when his fingers slipped down into her warmth. When he touched her sex, Suzanne gasped out, "Oh my goodness."

Her hands found the waistband of his underwear as she traced her fingers over the length of him from the outside. Alex groaned again before she pushed his underwear down. As she gripped him, Suzanne hitched a breath when she looked at his length. "You're so big," she murmured, and Alex was tempted to move inside of her at that very moment.

However, he forced himself to slow down. Alex pushed her panties off. Then he removed his underwear, pulling her close against him. He leaned down and feasted on Suzanne's neck again, peppering kisses down her shoulder to her breasts again. When he pulled a nipple into his mouth again, Suzanne cried out in bliss. Alex lapped at it with the rough pad of his tongue before moving to her other breast. His hand dipped between her legs again, and her lower body rose when his fingers found her seam.

"Oh my god," she moaned as his fingers traced her from front to back. "Alex," she mumbled.

Alex reveled in her expressions and he whispered, "I'm here, baby. Right here." He slipped a finger inside of her, and he watched her as she moaned louder. Alex added another finger, and she whispered, "I feel like I'm going to come."

Alex moved his fingers back and forth inside of Suzanne while making sure the heel of his hand touched her clit. She was gasping and writhing in pleasure, tossing her head back and forth. Seeing Suzanne's orgasm was one of the most pivotal moments in his life. Alex knew at that moment that he was in love with her, and he wanted to make her come many more times. Alex leaned over and kissed her deeply as he rode out the final twinges of her climax.

Suzanne immediately leaned up. "My turn." She grasped him, and he groaned loudly as she gripped him in her hand. Her fingers touched his balls in just the right spot. Alex moaned again, bucking against her hand. One of his hands remained on her breast, and he squeezed it in the same rhythm as she stroked him, making her moan in pleasure.

Suzanne took him completely by surprise when she leaned down and licked the length of him, causing him to writhe in her hand again. When she took him into her mouth, Alex whispered, "Just for a minute. Don't want to come too soon." Her mouth stroked him, and her tongue followed behind. Finally, Alex pulled back and said, "It's time for me to be inside you."

Suzanne gasped in anticipation and pleasure from his words. Alex took the moment to reach down and pull her breast into his mouth again, torturing her just as she had done with him. When Alex pulled back, he reached into his drawer to pull out a condom. "Are you ready?" he whispered.

"Absolutely," Suzanne moaned with shining eyes.

Alex moved to where he was positioned between her legs. He opened the condom and Suzanne helped slide it onto him. Alex moved until he was right at her opening. Before sliding inside her, Alex looked deeply into her eyes. "I love you, Suzanne."

Tears sprang into Suzanne's eyes, and she said, "I love you, too."

They both groaned loudly as Alex slid partially inside of her. "Are you okay? I'm not hurting you, am I?"

"No, it's wonderful," she moaned.

"Take some deep breaths," he whispered. When she did, he pushed in all the way. He groaned loudly at how tight she was, and how right it felt to be inside of her. "Shit, Suzanne. Baby, this is wonderful."

Suzanne was moaning his name repeatedly when he said, "Open your eyes and look at me." When she did, he groaned again as he began to move and increase his thrusts inside of her. Suzanne widened her hips more. She was moaning and crying out in ecstasy.

Alex leaned down and lapped at her breast, pulling her nipple into his mouth at the same speed as he was thrusting. "Oh my god, Suzanne. Shit! Nothing has ever felt so good!"

Suzanne was thrashing her head and moaning incoherent thoughts. Alex touched her chin to bring her gaze back to his as he increased his speed, hitting the exact right spot inside of her. "Alex," she gasped. "I'm going to come...oh god!"

"I'm here, baby," Alex felt her orgasm as her muscles squeezed. "Come for me." Her expression made his balls tighten, as his own orgasm raced up his cock. He yelled loudly as his release flowed out. Exhausted, he buried his face in Suzanne's hair, breathing in the flowery smell.

The two of them lay there, completely spent. Alex wasn't sure how much time passed before he finally lifted, giving her a chance to take a full breath. "Sorry, baby. Didn't mean to suffocate you."

Short of breath, Suzanne giggled. "It's fine." Her hands were caressing up and down his back.

Alex leaned in to kiss her softly before he leaned back and studied her. "God, you're gorgeous!" Her hair was laying across one shoulder, the curls fanning out away from her face. Her dark brown eyes were soft with satisfaction. Alex kissed her neck and shoulder before pulling her close against him.

"I meant what I said, Suzanne." he whispered against her hair.

"Meant what?"

"I have fallen in love with you. You are the most wonderful woman I have ever known. I love you!" Alex buried his face in her neck, breathing in her perfume along with her scent. He hoped to follow in Pastor Brian's footsteps if Suzanne was actually the one for him. Alex was flabbergasted that the normal fear was nonexistent at the present moment.

"Oh Alex, I love you too," Alex heard tears in her voice, and he leaned up to wipe them away before kissing her passionately.

After getting them glasses of water, Alex and Suzanne made love a second time, unable to keep their hands off of each other. Sex with each other was the final push for them into a full-blown relationship as boyfriend and girlfriend. In Alex's eyes, Suzanne was the one for him. He would enjoy every moment they had together.

Alex worshipped her body a third time before they fell asleep, exhausted and completely sated.

***

His gut burned with rage. She was in there with him! He watched them go on their date and followed them to the restaurant, sitting in his car, waiting. The way Alex sat beside her in the booth irritated him, and he wanted nothing but to punch his lights out.

When they walked out, his anger churned even more when he saw the willingness in Suzanne's eyes as Alex leaned over and kissed her.

He repeated the action many times during dinner, and again as they walked outside to his car.

Stephen followed Alex's car and parked on the side of the street so that he wouldn't be seen. When Suzanne went into his apartment with him, Stephen knew it was time to up his game. Being with Alex was a mistake. She was meant for him, and one day she would come to understand it. Stephen would do all that he could to prepare for when she was ready.

Chapter 7

Monday morning, Suzanne melted into Alex's arms when she saw him waiting for her. The two of them walked arm in arm into the dining hall.

"I missed you yesterday," Alex whispered. He had driven Suzanne back to the dorm early in the morning. Then he went home for his mother's birthday. Alex drove his mom to church, and he took her to lunch afterward.

"I missed you, too." Alex didn't realize Suzanne had similar thoughts about a serious relationship. She knew he was the one for her as well. Suzanne had been so overwhelmed by their time together that she didn't say it out loud. She hoped for an opportunity where she could tell him.

"What did you do?" Alex leaned away to look into her eyes as they waited in line for breakfast.

"I spent most of the day at the library. I have a research paper due soon, along with a gigantic project," Suzanne said. Suzanne's heart skipped a beat as she thought about seeing Stephen in the library at the same time as her. However, other than speaking to her, Stephen moved off by himself. *Guess Hannah's thinking is wrong, and he really needs help,* Suzanne thought to herself.

Alex nodded and said, "I need to spend most of the afternoon there until basketball practice."

"Can I come and watch you tonight?"

"Baby, you don't even have to ask me that."

Suzanne's heart skipped every time he used that term with her. She blushed as she recalled his use of it during their time of intimacy. Suzanne gave him a soft smile before she reached for a tray, and they moved through the line.

Once they had the food they wanted, they joined their friends at the table near the windows. Suzanne thought about the automaticity of sitting with this group that she was now a part of. She glanced over and saw Michael and Hannah absorbed in each other. Suzanne also couldn't help but notice Danny and Michelle talking together. Michelle was smiling and blushing.

The week before, Danny surprised Michelle at basketball practice. Hannah confided in her that Danny sought her assistance to help break the ice in his desire to get to know Michelle better. One night at basketball practice, Michael crooned the words to a love song. Then, Alex and James carried a banner out with Danny in the middle. The banner said, *Michelle Walters, will you go on a date with me on Friday?*

Alex leaned closer, noticing her silly grin. "What's on your mind?"

"Look at that," she whispered, pointing out the connection between Michelle and Danny. "He really likes her."

Alex nodded slowly and quickly averted his gaze when Danny glanced their way. "It's nice to see the two of them finally together," he agreed. His arm went around the back of Suzanne's chair, and his fingers feathered through her hair. He must have noticed desire crossing her face. Alex took advantage of the moment as he leaned over and kissed her softly.

"What was that for?" she asked.

"Because I love you and I wanted to," Alex said, gazing deeply into her eyes.

Suzanne nestled closer to him as she finished the food on her plate. She couldn't help but notice Alex's eyes on her, and she wondered if there was food on her face from the way he was gazing at her. However, Michael spoke, and Alex turned his head. He laced their fingers together as he answered Michael's question. Suzanne always felt so safe when she was with Alex. The only other men who made her feel that way were her dad and her grandfather.

As the two of them walked out after breakfast, he walked them to a secluded part of the student center. His arms went around her waist as he pulled her close. Then he kissed her passionately, expressing his feelings with his mouth on hers.

Suzanne pulled back, gasping for breath. "Wow!" She repeated her question from earlier. "What was that for?"

Alex peppered kisses along her cheek and into her hairline. He repeated the line he used earlier. "Because I love you and I wanted to."

Suzanne beamed at him and said, "I love you, too."

"I can meet you for a quick lunch before I have to go to the library."

"Okay, I will wait for you here."

Alex walked her as far as he could before giving her another soft kiss. "Bye, gorgeous."

"Bye," Suzanne whispered.

Suzanne walked into class and situated herself at the desk where she normally sat. She glanced up as Stephen walked into the classroom.

His eyes lightened as he spotted Suzanne. "Good morning."

"Good morning, Stephen," Suzanne said, glancing at him before arranging her textbook and notes to prepare for class.

"Did you have a good weekend?" Stephen asked.

"I did." Suzanne elaborated no more. "Did you have a pleasant weekend?"

"Yeah, if you count working as something nice."

Suzanne chuckled. "Where do you work?"

"I work the counter at the Chicken Shack. I quit to commit to classes here at school, but I need the money. I'm back working part time now."

"How many hours do you work?" Suzanne was looking at him.

"I work about twenty-five hours a week," Stephen smiled at her.

Suzanne studied his face for a moment. She had noticed that Stephen only smiled when she was around. Every other time, it looked as if he didn't want to be there. Suzanne wondered if Hannah's doubts were correct. "So have you been working on the term paper for our foundation class?"

Stephen said, "How was your time at the library?"

"It was a tiring afternoon!" Suzanne said. Stephen glanced down. Suzanne thought he was tempted to touch her hand when Hannah walked in the door and made a beeline for their table. Suzanne's stomach eased. The thought of Stephen touching her made her immensely uncomfortable. This time, she was thankful for Hannah's doting.

***

Alex was waiting for Suzanne at the spot they talked about meeting for lunch.

"Hi," she whispered as he leaned down to kiss her. Alex noticed a guy and Hannah behind Suzanne as he pulled back. The guy was watching him strangely.

"Hey, I'm Alex," he said, reaching out his hand.

Stephen's handshake was loose and not a firm grip at all. "Stephen," was all he said.

Alex realized it was the guy he observed sitting in the car after their first date. His stomach dropped as he wondered if the guy was watching Suzanne walk inside that night. It seemed as if he was watching her now.

Alex frowned as he placed his arm protectively around Suzanne's shoulders. Alex shouldered her backpack and held the door open for her. He pushed the worry over this guy away in order to focus on Suzanne.

Once Alex and Suzanne were seated, he looked at her with a thoughtful glance. Slight paranoia filled Suzanne as she looked at Alex and asked, "What are you thinking?"

"I want you to meet my mom," he commented. "How about we plan a weekend where we go for a visit to my house?"

"I would love that," Suzanne said, smiling at him. She glanced at the table.

"What is it?" Alex asked.

Suzanne gazed at him. "My parents are coming next Saturday and they want to meet you."

Alex paused as his gut tightened. Meet Suzanne's parents? Was he ready for that? Then he saw her vulnerable gaze.

"I would love to meet them," he said as he kissed the top of her head.

Suzanne let out an enormous sigh. "Thank you. I promise I won't let my dad be intimidating."

Unable to help himself, Alex smiled back as he leaned close and kissed her softly. "Thank you, pretty lady," he murmured against her lips.

Suzanne blushed. He loved when his words and touch caused her to turn red.

***

Stephen watched Suzanne as she came into the library.

"Hi," she said.

Stephen appeared to look up with a surprised glance. Suzanne did not know it was just an act. He knew she was coming to the library, and he timed it to seem like he was already there studying. "Hey Suzanne,"

"Working on your paper?"

"Yeah, the topic Professor Dahl gave me is tough."

"I know! When are we ever going to use information on the philosophy of teaching when we are actually in the classroom?" Suzanne's face was adorable with her slight frown as she complained. Stephen wanted nothing more than to trace his fingers over her wrinkled brow.

"Well, good luck," she murmured as she walked to the back of the library.

Stephen pretended to complete his work as he watched Suzanne from afar. She moved back and forth from a shelf in the library devoted to educational topics. Every time she moved, he watched the soft movement of her hips, completely mesmerized. Whenever she looked up, Stephen pretended to be completely engrossed in what he was doing.

A couple of hours later, he was going crazy just sitting there, but he wanted to time his exit with hers. Finally, she gathered her belongings and walked in his direction.

"Can I walk out with you?" he asked.

"Sure."

"Did you get a lot done?"

"I think so. Most of my research is done, so now all I have to do is write it."

"Me too," Stephen said, as he gave her a soft smile. "I was wondering if we could study together for the next test in our math class."

"That sounds great," Suzanne said. "I will ask Hannah if she wants to join us."

Irritation ran through Stephen. He wanted to protest and say that he didn't want Hannah to join them. Afraid of any suspicion, Stephen nodded and said, "That sounds great."

"Bye, Stephen."

"I can walk you back to your dorm," Stephen said.

Suzanne hesitated before nodding. "Okay."

As they walked, Stephen asked about her family and where she was from, even though he knew the details. He followed her family when they came to visit. They came the Saturday after he first saw her. Stephen had even made the drive to her hometown and knew her home address. He wanted to pump his fist when she asked about his home. Stephen talked about his dad leaving when he was little and living with his mom. He didn't mention her drinking or ignoring him most of his life.

"Alex's dad also left when he was little," she commented.

Rage filled Stephen at the mention of Alex's name. Without thinking, he reached out and grabbed Suzanne's arm, gripping it tightly in his. Shock filled her face at how hard he was squeezing it. "Sorry," he mumbled, letting it go. "It makes me angry to hear that he struggled like I did." He came up with a lame reason, and he was relieved to see Suzanne's face fill with empathy and understanding. They were at her dorm.

"I will see you tomorrow, Stephen."

"See you," he said, and he rubbed her arm where he squeezed it a moment ago. "Sorry, again. It just brought up some tough feelings."

"I understand," she said. A light filled her face. "You could go to the counseling center and talk to someone. Mark is who Alex sees when he needs a listening ear. He also speaks with his youth pastor from his hometown, but Mark seems to know how to help people."

"I'll look into that. Bye Suzanne." Stephen waved as he stepped away. She didn't see him roll his eyes at the thought of getting help from some stranger.

***

Saturday arrived. Alex and Suzanne went to another movie, but all they did was share kisses. Michael was at the apartment, and Suzanne didn't want to be with Alex while Michael was there. Alex was honest about admitting he hated it when Michael and Hannah were in his room while he was home.

Alex drove to Suzanne's dorm. He saw her standing beside two older adults, and Alex knew it was her parents. Alex blew out a breath before exiting the car. "Here goes," he murmured.

Suzanne's eyes lit up when she noticed Alex. She gestured toward him. "Mom, Dad, this is Alex. We've gone out several times. When I asked him about meeting you, he was fine with it."

Alex shook her dad's hand. Then he smiled at her mom. "It's very nice to meet both of you. Suzanne has become a wonderful friend."

Suzanne shared the evening before about deflecting their relationship. Alex frowned slightly at the idea. When she talked about how overprotective her dad was, Alex agreed. But deep down, he wasn't sure he truly liked the idea. Was Suzanne embarrassed by him? Was he not good enough to appear as her boyfriend?

"Well, Alex, it's nice to meet you," her mom smiled at him. "Suzanne has mentioned you, and we are glad to put a face with the name."

Suzanne's dad remained quiet, but his arm rested around Suzanne's waist.

Suzanne said, "Would you like to come to lunch with us? The girls are coming. We could also invite Michael if that would make you feel better."

Alex felt as if he couldn't say no. "Sure. Michael is at the apartment. I can go ask him and drive him back over here."

Suzanne beamed at Alex. "Great," she said.

Michael agreed to come with them after teasing Alex about meeting her parents. "Shut up," Alex said.

"It must be getting serious," Michael said with a grin on his face.

Alex thought so, but after meeting her parents, many thoughts were racing through his mind.

Suzanne's father pulled into the parking lot of the Mexican restaurant in town. Alex walked around to open Suzanne's door to help her out of the car. Manners were ingrained in him by Pastor Brian and his positive influence on Alex. Alex couldn't help but notice the respect on the face of Suzanne's mom. He blew out an inward breath, thankful to have scored a few points.

Michael and Hannah drove in his car. Jackie, Michelle, and Jessica followed in Jackie's car. Once everyone was seated, the server came and took their drink orders. Another employee brought out chips and salsa. Although their friends were relaxed and laughing, Alex felt the tension in his neck and shoulders. It increased with the many questions Suzanne's parents asked him.

"So, Alex, where did you grow up?"

"Tell us about your family."

"Suzanne tells us you grew up in church. Tell us more about it."

Suzanne rolled her eyes with each question. "Mom, Dad, let Alex enjoy his lunch."

"We're just getting to know him," her mother said.

"You're giving Alex the inquisition, not just getting to know him." Suzanne said.

Alex touched her knee under the table. "Suzanne, it's okay. They can ask me questions."

Alex was pleased to see a small gleam of respect in her father's eyes when he said those words. He cleared his throat and said, "I grew up in a small town about thirty minutes from here. It's called Longfield. My mother is wonderful. She raised me on her own after my father left."

"You don't know your father?" her dad asked.

Alex raised his eyes from the table to glance at Suzanne's father. "No, sir. But my mom is a wonderful lady. She worked hard to give me a wonderful life."

"I'm sure she did," Suzanne's mother said.

Alex's voice sharpened. "She raised me just as you did with Suzanne. My mom took me to church on Sundays, and she disciplined me when I needed it."

"What about your grandparents?" Suzanne's father asked.

"Her parents died when I was young, so I didn't have many years with them. I recall a few memories of riding in my grandpa's truck to get ice cream." Alex's face creased into a smile. "I know my mom loved them, and she misses them." Alex explained about his older siblings. The last thing he said was, "Pastor Brian was my youth pastor. If I ever needed a man to speak with, he was always available. For reasons I don't understand, Pastor Brian took a special liking to me. Probably because I was an obnoxious preteen who needed a male influence."

The group laughed.

Suzanne cleared her throat. "That's enough, Mom and Dad. Alex told you his life story. Let him enjoy lunch."

Suzanne's mother turned questions toward Hannah, Jackie and Michelle.

Suzanne was gazing at Alex with shining eyes. She leaned toward his ear. "Thank you. I know they can be a bit much at times."

Alex grasped Suzanne's hand under the table. "They are looking out for your best interests." Alex hoped his eyes were genuine. He swallowed hard, hoping the small doublets flowing through his mind would dissipate. Thankfully, Suzanne didn't seem to notice.

The rest of their lunch ended on a much lighter note. Suzanne's parents seemed to like Hannah, Jackie, and Michelle. Michael teased him twice. Alex knew he noticed his discomfort. It was Michael's way of showing support.

Chapter 8

Hannah, Suzanne, Michelle and Jackie walked out of the dining hall toward the school gym to watch the guys practice for their upcoming game on Thursday. It had been two weeks since Suzanne had spent the night at Alex's place. The two of them went out twice more, but he dropped her off at the dorm. Suzanne loved the kisses Alex gave her before saying good night, but their busy schedules didn't allow another night at his apartment.

Jackie and Michelle strolled ahead of them as Hannah said, "I saw you walking with Stephen this afternoon."

"He walked me back to the dorm," Suzanne said. Stephen began escorting her back to the dorm after developing a habit of studying separately in the library. Suzanne marveled that Stephen was always there at the same time she was.

Hannah was quiet before she spoke again. "I don't want to come across as a nag, but please be careful with him. I get strange feelings when we are with him. You didn't see, but he frowned when Alex put his arm around you as you walked into lunch today."

"Really? I wonder what that was about." Suzanne frowned slightly. "I think he has some emotional issues. His dad left him when he was little. He talked about it when we walked together. Stephen became so upset that he grabbed my arm the other day. I think the memories were painful for him to talk about."

Hannah stopped and looked at Suzanne. "He touched you?"

"I don't think he meant to. His thoughts focused on his traumatic years of growing up." Suzanne's eyes widened.

"This is the last time I will say it, but please be careful with him. His having touched you like that makes me not want to trust him even more." Hannah gently touched her arm.

"I'm sure everything will be fine," Suzanne said, waving her hand in denial.

They walked through the doors of the gym, and Suzanne's heart jumped at seeing Alex in his practice clothes. He filled out the t-shirt extremely well, and his calf muscles bulged as he ran up and down the basketball court. When Alex turned and spotted her, his face lit up and he waved in her direction.

"Let's sit over here," Michelle said, leading the way to the bleachers behind the bench piled with their gear. She failed to notice Danny's longing glance at her. Suzanne observed it, and she thought about how cute they looked together. She remembered they had their first date, but Michelle didn't share many details about it. Suzanne noted the dreamy expression on Michelle's face, but she said nothing about it.

Fifteen minutes later, the guys took a break. Michael and Alex made a beeline for Hannah and Suzanne. Michael grabbed Hannah and planted a sweaty kiss on her while she giggled. Alex wiped his face with his towel before he leaned, and kissed Suzanne. He was thoughtful enough to make sure his sweat didn't touch her. As he entwined their fingers, he said, "How was your afternoon?"

"It was long, but I finished the research for my paper. Now all I have to do is write the words. What about you?"

"After my last class, I studied for a couple of hours, trying to make sure I am ready for the exam on Friday." Alex smiled down at her as he pushed a stray strand of her hair behind her ear. He leaned in to whisper in her ear. "You're beautiful standing there."

Suzanne blushed. "Thank you. You look great in basketball shorts."

Alex pressed a gentle kiss on her lips, but he lengthened it. Suzanne enjoyed his soft lips. The whistle blew, drawing him back to the present. "Wait for me, okay? I will drive you back."

"Okay," Suzanne whispered as he squeezed her hand. When Suzanne turned, she took note of Danny and Michelle talking together. Michelle was smiling and blushing. Suzanne wanted to pump her fist, but she simply walked back to where the girls were sitting.

***

Two more weeks flew by. Alex and Suzanne dated and spent as much time together as possible with their busy schedules. Fall break drew near, and when they returned, the schedule would be insane as they prepared for the weeks before the end of the semester.

Alex was on the way to pick Suzanne up for dinner. He told her he was taking her somewhere they had never been, and that it was a surprise. Then she was going back to his place. Hannah and Michael were out of town, visiting his hometown.

Alex had his hands shoved in his pockets, gazing at the floor when Suzanne walked from her hallway into the lobby. When he looked up and saw her, desire raced through him. Alex pulled her against him and kissed her hungrily, pleased at the desire on her face. "Shit, you're gorgeous tonight!"

She wore a lovely crimson dress made of velvet. The skirt stopped just above her knees. The way she smiled at Alex gave him the idea that she knew it would make him crazy. It pulled tight over her torso, showing off her curves. The dress flared out into a full skirt.

Suzanne chuckled against his lips. "Thank you. You look amazing, too." He wore a button-down shirt, a navy blazer and dark brown corduroy pants. The weather was cold enough for them to wear winter clothing.

Alex gently took Suzanne's coat, and he held it out for her. Once she pulled it on, he helped pull her long hair out from under it. Suzanne shivered as his lips grazed her neck. "We won't make it to dinner if you keep going like that." She whispered as his mouth traveled up to her ear.

"You bring it out in me," he whispered. She turned to face him, and he kissed her gently before tucking her hand into his elbow and escorting her outside.

The drive took a while. Alex wanted the location to remain a surprise. She gasped in delight as he pulled into the parking lot of a building decorated with twinkle lights. The restaurant sat beside a lake, and the lights sparkled and reflected on the water. "It's so beautiful," she whispered.

Alex lifted her hand to his lips and kissed each finger. He hadn't let go of it the entire drive. "Yes, it is." He gazed at her as he spoke the words. She dipped her head down in embarrassment as he walked around to open her door. Alex never grew tired of seeing the crimson blush creep up her face, knowing he put it there. It gave him a powerful emotion. Alex said, "Michael and Hannah recommended this place. They found it a few weeks back and told me we needed to come here."

The host seated them, and Alex sat beside her in a booth. His arm wrapped around her shoulder, pulling her against him as they gazed at a shared menu. Alex's lips kept kissing her head, her cheek, and her forehead. Suzanne leaned into his arm, and Alex absolutely loved it. Her soft and feminine mannerisms turned him on, and his hands continued to touch her.

Once they placed their order, Alex took her hand with his other one and kissed her fingers again. "The way you look tonight, I can't stop touching you." He mumbled.

Finally, Alex pulled back slightly. He looked at her and said, "Would you like to come and visit me the weekend after Fall Break? I told you I would like you to meet my mom."

"Yes, I would love that."

"You can stay in my room, and I will sleep on the couch," Alex said. His mom's house was small, with only two bedrooms.

"I don't want to put you out of your bed." Alex put a finger to her lips to silence her.

He said, "It will not put me out. The couch has a pull-out bed, and it will be fine for a couple of nights. You can come to church with me and meet Pastor Brian."

Suzanne smiled at him with love. "I would like that."

The server brought out their salads and bread. A few minutes later, their entrees also came out. The two of them talked and relaxed, enjoying the time to catch up. Once they finished dinner and dessert, Alex stood and held out his hand.

Suzanne allowed him to help her out of the booth, and he led her to the small dance floor. A band played soft jazz music. Alex pulled her so closely against him, and they swayed together, eyes closed, caught up in just being together. The two of them danced until their feet hurt.

When Alex pulled out of the parking lot, Suzanne said, "Thank you for this magical evening."

"It's selfish of me." Suzanne's eyes had questions in them as she glanced over at Alex. "But I don't like the thought of not seeing you for an entire week." She chuckled.

"I'm thinking the same thing. I will miss you, too." She squeezed his fingers clasped in hers.

Half an hour later, Alex pulled into his driveway. He helped her out, took her overnight bag in his hand, and he led her into his apartment. The moment he dropped her bag on the floor in his kitchen, he tugged Suzanne in his arms. She pushed into his embrace. Alex walked her into his bedroom and shut his door. The two of them made love several times during the night. It had been a month since they had been together last, and they made up for lost time. They spent all of Saturday together, even going to the library and studying beside each other. Alex ordered pizza. They sat and watched movies, laughing and enjoying the time together. After the movie, Alex turned on soft music and pulled Suzanne up to dance with him again. Half an hour later, he picked her up in his arms, and carried her to his room, where they made love again.

***

Suzanne spent Fall Break with her parents. Many of the days involved traveling to both grandparents' houses. She ate lunch with her grandmother and enjoyed another dinner with her grandparents. She dedicated all of her time to catching up with family. Suzanne didn't realize how much she would miss Alex. They talked on the phone every night, but she counted down the hours until driving to his home on Friday.

She told her parents, and of course, her mother had a million questions. At one point, Suzanne called Alex to introduce her parents to his mother. She understood the phone call comforted her mother, but annoyance filled her.

"Really Mom? Is this necessary?" Suzanne protested against her mother's ridiculous coddling. Suzanne pressed the mute button as she asked the question.

Her mother's face tightened. "Suzanne, it's my job to take care of you. Even at this age."

"Mom! I'm almost nineteen years old! It's time for you to let me decide who I would like to date!" Suzanne wondered if steam came out of her ears at the moment.

"I know your age, Suzanne! But right now, it's like I'm dealing with a five-year-old! You are acting extremely childish!" Her mother shouted at her.

Tears filled Suzanne's eyes. "Maybe it's time for you to trust my judgment. That's why this bothers me. You don't think I can make wise decisions for myself!"

It was the only time Suzanne could remember that the two of them had raised their voices at one another. Now that she was eighteen, her mother couldn't ground Suzanne, but Suzanne sensed she might want to.

Her mother rushed out of the room, covering her mouth with tears in her eyes. Guilt rushed through Suzanne's gut. She owed her mother an apology after she finished talking to Alex. Thankfully, Suzanne pushed the *hold* button and Alex didn't hear their argument.

Suzanne tried to steady her voice. "Sorry about that."

Alex whispered, "It's okay. I miss you so much."

"Me too," she answered. "This week has gone by so slowly."

Suzanne recalled the previous weekend they had spent together. Falling asleep in Alex's arms comforted Suzanne. He was so gentle with her. For the millionth time, she thought about how his treatment of her differed from anything she'd ever experienced. Alex treated her like a princess, and she fell deeper in love with him. Suzanne wished she had more experience with boys and dating. She understood her innocence as a weakness, and Suzanne always thought about how she wished she knew more about love and sex. Her parents thought they were protecting her, but it made everything worse that they didn't teach her how to navigate her life in this area.

"I agree. What time are you leaving on Friday?" Alex's voice brought her out of her daydream.

"Around nine." The drive took an hour from Suzanne's hometown. "I will be there at ten."

"Baby, I can't wait to see you. I've missed your beautiful face!" Relief filled Suzanne that he didn't see her blush over the phone. She wondered if they remained together for twenty years, if she would react this way to the words he spoke to her.

"I've missed you, too. I can't wait to get there."

When Suzanne moved back into the kitchen, her mother sat at the table. "Honey, please wait. I want to talk to you."

Suzanne rolled her eyes. "What is it, Mom?"

"Don't roll your eyes at me, young lady. I'm your mother, and I am allowed to ask you questions," she snapped.

"Mom, I realize this has to do with Alex and my going to his house," Suzanne said, looking into her mom's face. "I can see from your face that I am right."

Suzanne's mother touched her arm. "I'm sure it seems as if we are overprotective, but it is our job to keep you safe. It was lovely talking to Alex's mom, but I want a few more details. Where will you sleep when you're at his house?"

Suzanne refrained from rolling her eyes. She sighed. "Alex said I can sleep in his room. He will sleep on the pullout couch in the living room."

Her mom nodded. "Okay, that sounds acceptable. I also need you to write the address and phone number where he and his mother live."

"Mom, I'm sorry for yelling at you. It was childish. I just want you to recognize that I am almost nineteen years old. But I don't think you need to know every single detail."

Her mother pulled her into a hug. "I'm sorry, too. It's difficult for us to let you go, but it's time to allow you room to decide for yourself."

Suzanne leaned back. "Thank you for caring about me so much. When I look back, I will be thankful for it someday."

Her mother touched Suzanne's cheek. "Can I please get the address and phone number before you forget?"

Suzanne sighed again, "I will get the address and phone number in my book upstairs."

Suzanne trudged up the steps, making sure her mother didn't see the rolling of her eyes this time.

***

Suzanne smiled as she pulled into Alex's driveway. The house where he and his mother lived was adorable. Her eyes lit up when she saw him open the door inside of his carport and walk outside.

The minute she stepped out of her car, Alex was beside her. He pulled her into a tight hug.

"Hey gorgeous," he murmured against her hair. Alex pulled back, but he didn't give Suzanne an opportunity to respond before he touched his lips to hers.

Breathless, Suzanne said, "Hi," before Alex kissed her a second time. She didn't complain as the desire for him filled her core. When Suzanne realized where she was, she leaned away from him. "I don't think it's appropriate to be making out in your mom's driveway." She glanced down shyly.

"She's in the back of the house, making sure my room is clean." Alex tipped her chin up to him as he caressed Suzanne's face. He gazed at her adoringly.

"I promise she doesn't need to go to a lot of trouble because she doesn't have many days off."

Alex kissed her nose and smiled. "My mom is excited to meet you, and she wants everything to be just right for when you are here."

Suzanne opened the back door of her sedan, and she pulled out her overnight bag. She also had her suitcase because the plan was for her and Alex to return to school on Sunday afternoon.

Alex gently removed it from her hand. Then he pulled her suitcase out and carried it into a lovely kitchen. A raised window blew a gentle breeze because of the mile weather. Suzanne noted a neatly kept yard with a birdbath in a lovely flowerbed that bordered the back fence. Flowers were placed in the center of a new-looking table, with lovely placemats in front of each seat.

Suzanne turned to see Alex watching her. His expression was guarded, and she noticed his nervousness about her seeing his house. "I love your house."

"It's not big," he said.

"I don't care about that. It's so neat and clean. I can see the backyard is so nicely kept with the birdbath."

Unable to stop himself, Alex pulled Suzanne into a hug with a grateful expression in his eyes. "Thank you. In the spring, Mom has flowers planted in every corner of the yard."

"Hello." A lovely woman entered the kitchen. She had brown curly hair that had been permed, and Alex had her deep brown eyes. She also wore a beautiful smile.

"Mom, this is Suzanne." Alex wrapped an arm around Suzanne's waist.

"Hello, Suzanne. I'm Tammy Fleming. It's so nice to meet you. I can see why Alex doesn't stop talking about you." Suzanne giggled as Alex murmured, "Mom," under his breath.

Suzanne's eyes turned teasing as she looked at Alex. "He can't stop talking about me, huh?"

Alex's mom laughed along with her. "I promise it's all been good things."

"I love your home," Suzanne said.

Tammy gazed around. "It's not much, but it works for the two of us." Her eyes filled with warmth when she looked back at Suzanne.

"Well, you've done a wonderful job turning it into your home."

"Thank you, sweetheart. I can see why Alex cares for you so much." Tammy gently hugged Suzanne, and her heart melted at his mom's acceptance of her so quickly. When Alex's mom pulled back, she said, "Alex's room is all ready for you."

Alex picked up Suzanne's bags and led the way down a short hallway. Suzanne smiled when she entered. He decorated his room with Star Wars posters and with rock band posters, similar to his apartment.

Suzanne turned toward Alex. "This looks like your room."

Alex's mom laughed. "My son is rather predictable in his room decorations."

"Okay, okay," Alex murmured in embarrassment, but he exchanged a deep look with Suzanne. She knew he would pay her back later for her teasing. Her stomach flip-flopped as she anticipated what he might do to her.

"I have to work tonight," Alex's mom said. "But I have a casserole ready to put in the oven for dinner before I have to go."

"That sounds wonderful."

"Well, I will let you get settled. I have some other chores to get done before I go."

"Thank you for having me, Mrs. Fleming." Suzanne said.

"Please call me Tammy," Alex's mom said with a smile as she exited the room.

Alex sat on his bed as Suzanne unpacked a few things, including her dress for church on Sunday.

Suzanne admired him as he laid back against his pillows. She had missed him more than she could even say. The time with her family had been wonderful, but Alex was such a part of her now that her heart ached the entire time she was at home. The way he looked at her made her wonder what was actually going through his mind. Suzanne turned her back as paranoia overtook her thoughts. She pulled her clothing out in a neat stack before turning to place it on the chair across from the bed. Suzanne could not stop her eyes as they drifted toward Alex a second time.

Alex caught her staring at him, and he grinned slowly in his sexy way. "Why are you staring at me?"

"I just missed you."

"Well, come here." Alex grabbed Suzanne's hand, pulling her so that she stumbled and fell on top of him.

"Alex, I'm not sure this is appropriate with your mother at home."

Alex silenced her protest with a deep kiss, and then he pulled away. "Until tonight, then.. The look in his eyes filled with promise causing Suzanne's gut to somersault. Alex's eyes narrowed, and he had an impish look on his face. Before Suzanne moved away, he tackled her and tickled her, causing her to gasp and squeal. As much as she tried to wrestle free, Alex had her pinned down on his mattress and somehow he wound up above her. "That's for earlier with my mom." His eyes became serious as he gazed at Suzanne. Her heavy breaths were causing her chest to rise and fall. His eyes drifted down her torso. Suzanne's eyes were filled with longing, but she whispered, "Your mom."

Alex nodded, and he stood up, reluctantly. Holding out his hand to Suzanne, he helped her to her feet. Alex kissed her gently before saying, "Come on. I will drive you around my little town."

"I would love that." Suzanne grinned at him, happy to be here with him.

He entwined their fingers and called out, "Mom, I'm going to drive Suzanne around. We will be back in a little while."

"Okay." His mom stepped out from her bedroom with a basket of clothes in her hand. "Dinner is at six."

"Bye, Tammy," Suzanne called, and she almost choked at saying her name. It would definitely take some time to get used to it. Suzanne came from a generation of adults where she was trained to call them *Mr.* or *Mrs.* Her mother would be appalled to hear Suzanne call Alex's mom by her first name. Shrugging off the negative thought, Suzanne thought, *I'm growing up, so Mom needs to understand.*

Alex drove Suzanne by all the schools he attended from elementary grades up through high school. He drove her to his church, but Pastor Brian's car was not in the parking lot. "We will see him on Sunday. He went out of town with his family to Dallas for a few days."

"I'm so happy I can meet him," Suzanne said as Alex smiled at her, squeezing her hand.

Alex stopped by a video rental store so that they could choose a couple of movies for the weekend. He pretended to gag when Suzanne picked a romantic film. She mimicked him when he chose an action movie. Suzanne didn't care because they were happy to just be together. Alex drove them back to his house with an hour to spare before dinner.

Tammy was in the kitchen sliding a delicious-looking casserole into the oven. "Just in time. This takes about forty five minutes to cook."

Suzanne stepped forward. "Can we help in any way?"

"Thank you, sweetheart. Maybe around five thirty, you can help make the salad."

"Yes, ma'am, I will be happy to help."

Alex tugged her hand into the living room. "Do you want anything to drink?"

"I wouldn't mind some water."

"Coming right up. I will find a snack for us as well."

When Alex returned with the drinks and some chips, he grabbed the remote control from the coffee table and flipped it on, scrolling through the channels. A classic movie was playing, so he put down the remote to watch it.

His mom had gone into her room to get ready to go to her shift at work that evening. Alex wrapped his arm around Suzanne, pulling her close. She snuggled against him in the way he loved, and his arm tightened. Suzanne started to get drowsy as Alex's fingers were softly sifting through her hair. She felt completely relaxed, and she wound up dozing on his chest for a few moments.

Suzanne awoke to Alex's mom calling him into the kitchen. She was shocked that thirty minutes had passed. As Suzanne followed him into the kitchen, she noticed the makings for the salad on the counter beside the refrigerator. His mom also set out a bowl, and Suzanne began chopping lettuce and vegetables to go into the salad.

Ten minutes later, the three of them set the table and sat to enjoy the delicious taco casserole that his mother had made.

"Tell me more about your family, Suzanne."

Suzanne talked about her parents and how she was an only child. She also told her about both sets of grandparents living nearby.

"That must be wonderful," Tammy commented. "You and Alex are similar in that he is almost like an only child. My older sons have lived on their own for about ten years. It's just been Alex and me for that time together. He spent a few years with my parents, but they both passed away in a car accident."

"I'm so sorry," Suzanne said. Tammy touched her hand.

"Thank you, sweetheart," she said.

"I would have loved having a brother or sister," Suzanne commented, feeling the normal tightness that came on when she thought about it. She smiled at Alex and said, "Do you see your brothers very much?"

Alex explained they spent holidays together, but that was about it. His brothers lived in the Dallas area, where one worked at a large accounting firm and the other one worked for an airline company. Alex's expression was closed off as before when she first saw his house.

Suzanne relaxed and thoroughly enjoyed her time with Alex's mom. The dinner was delicious, and she welcomed Suzanne. Suzanne insisted that she and Alex wash the dishes so that his mom could rest for a few more minutes before heading out to work. She covered shifts at a diner as her second job. Suzanne had a significant amount of respect for how hard she worked. She was a secretary for an attorney's office during the week, and she worked at the diner four nights a week (mostly on the weekends). Suzanne knew that Alex's part-time jobs in high school had also helped. His mom didn't want him to work during college so that he could focus on his classes and maintain good grades. It was clear she adored her son, and that he also loved his mother.

***

Twenty minutes later, Alex's mom waved goodbye as she walked out, got into her car, and drove away.

"Finally," Alex murmured as he drew Suzanne into his arms and kissed her passionately, excited that he had a few hours of Suzanne to himself. Suzanne enthusiastically returned his kiss. Alex pushed her back onto the couch while continuing to kiss her. His hands caressed the hair back from her face as he peppered kisses all over her face and down her neck. Suzanne was gasping with pleasure everywhere his lips touched her.

Alex moaned at her responsiveness. He moved her hair back away from her neck so that he could feast on it with his lips and tongue. "I've been looking forward to this all week. I knew my mom had to work tonight, and I couldn't stop thinking about being with you." As he spoke, his lips feathered across her cheek and down her neck. Alex loved the silkiness of her skin.

"Oh, my," she whispered again. Then she turned the tables on him, shoving her hands up under his shirt. Her eyes darkened when he gasped. Suzanne's fingers trailed up to his chest and back down to his waistband.

Alex pulled back, and his eyes were heavy with desire. "Do you want to go to my room?"

Unable to speak, Suzanne nodded. Alex lifted Suzanne, wrapping her legs around his waist. Alex grasped her rear, caressing it. Alex shut his door and locked it before kissing Suzanne again as his hands slid up under the sweatshirt she was wearing.

He reveled in her soft skin. As his fingers traveled over her stomach and up to her breasts, she was inhaling and exhaling loudly. "Oh, my."

Alex walked them to his bed and fell on top of her. As he did, he shoved her sweatshirt up and over her head. Alex gazed at her in her bra, he never tired of seeing her like this. Alex didn't think he would ever grow weary of seeing her beauty. She was not vain, and that turned him on even more.

After removing the rest of their clothing, Alex pulled a condom from his bedside drawer. He set it beside him on the table. Alex pulled Suzanne's breast into his mouth, and he sucked on it. She gasped and arched her back as he moved to the other breast.

Suzanne's hands traveled down to his torso, and she gripped him, caressing him in the way he loved. It was hard for him to remove his hands from Suzanne, but he shredded the wrapper of the condom. Suzanne helped him roll it onto his length, and Alex closed his eyes in pleasure.

When he pushed inside of her, Alex paused. He groaned from the sensation washing over him. All he knew was their connection was stronger than ever when he was making love to her. Before beginning to move, Alex took a moment to kiss Suzanne deeply. He lapped at her breasts, making the nipples as tight as possible before beginning to move inside of her.

Suzanne thrashed and moaned in ecstasy.

Their time of making love was a beautiful expression of their feelings for one another. Once they finished, Alex held Suzanne close and whispered, "I love you."

"Oh, Alex, I love you, too."

As much as Alex would have loved to stay in his bed with Suzanne all evening, he knew it was probably not a good idea. Alex suggested they get dressed and watch a movie. They relaxed on his couch in a tight embrace as he enjoyed the romance film that she had chosen. Alex embraced her from behind, so he spent plenty of time nuzzling her neck and ear. At one point, he reached down and kissed her tenderly because he could see the goosebumps standing on her arms.

***

She visited his house. Suzanne was spending the weekend with that scumbag, Alex.

Stephen pounded on the steering wheel, growling with narrowed eyes. He tried so hard to be patient and get to know Suzanne. His original plan wasn't working. His plan needed revision.

Stephen spent a day watching Suzanne's house, so he was there when she loaded her car and drove to Alex's home. Suzanne never knew he followed her. Stephen knew to stay several cars behind.

Thankfully, there wasn't any awareness on her part. He could use her naivety to his advantage. A sinister smile filled his face as he thought about knowing where she was. One day, she would thank him. He was like her guardian angel. Once she was truly his, she would be so grateful for his constant protection of her and the sacrifices he was making for her.

However, he needed to deepen their friendship. As he did, he would plant seeds of doubt in her mind about her jerk of a boyfriend. Stephen kept his car several lengths behind hers. Stephen stayed behind her until she pulled into Alex's driveway. He drove past Alex's house and turned back toward where he had come from. As he started his drive back to his home, he formed a plan of what he could do to get Suzanne away from Alex permanently.

Chapter 9

The weekend flew by quickly, and it was Saturday evening. Alex's mother took them out for dinner before her shift that evening. She worked early hours on Saturday evenings in order to rest up for church on Sundays. So the meal was actually in between lunch and supper.

Suzanne fell deeper in love with Alex from the time spent with him and his mother over the weekend. The two of them drove to the mall on Saturday, enjoying some shopping and being together. Suzanne found early Christmas gifts for both of her parents, and he found something for his mom.

The two of them made love again on Saturday evening after his mother left for work again. Afterward, they watched the action movie Alex chose while wrapped in each other's arms. Alex and Suzanne realized that the time back at school would be scarce, as Thanksgiving was quickly approaching. After that, the semester would wrap up as they completed projects and final exams.

Suzanne turned to Alex after the movie ended. "Would you like to come and visit my home over Thanksgiving break? I talked to my parents about it, and they are fine if you can make it." Uncertainty flew through her at the thought of him saying no. Part of her wished to withdraw the question.

Alex's eyes softened, and Suzanne breathed an inward sigh of relief. "Baby, I would love that. But only if you agree to come see me during Christmas break."

The smile in Suzanne's eyes made Alex lay her back against the couch, and he twisted until they were lying face to face. They spent fifteen minutes making out before Alex sat up and suggested they find something else on television.

***

On Sunday morning, Alex, Suzanne, and his mother made the short drive to their church. As soon as Alex parked the car, his mother waved goodbye as she walked toward her Sunday school class.

Alex wove their fingers together, and he pulled Suzanne closer to him as they walked into the youth and college building.

Suzanne noticed a very good-looking gentleman over to the side as they entered. The man's eyes lit up when he saw Alex, and he made a beeline over to shake Alex's hand.

"Pastor Brian, I want you to meet Suzanne Marks, my girlfriend."

"I guess this is the reason you haven't visited in a while." Pastor Brian's eyes twinkled as he took Suzanne's hand into both of his, and she couldn't control the blush creeping up her neck to her face. "It's very nice to meet you, Suzanne. Welcome to our church."

"Thank you. It's wonderful to meet you. Alex has told me so much about you."

The three of them talked and visited for a few moments before someone called Alex's name. A female someone.

As Suzanne turned, she spotted a gorgeous blond girl walking toward them, her eyes only on Alex. Jealousy shot through her, and

Suzanne didn't realize she had stepped back until Kayla leaned in to hug Alex.

"Hi Kayla! It's wonderful to see you!" Alex said as he returned her hug.

"You haven't called me in such a long time, you goober! How are you?" Suzanne stood awkwardly to the side.

Alex's eyes widened, and he gently tugged Suzanne back toward his side. "Kayla, I would like you to meet Suzanne Marks, my girlfriend." When he glanced at Suzanne, he said, "Suzanne, this is Kayla Bradford, an old friend."

Kayla's eyes shone with friendliness. "It's nice to meet you, Suzanne." She fixed her eyes back on Alex. "That explains why I haven't seen you in so long. I didn't realize you were dating anyone." Teasing sparkled in Kayla's eyes.

Suzanne whispered. "It's nice to meet you, Kayla." But it seemed she was invisible at the moment. Her old awkwardness returned in a flash.

Alex laughed in his easy-going manner. "So sorry to keep you in the dark, dear Kayla. I didn't realize you needed to know my every waking move."

Kayla chuckled as she grinned at Suzanne. "Where are you from, Suzanne?" Suzanne answered in a shy voice. At the moment, she couldn't comprehend her unpleasant emotions. It was almost as if she had intruded on their moment together. Suzanne gritted her teeth at her ridiculous reaction. Kayla was showing nothing but friendliness toward her.

Someone called Kayla's name, and she said, "It's nice to meet you, Suzanne. We need to get together so that I can give you tons of blackmail information about Alex." Kayla glared at Alex, and Suzanne giggled.

"I would love that," Suzanne said.

"Alex, call me soon!" Kayla dashed over to the group of friends in the back of the room.

"Will do," Alex called as Pastor Brian cleared his throat.

As they walked to some chairs, Suzanne asked, "Is she an old girlfriend?" Inwardly, she admonished herself for sticking her foot in her mouth with that comment. Suzanne observed clearly that Kayla saw Alex as a friend.

"Who, Kayla?" Alex asked. "No, we're just old friends."

Suzanne looked over to see Kayla deep in a conversation with another guy. "Well, that's a relief," Suzanne said as Alex entwined their fingers together.

He leaned toward Suzanne. "You're not jealous, are you?" Alex's eyes had a dangerous glint in them.

"Why on earth would I be?" Suzanne asked, waving her hand at him. "And I would love to learn juicy information about you." Suzanne's eyes flashed flirtatiously. Her chest expanded when Alex's eyes darkened toward her.

Pastor Brian chuckled. "I like her, Alex. Don't let her get away from you." He pointed at Suzanne and said, "Hopefully, Alex won't drive you too crazy."

Suzanne chuckled as Alex led them to seats at the front of the room for their class to begin.

***

After church, Alex's mother cooked a spaghetti lunch that was absolutely wonderful. Suzanne commented over and over about how good it was. She said she was stuffed and probably would not eat any dinner once she got back to school. Her plan was to get ahead in studying for their upcoming midterm exams. She and Alex had already discussed the need to work that evening.

Both of them were dreading the upcoming separation for Thanksgiving, but neither of them approached the topic. Plans were made to visit each other during those times. Alex breathed a sigh of relief that they would go too long without seeing one another. He did not know how to navigate a long-distance relationship, but Alex wanted to try with Suzanne.

The two of them talked about spending the next few weekends together. They decided that even if it was cheap and just hanging out together, they would make the most of their time left. Alex planned to surprise Suzanne with dinner at the lovely restaurant by the lake where they visited before fall break.

Alex learned that making love to Suzanne was like a drug to him. She was completely addictive. He planned to have her stay with him at least once more before Thanksgiving. However, if she wanted to focus on her studies, Alex would respect her and wait until they would be together again.

Alex helped Suzanne carry her bags to her car. He walked back to his mother and pulled her into a hug. "Bye, Mom."

"Call me when you get back," his mom said.

Alex nodded, and she hugged him tightly one more time before pulling Suzanne in for a warm hug as well.

"Thank you so much for inviting me. I had a wonderful time." Suzanne smiled at Alex's mom.

"You are welcome to come back and visit anytime, sweetheart."

After commenting on it several times, Alex's heart soared at how Suzanne had fallen completely in love with his mother. He hoped that if the two of them continued to date, they would develop a close relationship.

Alex walked her to her car and held the driver's door open for her. "Follow behind me."

Suzanne nodded, and she touched her hand to her lips to blow him a kiss. Alex pretended to catch it against his own hand, causing Suzanne to giggle at his silliness. His mom stood in the carport as they pulled out. When he stopped his car to wait for Suzanne to pull out, he observed Suzanne waving vigorously. His love for her deepened from that moment.

Thirty minutes later, Alex pulled into the parking place beside where Suzanne parked her car. He smiled at her gently as he helped take her bags out of her back seat. Alex placed them on the ground, and he pulled Suzanne into his arms. As Alex gazed into her gorgeous eyes, he said, "I'm going to miss you."

Suzanne laughed. "You will see me tomorrow morning."

"It won't be the same as being at my house with me."

Her eyes quickly became serious as she thought about how quickly the three weeks would fly by. "I know."

Alex pulled her into his arms, and he put all of his feelings into his kiss. Suzanne returned it, causing him to pull her even tighter against him. She didn't open her eyes when he pulled back. As Alex caressed her cheek with warmth in his gaze, she opened her eyes. "I love you, Suzanne Marks."

"I love you too, Alex Fleming. Thank you for inviting me to your home. I loved learning about you, and I love your mom."

"If I call you before bed, will that give you enough time to study?"

"Yes," she moved to say more, but Alex leaned in to kiss her, stopping the words she was going to say.

"Bye, gorgeous."

"Goodbye, and don't forget to call your mom," she whispered. Then she picked up her backpack, her suitcase, and walked inside the dorm.

Alex stood and watched her before moving back to his car to drive back to his apartment. Michael was lounging in the living room when he walked inside.

"Hey man, how was your fall break?" Michael asked.

Alex fist-bumped him before saying, "It was wonderful. How was yours?"

"Good," Michael shook his head, "but I missed Hannah more than I thought I would."

"I get it, man. The thought of being separated from Suzanne for Thanksgiving and then two weeks of Christmas is killing me. She came to see me on Friday, and it wasn't so bad for this break." Alex walked his bag into his room and returned to slump in the chair as his roommate surfed channels. Michael stopped when he came across a football game.

"Hannah is driving up to my house before she comes for the month-long January session. But I get it. Separation is difficult from the one you love."

"We've made plans to visit each other as well. Suzanne invited me to come to her home."

"Why do you sound so worried?" Michael asked. "I would think that would make you happy."

"I'm not sure," Alex murmured as he stared into space. "Her family is perfect. I'm afraid her parents won't like me and where I come from. You saw how they questioned me when they came for lunch a while back."

"I thought the same thing when I first traveled home with Hannah. But it worked out, and I really like her parents. Maybe it will be the same for you. If it makes you feel any better, Hannah's dad asked me a million questions as well."

Alex was listening. The doubts continued to rush through him. Alex watched Suzanne when she first arrived. She was lovely in her compliments, but he wondered how small and drab his home looked compared to the house she grew up in. Alex had not been to her home, but he was certain it was larger than his. "I hope so. Well, I need to get some homework done. I think I'm heading to the library."

Michael continued lounging as he said, "I'm waiting until tomorrow. I will probably study a little before bed."

***

He smiled as he watched Suzanne walk into her dorm. As he stood behind a tree so as not to be seen, Stephen finally had a plan in place. Hopefully, her stupid friend Hannah wouldn't interfere. It would start with a phone call this evening. Stephen sat in the parking lot of a truck stop on the edge of town, waiting until Suzanne's car entered back into town. He ignored Alex's car, which was right in front of her, as he followed behind her all the way to her dorm.

As he walked back to his car and drove home, Stephen pondered his plan again. He wanted to sound desperate and in need of major help with their foundations class and the project they were having to complete. He understood what a soft heart Suzanne had. All it would take was sounding worried, and he knew she would offer to help him. That was why he knew Suzanne was supposed to be his girlfriend. He knew everything she did, and he was learning the way her mind worked.

Two hours later, he dialed her number. It rang four times, and Stephen wondered if she had left without him knowing.

"Hello," Suzanne sounded rushed.

"Suzanne, this is Stephen."

"Oh, hi, Stephen. How was your fall break?"

"It was boring-just my mom and me," Stephen said. "We did nothing."

"Well, I'm glad you got to spend it with her." Stephen sensed that she was about to cut off their conversation, so he interrupted before she could hang up on him. Irritation filled him at how complacent she sounded during this phone call. It was something he would change when they were together. If Stephen was going to take care of Suzanne's every need, the least she could do was listen when he wanted to talk.

"Listen, I know we just got back, but I'm really struggling with the project for our foundations class."

"Yeah, I just spent two hours working on that."

"I'm afraid that I'm going to fail it. I just can't seem to get my research right." Stephen moaned as if he truly cared.

"Do you want some help with it? I can meet you after lunch tomorrow."

"Would you mind, Suzanne?"

"I would be happy to help you out."

"Great. Also, I don't want to sound weird, but can it just be the two of us tomorrow? I know sometimes Hannah comes with us to work, but I'm kind of embarrassed about this and would rather that everyone in class not find out my business."

"I understand. Yes, I will meet you at one, and we can work for a few hours."

"Thanks, Suzanne."

"You're welcome, Stephen," Suzanne said, and then she ended the call.

***

Alex dialed Suzanne's number. Even though they had just spent a weekend together, he missed hearing her voice. Alex frowned when he got a busy signal. He hung up and called two more times.

"Suzanne?" Alex asked, feeling the temperature rising within him. "Where on earth have you been? I've been calling, and it's been busy for ten minutes."

"I'm sorry, Alex. Stephen called, and he wanted help with the project we are working on. I plan to meet him tomorrow."

"Oh," Alex said. "How long are you working with him tomorrow? I wanted us to hang out for a while before dinner, maybe play some ping-pong or something." Alex tapped his fingers on his bedside table.

"That sounds like so much fun, but I promised Stephen I would help him."

"I guess he's more important than your boyfriend," Alex said, with a sharpness in his tone.

Suzanne said nothing. She lowered her voice. "Alex. He asked for my help. What did you want me to do? You never mentioned hanging out tomorrow."

"Suzanne, we do it all the time, so I didn't realize I would need to squeeze myself into your schedule." Alex's voice rose in volume to match the heat rushing through him.

"Alex! What is wrong with you? I'm helping a classmate who asked for some help."

Alex raised his voice louder. "I just assumed we would hang out like we do every Monday! You realize we won't have much time together before Thanksgiving."

"You know what? I don't want to be with you if you're only going to yell at me," Suzanne retorted.

"I guess we won't. Go be with this other guy!"

"Fine, I will. And you can forget about my coming to your game tomorrow night!"

"Suzanne..." Alex began, but she interrupted.

"I need to go. Good night, Alex!" Alex heard tears in her voice as she slammed the phone down on its base. Alex winced at the loud ring that reverberated in his right ear.

Alex growled as he dialed Suzanne's room number again. Jessica said, "Hello."

"Hey Jessica," Alex tempered his voice. "Is Suzanne still in there?"

"Let me check." Alex listened as Jessica knocked on a door, probably the bathroom. Suzanne, the phone is for you." Jessica said. She must have just come into the room since Suzanne hung up with Alex.

"Who is it?" Suzanne asked.

"Oh boy," Jessica said. "It's Alex, but I'm guessing he messed up, based on your expression. He must have done something boneheaded."

Alex rolled his eyes. The girls didn't seem to care that he eavesdropped on their conversation.

"I don't want to talk to him," Suzanne said. "Tell him that."

"Suzanne..." Alex tried calling through the phone, but Jessica was ignoring him.

Jessica whispered softly to Suzanne, so Alex didn't hear the words.

"Jessica," Alex said. "Jessica..." he repeated.

"Yes?" Jessica answered.

"I need you to tell Suzanne that I'm coming over there if she won't talk to me," Alex said.

"Just a minute," Jessica said. Alex listened as she told Suzanne what he said. "Alex, I'm not sure what you did to upset my roommate, but let me warn you. Do not continue being a jerk. Do you hear me?"

Alex rolled his eyes. "Yes, I hear you." Even though her words aggravated Alex, he was thankful Suzanne had such a good friend in Jessica. "And I changed my mind. Please tell Suzanne I'm on the way over there." Alex hung up the phone before either girl could protest.

When Suzanne hung up on him, Alex realized he had screwed up big time. Why did he overreact and get so angry? Alex blew out a breath, knowing that he wouldn't be able to sleep until he worked this out with Suzanne. Alex pulled on some sweatpants and a sweatshirt. He glanced at his watch, and saw it was late. But he needed to apologize and fix things with Suzanne immediately. He dashed to his car and drove to her dorm.

A few moments later, Suzanne walked out of the hallway where her room was located. Alex saw the look on her face, and shame washed over him a second time for becoming so angry with her. He grabbed her hand to walk outside, and he felt a sting of rejection when she pulled it away. Instead, she folded her arms across her chest as she followed him outside. Alex led the way to a bench in front of the dorm.

"Suzanne, I'm really sorry. I realize I overreacted to your plan to help Stephen with his project tomorrow."

Suzanne didn't answer. She kept looking at her feet.

Alex gently touched her arm, but she wrenched it away. "Baby, I didn't mean to get so mad on the phone. Please forgive me?"

"Why did you get so angry and yell at me?" Suzanne finally asked, keeping her arms folded over her chest.

Alex looked down at his feet. "I'm not sure. I guess because we have so little time together before we are separated for Thanksgiving week. Then we have only three weeks before the Christmas break. I don't like the idea of being apart from you, so I guess I wanted to take advantage of every second with you."

Suzanne glanced at him. Her eyes softened. "I'm not excited about that either. But we both know we're going to have to get our assignments completed. It's going to be crazy."

Alex looked at her with humility on his face. "I understand. It could just as easily have been me needing time. I'm sorry, baby."

"You've never yelled at me like that before. It scared me how angry you got." Alex hated the uncertainty he heard in her voice.

"Suzanne, I'm really sorry that I scared you. To tell you the truth, I have a temper. I've spoken to Mark about it a little, but I can see that I need to work on it some more."

Suzanne studied Alex's face. "I just don't want to always be the one you become angry with. Alex, now that we're in a relationship, we're going to disagree sometimes. But the way you spoke to me was so hurtful."

"I know, and I am sorry. I couldn't go to sleep knowing how I spoke to you." Alex took her hand again, and this time she didn't pull away. "Will you forgive me if I promise to schedule a meeting with Mark at the counseling center?"

"Of course I will."

Alex dipped his head to smile into Suzanne's eyes. "Can we kiss and make up now? I hear that's the best part of an argument."

Suzanne chuckled as she allowed Alex to pull her into his arms. She snuggled against him, resting her face against his chest. Alex loved how small she was because he could bury his face in her neck as she cuddled against him.

As Suzanne leaned back, Alex gazed at her without speaking. One of his hands cradled her face, and his fingers feathered along her cheek. He leaned forward and kissed her softly. Alex made sure that his kiss was filled with how sorry he was that he had behaved like such an ass. He deepened the kiss and urged Suzanne's mouth open. As she did, his tongue dove in, and it caressed hers. Suzanne gasped with pleasure as she returned his kiss. By the time he pulled back, she was practically sitting on his lap. Alex continued to hold her tightly, not letting her move away.

Alex smiled at her and said, "Thank you for forgiving me."

Suzanne smiled back. "You're right. Making up was the best part of fighting."

Alex laughed as he kissed her once more before putting his lips against her forehead. He walked her back to the dorm, and they embraced a last time before he said, "Good night, beautiful. I love you."

"I love you, too." Suzanne kissed him before she walked inside.

Chapter 10

Alex treated Suzanne wonderfully after their argument the night before. Suzanne's heart skipped with love when he offered to carry her backpack to her next class for her. As they walked, she said, "I can make it to your game tonight. Stephen and I should be finished by four this afternoon."

Alex bent down to kiss the hand he was holding. "Thank you, beautiful."

Suzanne didn't stop her smile from how he made her feel at the moment. "Can I ride with you back to the dorm tonight?"

"I planned to ask you, so the answer is yes."

"Thank you for carrying my backpack," Suzanne smiled into his eyes.

Alex kissed her softly. "Anything for my girl."

Suzanne took her bag and placed it evenly on both shoulders with Alex's help. "I will see you later."

Alex touched her lips a final time. "I love you, Suzanne."

"I love you, Alex."

When Suzanne walked into class, she noticed Stephen wasn't there. He usually arrived before her. She pursed her brow and wondered if he still needed her help. Irritation filled her as she thought about how she cancelled plans with Alex to help him. He should have called her to tell her he wouldn't be in class today. Suzanne wondered if something happened at the last minute. Her thoughts halted as she noticed Hannah walking into class.

"Hey friend," Hannah moved to sit beside her.

"Hi." Suzanne smiled at her friend.

"I'm glad we are having a few minutes. It's been busy since coming back from fall break. I feel like I haven't talked to you at all."

"I know," Suzanne agreed. "It will get even crazier, I'm afraid."

"Do you want to study together this afternoon?"

Suzanne paused, wanting to include Hannah. But she remembered Stephen's request not to ask Hannah to join them. However, he wasn't here at the moment.

"I promised Stephen that I would help him at the library, but he's not here today."

Hannah stayed quiet. "Just the two of you?"

Suzanne frowned. "Yes, he called me and told me he was having trouble with the project. I promised to help him."

"I'm glad he's not here today," Hannah said. "You know I've told you that there's something weird about him. And I just don't trust him."

Suzanne shook her head in annoyance. "Well, I guess you don't need to worry about it since he isn't here."

The two girls talked until the professor arrived. Both of them were rule followers, so they focused and took part in the discussion for the day.

When Suzanne walked out of the class an hour later, surprise filled her upon noticing Alex waiting by the building. "What are you doing?"

Alex gently took her backpack while saying, "I decided that I'm going to take advantage of every minute that I can with you. I know we have crazy schedules, but I can at least come and walk with you."

Suzanne reached up and kissed him, surprising both herself and Alex. He returned her kiss. "Stephen wasn't in class today, so I'm not sure if he needs my help at all anymore."

Alex frowned. "That's strange. He called to ask for your help, and he didn't even show up to class today."

"Yes. But I'm thinking something must have come up."

"Do you want to grab some lunch?" Alex asked.

Suzanne grinned and teased, "I would love to have lunch with you." She batted her eyelashes at Alex.

Suzanne could tell that Alex was aroused by her flirting because he pulled her into a dark corner of the student center. He pulled her tightly against him to kiss her.

"Wow!" Suzanne said when she came up for air. "What was that for?"

Alex rubbed his nose against hers. "It's because we're still making up from last night. And I love you." He kissed her tenderly again.

Suzanne caressed his face. "I love you so much."

Alex entwined their fingers, and he pulled Suzanne close before they walked into the dining hall. As soon as they got inside, she saw Stephen over on the other side of the dining hall.

"Stephen is here. Will you give me a minute to ask him if he still needs help today?"

Alex frowned when he spied Stephen. "He's at lunch, but he wasn't in class? That seems weird."

"I agree," Suzanne said. "Give me a minute to talk to him."

Alex promised to wait for her before going through the line. He walked to their seats and placed their bookbags on each of the chairs.

Once Suzanne reached Stephen, she said, "Stephen, I noticed you weren't in class today. Do you still need my help?"

Stephen's eyes widened, and Suzanne wondered his thoughts. "Yeah, my car broke down, and I had to get it towed."

Suzanne frowned. "Okay, yeah. That's a good reason."

"I'm sorry to have caused you worry. But I would still like your help if that's okay with you."

Suzanne nodded. "Yes, but I'm going to get some lunch first. I will meet you there in an hour. Also, I need to be done by four today."

"You have something planned tonight?"

"Yes, I'm going to the basketball game."

Stephen said, "Sure, that's fine. Meet you in an hour."

Suzanne walked back to Alex.

Alex and Suzanne joined their friends. Hannah sat beside her, and Michael moved across from Hannah so that he could talk to Alex.

"I saw Stephen," Hannah said. "He's at lunch, but he missed class?"

"He had car trouble," Suzanne said. "I told him I wanted to eat with Alex first and that I needed to be done by four in order to get ready for the game tonight."

Hannah became still. "Suzanne, please don't study with him by yourself. I told you I don't trust him."

"Trust who?" Alex asked as he heard what Hannah said. Michael also turned in their direction. He was rather protective of Hannah after the trauma she went through. Anytime she spoke with concern in her voice, he immediately tuned in to her.

"Hannah, it will be fine." Suzanne looked at Alex. "Hannah is worried that I shouldn't be with Stephen one on one."

Alex frowned. "Hannah, why does that worry you?" Alex was good friends with Hannah, and Suzanne understood he trusted her judgement. She pursed her brow, wondering if Alex trusted her.

"There's just something about him that bugs me," Hannah said. "I can't put my finger on it, but he seems to want to be with Suzanne only."

Alex took Suzanne's hand. "Baby, are you sure you should work with him?"

"Nothing is going to happen!" Suzanne raised her voice. "We are going to the library. It's a public place where plenty of people will be around." She turned toward Hannah. "Hannah, I realize you went through a terrible situation with Rhonda. But that will not happen to me. All we are doing is studying in the library." Suzanne wanted to cringe at the hurt in Hannah's eyes. However, learning to be independent meant standing up for herself.

Alex touched her cheek. "Please be careful. After what happened with Hannah, I don't want anything to happen to you."

"I will be fine," she said.

Alex studied her face. "Can you do one thing for me?"

Suzanne nodded, knowing she couldn't deny Alex anything. Part of her wondered why she didn't argue with Alex like she did with Hannah.

"Will you work with him out in the open and not in a study room in the back?"

Suzanne nodded a second time. "That's what I already had planned. I don't want it to appear as if I'm cheating on you."

Alex kissed her forehead. "Thank you. I wish I could be there with you, but I have my afternoon class."

Hannah said, "I know you told me he's embarrassed, but I'm going to be there. I won't sit with you, but I'm going to sit where I can monitor the two of you." She looked straight at Suzanne. "Suzanne, I don't want to hover over you or compare you to what happened to me. I just have a funny feeling about Stephen, okay?"

Suzanne rolled her eyes. "Okay, okay."

"Hannah," Michael said. "You need to be careful if this guy has problems. Maybe I should come with you."

"Do you have time?" Hannah leaned across the table, and she placed a hand on Michael's arm.

"I planned to study in there, anyway."

Hannah smiled into Michael's eyes. "It's a date, then."

Michael kissed her softly.

"That will make it look more normal," Hannah said, turning back to Suzanne. "It will appear as if Michael and I are studying together. That way we can watch out for you."

Suzanne rolled her eyes again. "Okay, but I think you are stressing over nothing."

***

His plan worked. The tap he placed on Suzanne's phone proved to be a brilliant move. The evening before, he listened in on their fight. However, he must have missed their makeup session when he made dinner for himself because this morning they were all lovey-dovey in the dining hall. Stephen wanted to punch a wall when he saw Suzanne walk up to Alex and kiss him. He stayed out of sight as he followed them into breakfast. Stephen wanted to slap Alex's arm away from Suzanne as his gut burned.

Stephen knew he needed to increase the doubt in Suzanne's mind. It might take some sleuthing on his part before he met her for their afternoon study session. He didn't bother to think about how missing class might raise some red flags. After breakfast, he walked over to the registrar's office. Stephen told the secretary that he was waiting for a friend, and he sat in a chair in the waiting area. Thirty minutes later, the two women asked him to leave in order to take their break. Stephen hid in the bathroom until they walked past, and he slipped through the door of the office. He spent his entire life blending in and being invisible. Stephen walked to the filing cabinets and found *Alex Fleming* on one of the manila folders. He wouldn't have enough time to peruse the contents in the office, so he shoved the folder into his backpack before exiting the office. Stephen ran to his car and locked himself inside. Thankfully, there wasn't anyone around to notice him. Excitement filled him as he read personal information about Alex, his background and being raised by a single mom.

He grimaced to himself as he thought about Suzanne questioning why he wasn't in class. Stephen realized he couldn't do anything like that again or it might arouse suspicion.

Stephen smiled, deciding how to mention minor facts to Suzanne during their time together. It was essential that he meet with her again, so he planned to use his struggle to get her to help him the next day. Slowly, he would continue planting seeds of doubt in Suzanne's mind, and she would totally believe him.

Stephen was distracted by his thoughts when the door opened, and Suzanne stepped inside.

Stephen's eyes drank Suzanne in as he watched her sashay toward him. "Hey. Do you want to go into a study room?"

Suzanne paused where she was standing. "Why don't we sit out here? That way, if there is research we need to find, it will be right here."

Stephen's eyes narrowed in anger, and he wanted to demand that they go into a room. "Okay." That was all he said.

Suzanne studied him for a moment. Stephen became paranoid, afraid she read into his anger. "You're right. This will be much better."

Stephen moved to a table. When he sat down, Stephen noticed Hannah and her boyfriend, Michael, coming into the library. Neither of them came toward where he and Suzanne were sitting. They bypassed them and moved to another table in a different section of the room. Stephen almost sighed with relief as he realized they were there to study together.

Stephen wanted to sound upbeat, so he said, "Thank you for agreeing to help me today."

Suzanne smiled, and Stephen almost gasped at her beauty. "I'm happy to help a friend."

Stephen pulled out his project and pretended to focus on what Suzanne pointed out. He wanted nothing more than to lean over and kiss her. However, he refrained. That she called him her friend enraged him, but he schooled his expression so it wouldn't show.

At one point when they took a break, Stephen said, "So you and Alex Fleming are pretty serious, right?"

Suzanne smiled dreamily. "Yeah, we are."

Stephen waited a few moments. He made sure he appeared to study his notebook, scribbling words before he commented. "You realize he was abandoned by his dad, right?"

"Yes, I visited him and his mom over fall break."

Stephen smiled at her. "I'm sure that was nice. But please be careful with him. He got into trouble a lot with his teachers in school. He had some anger issues. Probably because he didn't have a male figure in his life."

Suzanne frowned slightly, and a worried expression came into her eyes until she shook her head. "Thanks, Stephen. But Alex and I are fine."

"Yes, I know. I'm happy for the two of you. And I just wanted you to know." Stephen led the conversation back to the project. He smiled inwardly, knowing that Suzanne was worried. Stephen could see it on her face. He hoped their argument caused her to doubt.

They packed up their books at three thirty, and Suzanne moved to walk out of the library.

"Suzanne, wait." Stephen put a hand on her arm. "Can we meet again tomorrow? After our one o'clock class." Stephen could see indecision in Suzanne. Finally, she smiled at him and said, "Okay."

"See you tomorrow in class."

That night, Stephen rifled through Alex's folder. The folder was still in his possession. He would find a time to sneak into the registrar's office and return it in case someone discovered it was missing. There were two pictures of Alex playing basketball. His expression looked intense and angry. Stephen drove to the photo store in town, and he paid to have an extra proof made of it. The other picture he would use was one of Alex getting physical with a player on the opposite team. Alex's arms were extended as if he were going to push the other player. Stephen smiled as he imagined the fear and horror on Suzanne's face when she saw it. She was so innocent that Stephen knew she would believe it. That was why she needed to be with him and only him.

Stephen found his binder containing the research for the project Suzanne was helping him with. He pushed the copies of both photos down into the plastic sleeve inside the front cover. Stephen pushed the notebook securely into his book bag, ensuring the pictures would not fall out. He braced his books on either side of the notebook. Then, he placed the original photos back into Alex's folder.

It wouldn't be much longer, and Suzanne would be his!

Chapter 11

Suzanne and her friends walked to the basketball game to cheer on Alex, Michael, and Danny.

Suzanne sat between Michelle and Hannah, while Jackie sat on the other side. The four of them discussed final exams and the intense study schedule that had to be put in place. They kept up with the game, but enjoyed a time of catching up as they did.

"I'm going back to the library tomorrow," Hannah said. "It seems like I should move in there from all the time I have been spending in the place!"

Her friends chuckled. "We will bring meals so that we can all share." Michelle said.

Jackie piped in. "We need to take pillows and blankets so that we can sleep in between studying." The three of them laughed at Jackie's joke.

Suzanne said, "I'm so ready for this project to be finished."

"So am I," Hannah said. "But I think I'm almost finished." She was distracted when Michael scored a three-point goal. Hannah cheered loudly.

"I'm about done, too, but I don't think Stephen has even started writing his research yet. Hopefully, I can encourage him to begin that tomorrow."

"Wait, you're going back tomorrow to help him?" Hannah asked.

"He's not finished yet, and I promised." Suzanne said.

Hannah stared at her. "You don't understand why I'm concerned, do you?"

"Not really."

"You don't see how he looks at you when the two of you are together. It's obvious he likes you, but he's like a peeping Tom in the way he gazes at you. It's so creepy because it's almost as if he is worshipping you. Yesterday, all he did was stare at you every time you moved from the shelves to the table." Hannah had a disgusted look on her face. "I think you need to stop helping him altogether."

Suzanne shook her head in denial. "I don't believe it. Why would he look at me like that? I'm no different from any of you."

Suzanne noted as Michelle, Jackie and Hannah looked at each other.

Michelle said, "You need to trust Hannah after what she's been through. When she has a strange feeling, it's something you should trust. This guy sounds like he's a creeper."

Suzanne realized they wouldn't drop the subject. "Okay, okay, I will be careful."

"Does that mean you will cancel tomorrow?" Hannah asked.

"I can't do that because we already agreed to meet."

"Then Michael and I will be there for you."

"We were already going there as well, so we will sit close by as well." Jackie said.

"All of you are worrying over nothing. Stephen just wants my help so that he can do well in that class." Suzanne argued.

Alex rebounded with the ball from the opposing team, and the four of them stood cheering. Suzanne was relieved that the conversation turned to other things.

*****

After the game, Alex persuaded Suzanne to come back to his apartment while he took a shower. He wanted to get a coffee with her before the night ended. Suzanne, always willing to spend time with him, agreed.

Once they got to Michael and Alex's apartment, Suzanne sat in the living room with one of her textbooks while she waited for Alex. Fifteen minutes later, he walked out looking as wonderful as always.

Alex pulled her up from the couch. "Come here," he said, and Alex kissed her thoroughly. "Mmm...that's much better. I couldn't kiss you when I was all sweaty." Alex's lips caressed hers, and he deepened the kiss until they heard the door open. Suzanne sprang back in embarrassment as Michael and Hannah walked inside.

"Did we interrupt something?" Michael teased. Alex pulled his sweaty towel out of his gym bag, and he threw it at Michael as they both laughed. Suzanne's face was buried in Alex's chest as Hannah joined in on the teasing.

Suzanne had an idea. "Do y'all want to go with us to get a coffee?"

Both Michael and Hannah agreed. The three of them waited while Michael took a shower. As soon as he was finished, the four of them drove to the diner right down the street. Michael and Alex held the girls' hands in theirs on the drive as Alex drove his car. The conversation was light, just what they needed.

When they were shown a booth, both guys wrapped their arms around Hannah and Suzanne. The two girls snuggled against them, enjoying something they had not really done before, a double date.

The four of them ordered a coffee, and the guys ordered dessert.

Alex spoke up. "We need to do this more often."

Michael nodded his head. "Let's plan something before we leave for the break."

"What about the bar we went to last month?" Hannah suggested.

"That was a great night!" Suzanne said.

Alex leaned over and kissed Suzanne softly. She could tell he remembered the wonderful night. It was the weekend of their first time together, and Suzanne would never forget it.

The server brought out the two desserts. Alex and Michael were happy to share with Suzanne and Hannah. Alex found the fact that Michael got chocolate all over his shirt to be extremely funny. He teased his roommate about his obsession with the stain. Michael kept smudging it, making it worse until Hannah dipped her napkin into her glass of water. However, she was laughing so hard that she had a hard time rubbing the exact spot. Michael began shrieking when water from her napkin dripped into his lap, wetting his jeans. "It's going to look like I peed on myself!" The four of them were doubled over with laughter. Suzanne hadn't ever laughed so hard. These memories with genuine friends were some that Suzanne hoped she would never forget. She finally felt as if she truly belonged.

After they finished, Alex drove Hannah and Suzanne back to the dorm. Michael and Hannah walked around to a small porch beside the dorm, probably to make out.

"That was so much fun," Suzanne said. "We definitely need to plan it before the semester is over."

Alex stroked her soft cheek. "I had fun, too. I always enjoy every moment I can spend with you."

"Well thank you, kind sir." Suzanne leaned against his chest.

"You know you're beautiful." His voice rumbled in her ear. Suzanne closed her eyes and sighed as he held her even tighter. She wasn't sure how long she stood in his embrace, but she finally pulled back to gaze into his eyes. Alex groaned as he noticed her expression. He leaned in to kiss her passionately. Suzanne wanted nothing more than to be with him, but she needed to review a little more before taking a shower and going to bed.

"I need to go in and study a little more."

"Okay, I will see you in the morning." Alex kissed her forehead.

"I love you, Alex."

"Baby, I love you, too."

***

When Suzanne walked into class the next morning, Stephen watched her smile from his normal seat in class. Stephen nearly kissed her hand when she smiled at him. "Good morning," she said. The other day, Stephen had to think fast about a logical answer when Suzanne asked why he was absent. Stephen smiled inwardly when she asked while they were studying, because it showed him she missed him.

Stephen sat there, frozen, and he finally realized he hadn't responded. "Good morning, Suzanne. Did you have a good night?" Stephen knew about it already, having followed her after the game. He watched her leave with Alex to go to his apartment. Stephen also saw them get in the car with Hannah and Michael. Those two got on his nerves the day before because they didn't leave until after he and Suzanne finished. He had a strange sensation that they were monitoring him, and it made him angry.

"Yes, I had a break. Then, I studied a while longer before bed. How was your night?"

"It was boring. I went to work, and then I went home," Stephen said.

The two of them continued chatting as Hannah walked into the classroom. She spotted Suzanne next to Stephen, and she made a beeline to sit on Suzanne's other side. When she glanced at Stephen, he wondered if Hannah was sitting beside Suzanne because she didn't trust him. Stephen wanted to ask her to move her ass somewhere else. But he knew it would be a red flag for Suzanne. Stephen didn't mean to stick his foot in his mouth, but he said, "Hannah, are you and Michael going to be at the library again today?" Stephen wanted to kick himself.

"Yes, we are." Hannah looked at him evenly, and Stephen turned his gaze toward the front of the room. He didn't comment anymore about the situation in order not to arouse suspicion.

When the class ended, Suzanne leaned toward him. "I will see you at one, okay?"

Stephen wanted so badly to kiss her. "Sure, see you then."

Suzanne walked into the library right at one o'clock. Hannah and Michael filed in behind her. However, the two of them moved to the same table where they had sat the day before. As Stephen glanced around, Suzanne's other friends, Michelle and Jackie, were at another table on the other side of the room. It was almost as if they were surrounding the two of them in protection of Suzanne. Stephen's insides burned with anger. He would have to make sure they were studying when he shared the pictures he had of Alex. He was so close to finally having her all to himself without these busybodies.

Thankfully, the opportunity came when Suzanne's friends were intently focused on their assignments.

"I found something I wanted to show you," Stephen said as he opened up his binder again.

Curiosity filled Suzanne's features. Then, her expression turned puzzled when she saw the two pictures of Alex. "Where did you get these pictures of Alex?" Stephen studied her face. He wanted to slap the alarm off of it, but he refrained.

"Someone shared these with me. They know that the two of you are seriously dating, and they were concerned. Alex has a bit of a temper, and his reputation is pretty well known around campus."

Suzanne was quiet as she examined the two photographs. Her expression was closed when she looked at Stephen. His heart hurt, and he wished he could tell her how much he loved her. "I don't understand why you are showing these to me. If someone was concerned, they should have come to me and not given the photos to you. Who was it?"

"They wanted to remain anonymous because of Alex's anger issues." Stephen looked at his notebook, knowing that sounded so fake. Stephen touched the top of Suzanne's hand before she pulled away. Experiencing intense rejection from her, he said, "I just want you to be careful with Alex. You are my friend, and I don't want you getting hurt." Stephen wanted to take her hand back and force her to keep it in his. He found his hands clenching as he thought about it.

"Stephen, that's not really any of your business. I appreciate your caring about me, but my relationship with Alex has nothing to do with you." Suzanne pushed her chair back as if to stand.

Stephen's anger continued to build. One hand gripped her other arm. Suzanne looked at it in shock as he was squeezing her arm. "Stephen, what are you doing?"

Stephen withdrew his hand. "Sorry, I'm just concerned about you. Please be careful."

Suzanne studied him. "I need to go. I will see you tomorrow, Stephen."

Chapter 12

S uzanne walked to her dorm, not paying attention to where she was going. An alarm was going off in her as she wondered why Stephen had pictures of her boyfriend, a guy he hardly even knew. Her eyebrows were drawn closely together, and the corners of her mouth were pointing downward. Suzanne tried to tell herself that Stephen didn't know what he was talking about. However, the pictures were slightly alarming. The photos of Alex showed aggressive anger, more than would seem normal during a high school basketball game.

Suzanne was also concerned about Stephen having the photos. He and Alex had never even spoken, except for when Suzanne introduced them. Who would he have talked to that would have known about Alex being angry? Did this go back to Rhonda? Did Alex show anger toward her, and Suzanne just hadn't heard about it? Questions and fears continued rolling around in her head.

Suzanne was so lost in thought that she missed someone saying her name as she slammed into what felt like a brick wall. Suzanne yelped and clutched her chest. "Oh, sorry!"

"Suzanne, are you okay?" Alex steadied her to keep her from falling. "Baby, didn't you hear me calling your name?"

With widened eyes, Suzanne stared up at him as if in a trance. Suzanne shook her head. "I'm so sorry. You see I wasn't paying attention to where I was going. I'm also sorry for running into you."

Alex studied her without speaking. Then he drew her against his chest in a gentle hug. "You seem stressed out. Is there anything I can do to help you?" One of his hands rubbed her back in a soothing manner.

Suzanne took a deep breath as she snuggled against him. She closed her eyes and said, "No." Deep down, she decided there wasn't any need to worry about Alex. If Alex had anger issues, he wouldn't try to comfort her by giving her a back rub, or ask how he could help. When she pulled back, she said, "I'm fine now. I've been so stressed, but it's nice to see you, even though I ran into you, literally." Suzanne smiled up at him.

Alex chuckled. "You don't need to apologize for running into me. Any time I see you is a wonderful distraction, so you can bump into me as much as you want!"

Suzanne giggled. "You're the best person to bump into." She caressed his chest through his long-sleeved shirt, caressing his hard muscles. "I know I didn't really hurt you."

Alex's eyes grew dark from her hand on his chest. He cradled it while his other arm was still wrapped around her waist. Alex leaned down and kissed Suzanne gently. However, the gentle kiss soon turned into a passionate one as he tilted his head and deepened it. Alex pulled back slowly, taking his time. "Yeah, running into you was definitely the best part of my day."

Suzanne laughed again before he kissed her softly a second time.

When he stepped back, he said, "Can I walk you back?"

"I guess I can make time for that in my schedule," Suzanne teased. Alex shouldered her backpack and clasped her hand in his before they started walking again.

"I'm glad I ran into you. Michael and I talked about going on a double date on Friday. But I told him I want next weekend with you."

Suzanne's eyes narrowed when he didn't explain. "Why do you want next weekend?"

"I may have a surprise or two up my sleeve."

"Alex, what is it?"

"It's not a surprise if I tell you."

Suzanne clutched his arm, leaning against his shoulder, and gazing up at him with sad eyes. "Please tell me."

"Young lady, you will just have to wait." Suzanne laughed as Alex tried to pull away even though he didn't really want to.

Suzanne stopped, wrapping her arms around his waist. She kissed his cheeks, his nose, and finally his mouth. "Come on," she whispered. "You know you want to tell me."

"Mmm..., this is nice." It was a gratifying emotion to observe Alex weakening as she kissed down the side of his face and caressed his chest again. "Okay, okay, I will tell you part of it."

Suzanne looked up at him flirtatiously. "I'm waiting."

Alex groaned as he stared into her gorgeous eyes. "You realize what you're doing, don't you? I can't do what I would like because we have people all around us." Alex gestured at students walking and sitting in the near distance.

Suzanne continued drawing small circles on his chest while gazing up at him.

Suzanne laughed as he groaned. Then he said, "We're going back to the restaurant on the lake where I took you before Fall Break."

"I loved that place," Suzanne leaned up to kiss his cheek again. "Thank you for planning it."

Alex pushed her back with tension in his jaw as he swallowed convulsively. "You need to stop because I am afraid of what I might do to you right now."

Suzanne gave him a sultry look. "I could come back to your apartment with you."

Alex gazed at her momentarily before he shouldered her bag again and he took her hand, turning them toward his apartment. "Even if Michael is there, we can at least kiss like I want, but can't because we're in public."

"I love you, Alex." Her words made him tug on her hand to pull her to a faster gait to his place.

***

Alex finished his class, and he walked to his first appointment with Mark. He and his friends met with Mark after Hannah's abduction, but this was the first time Alex had met with him on his own.

When he walked into the center, Mark was standing behind the desk. The two of them shook hands before Mark said, "Let's go to my office."

Mark gestured for Alex to sit on the couch as he took the chair beside it. He picked up a pad and pen before looking at Alex. "Tell me what's on your mind."

Alex immediately wanted to flee from the question, but his angry response to Suzanne the other day kept him in his chair. "We've talked before about my anger issues." Mark nodded and Alex continued, "Recently, I reacted toward Suzanne. She and I started dating seriously, and I want to work on learning how to work through when I experience them."

Mark nodded as he jotted notes. "Let's start with your background. I know this may seem unnecessary, but it will help me understand where the anger is coming from. Do you understand?"

Alex nodded. "What would you like me to say?"

"Tell me about where you are from."

The tension eased in Alex's shoulders. "I'm from Talton, Texas. It's only thirty minutes from here. I lived there my whole life."

Mark wrote. "What about your family? Tell me about them."

The knot of tension returned. "It's just my mom and me. My dad left when I was three. I have two older brothers, but they are twelve and fourteen years older than me. I can recall a few years of them living with us when I was younger, but they moved out on their own before I was eight."

Mark's eyebrows raised. "That's quite an age gap. Do you have any memories of your dad?"

"No, I don't. One of my brothers was great about attending baseball and basketball games with my mom when I played. He often drove me to school because my mom worked long hours."

"So, you and your brother are close?" Mark asked.

"Yes, but he moved out of state about five years ago. He lives in Dallas with his wife, and they are about to have a baby."

"Do you visit him very often?"

"Not really," Alex answered. "My mom had a hard time with her job and making ends meet. He comes to visit twice a year, but that's about it."

"Are you and your mom close?"

"Yes, it's been just me and her for a long time," Alex said. "When I turned sixteen, I worked a part-time job to help her with rent, groceries, and any other expenses."

"That's quite a young age to take on that kind of responsibility. Did you have friends to hang out with?"

"Mostly at church. I dated a little, but most of my spare time was spent working to help my mom." Alex paused. "When I get my degree and begin working full time, I plan to continue to help her. I would love to help her buy the house she is living in or even something larger."

Mark raised his eyebrows again. "I'm glad to hear that you have a plan for the future. You sound like a wonderful son to your mom."

"She's done so much for me all my life. It's the least I can do to help her out."

"Alex," Mark paused. He looked at Alex. "Why do you feel you have to take care of her? It sounds like she knew how to take care of you."

Alex's eyes turned defensive. "I'm all she has now. Both of my brothers moved away, and one of them doesn't visit much. I've seen how tired my mom is and how hard she works. I want to help her."

The rest of the time was spent discussing Alex and his mother. Mark focused on it being just him and his mom. Alex's stomach tightened. He feared the time would run out before talking about his anger.

Mark wrote more notes before looking up. "I think that will be all for our first session."

Alex frowned. "We didn't even talk about my anger."

Mark looked at Alex. "I will tell you this one thing, and then I have homework for you before we meet again. It seems to me that you have too much responsibility on your shoulders. That, along with abandonment issues from your dad and siblings, anyone else would also struggle with anger." Mark reached out and touched Alex's shoulder. "You are a wonderful son, Alex. I will do my best to help you, but you may not always like it. I can tell you haven't liked this session very much. It's why we should to stop at this point to give you some time to process what was talked about."

Alex frowned again. Eventually, he nodded. "Okay."

Mark handed Alex a spiral notebook. "I want you to journal your thoughts every evening before bed. Write anything that comes across your mind from each day, and we will look at it together next time. Okay?"

Alex took the notebook and stood. "Okay."

They walked out, and he set up a time for the following week. Even though he felt frustrated by the session, he believed Mark wanted to help him. Therefore, he would come back again.

As Alex walked back to his apartment, he was delighted when Suzanne ran into him. After showing his concern about her stress level, her flirting completely turned him on. When she suggested they head back to his apartment, Alex realized he was pulling her into a run.

Thankfully, Michael wasn't there. Alex tugged Suzanne into his bedroom, and he shut the door before pulling her flush against him. He ravaged her mouth, even more aroused when she moaned.

Suzanne eagerly pulled her top over her head, and Alex groaned as he gazed at her.

Their time of making love was rushed because Michael could return at any moment. It was frenzied and filled with heat. Even though it was quick, it was still wonderful, as Alex pulled her against his side when they were finished.

He kissed the side of Suzanne's face and neck, breathing in her sweet scent. "Man, I love you."

Suzanne gazed up at him. "I love you, too."

Alex kissed her gently before he shared his news. "I went to see Mark today."

"I thought you said you had class."

"I did, but I wanted to wait to tell you about counseling after the session was over." Alex said, as his hand caressed down her back.

Suzanne leaned up to look at him. Alex was distracted as his gaze focused on her cleavage against his chest.

Suzanne said, "How did it go?"

It took several seconds for Alex to raise his eyes to Suzanne's face. "I like Mark. We all met with him during the group session after Hannah's abduction." Suzanne nodded. "It wasn't easy at first, but I think he can really help me." Alex shared the words Mark said, and Suzanne's eyes were shining at him. "What?"

She leaned closer and kissed him. "I'm proud of you, Alex. You've taken a big step."

Alex kissed her back. "Thank you, baby."

Suzanne cuddled against him again. "Maybe I should go see Angela sometime."

"Hannah's shared how much she enjoys sessions with her."

***

Suzanne surprised herself with her assertiveness when she kissed Alex on the sidewalk. She knew it aroused him because he was much more aggressive than he had ever been in the past. His movements inside her were rougher, but Suzanne found she enjoyed it. It made her feel desirable. Thoughts of his anger were at the back of Suzanne's mind, but she pushed them away.

After making love, Alex shared what had happened in his session with Mark. Suzanne's expression was open as she listened. When she told him she might go see Angela, she actually surprised herself. Her mind was totally mixed up with her worries over Alex's anger.

As they talked, she became drowsy. Thirty minutes later, she woke up lying on his chest, as Alex was caressing her bare back with gentle strokes. Suzanne jerked upright. "I shouldn't have fallen asleep. I have so much studying to do."

Alex gently pulled her against his chest again. "You know how wonderful you are to me, don't you?"

"Mmm-hmm..." Suzanne murmured as her eyes closed from his hypnotic touch. "I didn't mean to fall asleep."

"Apparently you needed the rest," Alex commented before he kissed the side of her head that was closest to his mouth. He was caressing her hair that had fallen over her shoulder. "I love your hair. Have I told you that?"

Suzanne hummed again. Alex tightened his arms. "I love you, Suzanne."

She lifted her head so that she could look into his eyes. "I love you, Alex." Then she moved to sit up. "But I need to go study some more."

Alex pulled her against him, holding her longer. "Okay," he said against her hair as his fingers sifted through the soft strands. "I will drive you back."

The short drive to the dorm was quiet. Alex was holding Suzanne's hand. "Everything okay?"

"I'm just considering all I have to do." Guilt washed over Suzanne about lying to him when her thoughts were on the photos Stephen showed her. And panic filled her mind about the lack of time to study and complete projects.

"Yeah, it's getting to be even crazier."

Alex pulled in front of the dorm, and he made her wait until he came around to open her door. Suzanne's thoughts focused on the fact that someone with anger problems wouldn't open a girl's door for her.

They kissed gently while Alex cradled Suzanne's face. "Thank you for a lovely afternoon."

"I enjoyed it, too." Suzanne smiled into his eyes.

"I will see you in a couple of hours at dinner."

"Yes, you will."

He touched her lips gently. "Bye, sweetheart."

"Goodbye." Suzanne shouldered her backpack and walked into the dorm.

***

Stephen watched them in anger. It built into rage as he remembered Suzanne's rejection. As much as he thought he had planted seeds of doubt in her mind concerning Alex, Stephen watched them walk to his apartment and go inside. Witnessing their obscene make-out session filled him with fury. The more he pondered on it, the more Suzanne must pay for how she treated him today.

He was trying so hard to help her see that she needed to choose him. Stephen had been more than patient. However, Stephen knew he couldn't show any aggression. As he walked to his car, Stephen considered his options to help persuade Suzanne. Maybe he needed to get her away from all of her friends. That would involve a lot of money.

Stephen planned to tell his boss to let him work extra shifts. As soon as he saved enough money, he would take Suzanne somewhere where it would just be the two of them. She would see how much she loved him when they could get away together. Meanwhile, he would also plan how to plant more fear and doubt concerning Alex.

His eyes clouded at the thought of separating her from her parents. They were filthy rich, and Stephen remembered how overprotective they were of Suzanne. His eyes narrowed at the thought of how Suzanne would be better off without them as well.

Chapter 13

Friday afternoon, Suzanne rushed from her last class to get ready for her double date with Alex, Hannah, and Michael.

Stephen had been in all of her classes, but they had spoken little other than to talk about assignments and their upcoming final exam. To Suzanne, he seemed distracted. She blew it off and focused on getting to her room. Hannah made her promise to come and get ready in her room. Suzanne dropped her bookbag, thankful for a night off of studying. She grabbed the outfit she had packed, shoes, and her makeup bag to walk down the hallway to Hannah's room.

Suzanne knocked on the door, and Hannah answered immediately. "Hi."

"Aren't you glad for a break tonight?"

"Yes, I need one," Hannah said as she led the way into her room.

"Where are Jackie and Michelle?"

"Jackie went to a movie with some friends, and Michelle's on a date with Danny." Suzanne smiled at the idea of her friends dating. Danny sat beside Michelle at meals, and they were getting to be an item. The two of them left the dining hall several times while holding hands.

The two girls talked lightly for a few moments. At one point, while Suzanne was styling Hannah's hair, Hannah said, "Stephen seemed quiet today."

"Yeah," Suzanne said.

"I wonder what was going through his mind."

Suzanne frowned slightly, and Hannah saw it in the mirror. "What's on your mind?"

Suzanne sighed. "The other day when you, Michael, Jackie and Michelle guarded me at the library, he brought out some old pictures of Alex."

Hannah had a puzzled look. "That's weird. Where did he get them?"

"He said someone else gave them to him, but he never said their name."

"What was wrong with the pictures?'

Suzanne sighed as they switched places so that Hannah could work on her hair. "It was close-up shots showing Alex getting angry during basketball games when he played in high school."

"What do you mean, *getting angry?*"

"I realize that people get aggressive when competing in a basketball game, but these seemed a little over the top when I looked at his expressions." Suzanne frowned.

"Suzanne," Hannah said, pausing. "You understand Alex isn't really like that."

"I know, but it was really weird and random when Stephen showed them to me."

"I told you I don't trust him," Hannah said. "Something about him is not normal."

"Maybe you're right. It seems the best idea that I tell him we can't study together for a while."

"Yes, I agree."

Suzanne smiled, thankful that Hannah was slowly becoming one of her best friends. As she pondered on it, Suzanne realized she hadn't spoken to her mom and dad in a while. Thankful that tomorrow was Saturday, she would call them in the morning. Even though she grew tired of their meddling in her life, she loved both of her parents.

Both Hannah and Suzanne dressed in soft, short dresses, accentuating their lovely curves. Adding the final touches to their hair, the two girls had just finished putting on jewelry when Hannah's phone rang.

Alex and Michael had expressions of awe on their faces when the two girls walked out. Hannah had on a deep red dress, while Suzanne's was a midnight blue. They glanced at each other before grabbing the girls' hands.

Michael led the way around to the small porch on the side while Alex drew Suzanne into the shadows of the front porch. Alex didn't wait a millisecond before his mouth was on Suzanne's, and he was kissing her passionately. Suzanne didn't have to look to know that Michael was doing the same thing to Hannah.

When Alex pulled back, both he and Suzanne were panting. "My word, you're gorgeous tonight!" Alex's eyes trailed up and down Suzanne's body as his gaze admired how the dress hugged her lovely curves. Suzanne's heart jumped with pleasure at his perusal of her body.

"Thank you." Suzanne beamed at him. "You always look amazing, too." The stubble on Alex's jaw gave him a rugged appeal.

The two of them stood staring into each other's eyes. Alex continued holding Suzanne close, and his hands caressed up and down her back.

"Are y'all ready to go?" Michael's voice interrupted, and they turned to see him and Hannah smirking at the two of them. Suzanne's face turned beet red.

Alex pulled Suzanne's hand to rest in the crook of his arm as he continued to gaze down at her. Then they followed Hannah and Michael outside. It was the start of a magical evening.

The time spent with Michael and Hannah on their double date enhanced the friendships already formed. The four of them relaxed and savored the night away from the stress of school, involving good food and dancing. It was planned for Hannah to go back to their apartment, so Alex took Suzanne out for a late coffee. Their time was special and intimate despite being in public surroundings. Suzanne snuggled up against Alex, and he kissed her often, but they kept their touches appropriate for the public eye. The time was spent sharing more intimate details of their years of growing up. Suzanne shared how hard it was being an only child. Alex talked about how he felt about not even knowing his father. Suzanne's heart broke at the raw grief in his eyes.

Another week passed, and Stephen remained strangely silent. He spoke to Suzanne in class, but Stephen left each class and he didn't linger behind to talk to her at all. Part of Suzanne wondered if she had offended him by telling him to stay out of her relationship with Alex. However, she was caught up in final cramming sessions with Hannah, and she couldn't stop to consider why Stephen behaved that way.

Suzanne was counting the days until her date with Alex, which was on Saturday night. He had arranged for her to come to his apartment afterward. Michael planned on taking Hannah to his grandparents' house a town away.

Suzanne had little anxiety in understanding what she learned. Since starting college, it became a strength. However, Suzanne was allowing it to overcome her thoughts aside from Alex. Her determination to learn independence was creating an obsession with her studies.

Suzanne hated being an only child because she felt like all the pressure was on her and her alone. Also, her lack of siblings made her lack in building relationships. She struggled with friendships during her younger years of school and up through high school because of social limitations. For most of her life, she was surrounded by adults. Her mother enrolled her in the church preschool, but Suzanne simply did not learn how to join in with other children. Suzanne understood her parents did the best they could within the circumstances of her life, but Suzanne often felt inept when communicating with her peers. Suzanne always wondered what was wrong with her and why she couldn't maintain friendships. She had a few friends from church, but she hadn't spoken to any of them since beginning college. The friendships she recently made in the past two months were absolutely precious to her, and she valued them more than anyone could imagine.

Suzanne followed up on her decision to make an appointment with Angela because of her stress over school. It was so bad that her hair was falling out, and her skin looked pale. Many days she forgot to eat breakfast or lunch unless she and Alex were meeting together. Jessica asked her several times if she was alright, so Suzanne realized her roommate noticed her anxiety.

That afternoon, she walked to the counseling center. Suzanne was happy to see Angela standing in front of the reception desk.

"Hello, Suzanne."

"Hi, I'm so glad to see you. I want to schedule an appointment with you."

"Are you busy now?" Angela asked. "I have thirty minutes available at the moment."

Suzanne thought about all she had to do. Her classes were completed for the day, and she needed to study. Instead, Suzanne said, "No, I guess not. I can meet for a few minutes."

Angela gestured for her to follow her back into her office.

Once Suzanne was seated, her nerves wracked her system. She wondered if she could back out now that she was actually in here. When Suzanne glanced up at Angela, she noticed the patience in Angela's posture. Angela's expression was soft, and one hand was lying on top of the other as she balanced a notepad on her lap.

"Having second thoughts?" Angela asked. Suzanne nodded. She had taken part in group sessions after Hannah's abduction, but this was her first time by herself.

Suzanne nodded with drawn brows and a tightened jaw. "Sorry, I've never really done this before, other than our group sessions after what happened with Hannah."

Angela leaned forward with an open expression. "Let's take it slow. How about you just tell me about yourself, and we can have a natural conversation?"

Suzanne blew out a breath and nodded. "I'm from Jeffersonville, which is only about an hour from here. I'm an only child, surrounded by my parents and all of my grandparents."

"Are your parents still married?"

"Yes, they are going on forty-five years of marriage in January."

"Do you get along with your parents?"

Suzanne nodded again. "We are very close, and I love them dearly."

"But..." Angela paused for Suzanne to continue.

"But they completely smother me! Not to mention all the attention from my grandparents. I have four cousins, but they are siblings to my two aunts and uncles."

"What do your parents do for a living?" Angela asked.

"My dad is an attorney, and he is the managing partner at a law firm in my town. My mom is a high school English teacher."

Angela nodded, and she jotted some notes. Suzanne fidgeted, wondering what she was writing. When Angela looked up, she said, "I'm only taking notes so that I can remember what we've talked about. I promise it's not anything bad about you or your family."

"I didn't think that," Suzanne said. Then she smiled slightly. "Okay, I guess I thought that."

Angela chuckled. "You aren't the first person who has wondered what I write on my notepad."

There was a pause before Angela continued. "Tell me what your childhood was like."

Suzanne talked about being raised in church, and always feeling like she could talk to her mother about anything other than when she began dating boys.

"Why was that a tough conversation?"

"My mom was uncomfortable even talking to me about when I developed into a teenager. She gave me many books to read about the development of my body and having sex."

"Most parents feel that way," Angela smiled. "What is your relationship like now? Do you talk to them often?"

"I try to call them every weekend, and my mom often calls me during the week. They were up here visiting me a lot in the beginning. I was so lonely. They recognized I didn't have many friends other than my roommate, Jessica. My mom hated my being alone so much, and she insisted they visit as much as they could. I finally told them not to as much, in order to learn how to stand on my own two feet."

"How did they take that?" Angela asked.

"They've always had a difficult time letting go, and I think my mom cried when they left the last time."

Angela nodded, and she jotted down a few more notes. "I have one more question for today, and then we will wait to talk more at your next session."

Suzanne nodded. This hadn't been too bad. She couldn't believe how much she had shared. Angela was really easy to talk to.

Angela pursed her brow slightly. "Tell me how you feel about being an only child? Is it hard for you not to have siblings?"

"I hate it." Suzanne said. "I feel like there's nobody else to take the lens off of me. I always feel like I am under a microscope with all the adults in my family."

Angela leaned forward and touched Suzanne's hand. "That is a completely natural feeling. When I speak to students with siblings, there is much discussion about sibling rivalry to work through. You are the opposite because you've never had someone to rival within your family." Angela paused. "Do you often clash with your mother?"

"Yes, I do," Suzanne said with wide eyes.

Angela nodded. "That's normal, too. Since you don't have siblings to fight with, your mother sounds like she is the choice for you to disagree with."

Suzanne nodded, but she was speechless as she felt amazed at Angela's intuition about her relationship with her mother. Nobody knew the yelling matches she and her mother had in her years of developing into a teenager.

Angela continued. "When growing up, you were learning to be independent and to make decisions for yourself. As your mother continued to guide you, it sounds as if you rebelled against her thoughts and opinions."

"Yes, that's exactly right," Suzanne said. "Her hovering became worse as I tried to step out on my own. My dad, too, but I think he was just trying to protect me because I am his little girl."

Angela nodded again, and she reached down on the bottom of her side table. Angela picked up a spiral notebook. She handed it to Suzanne. "Your homework is to write in a journal. I want you to write so much that it's almost like *vomit* from your mouth. Express your thinking about school, the change of becoming a college student, and your frustrations toward your parents. When you come back the next time, we will talk about what you've written."

Suzanne had an stunned expression. "That's it?"

"I think this is enough for now." Angela smiled. "For you to really trust me, we need to take things slow."

Suzanne nodded as they stood and walked out to the front of the center. As Suzanne walked toward the door, she noticed a girl with colored streaks in her hair. She remembered her as the girl who created a diversion when Hannah was abducted by Rhonda. Suzanne looked at her as she passed by without speaking. But the girl spoke up.

"You're one of the goody two shoes who is friends with Hannah, that girl that was abducted." The girl gave a sinister smile. "I should have known that all of you come for *counseling* to improve your lives." The girl pantomimed with her finger when she said the word *counseling*.

Suzanne didn't answer her, but Angela said, "Let's go on back, Vicki."

As Suzanne exited, she shook her head, thinking about how that girl was bad news. She quickly dismissed Vicki from her mind as her mind focused back on studying and preparing for her exam on Friday.

***

Stephen frowned as he watched Suzanne leave the counseling center. What on earth did she need to go in there for? Once she was his, he would put a stop to her talking to any of the idiots in there. Suzanne would thank him for it when she realized he was right. His love for her would be enough.

Stephen kept his distance behind Suzanne as he normally did. He knew she wondered why he had been so quiet lately. Stephen decided to lie low and play hard to get. Her longing glances at Stephen filled him with joy. She was becoming more interested in him.

Stephen had been working double shifts and saving money. He often worked late at night because he attended classes. Stephen stashed the funds where his mother would never see them. Once he felt he was more financially sound, he would work on enticing Suzanne to move in with him. He found a remote cabin on the edge of town, tucked back in the woods. It had a *for-rent* sign. Stephen knew it would be perfect for the two of them to start their life together. And Suzanne would be so excited to see all he had done to furnish it and make it just as she would love.

***

Suzanne and her friends walked to the basketball game that evening. They were spending time together before Thanksgiving break, when all of them would travel to their respective homes. As always, the four of them had a wonderful time. Suzanne had asked Jessica to join them, and it was nice spending time with her roommate as well.

Ever since the strange conversation with Stephen, Suzanne felt as if she was being watched. As the five girls walked toward the gym, Suzanne glanced behind herself and saw nothing. She shook her head at her crazy paranoia. Suzanne had said nothing to anyone because it was probably nothing.

Hannah caught her looking. "What's wrong?"

"Nothing," Suzanne shook her head, trying to dismiss her fears.

"Suzanne, I recognize paranoia when I see it. What's wrong?"

Suzanne sighed in frustration. Hannah had a sixth sense about herself ever since her situation involving Rhonda. "I can't explain it. Sometimes I feel like I'm being watched. It's probably nothing."

Hannah stopped. The others were walking ahead of them. "It might not be *nothing*. Why do you feel that way?"

"I'm not sure. I can't put my finger on it, but ever since the strange conversation with Stephen, our relationship seems off."

"I told you I didn't trust him," Hannah exclaimed loudly enough for their friends to look behind them.

"Shhh..." Suzanne put a finger to her lips. "I'm telling you because you already know about what happened with him. I don't want everyone to hear."

"Fine," Hannah said. "But I'm going to watch out for you." She turned in a circle, studying the buildings, trees, and the environment behind them. "Maybe you don't need to walk places by yourself."

"Why not?" Suzanne asked in exasperation.

"Jackie and Michelle walked with me when I was terrified of Rhonda. Michael did too, even though we were broken up. I'm thinking that would be a good idea for you. You definitely need to include Jessica in this since she's your roommate."

"That's crazy," Suzanne said. "Everyone is busy with their own life. I can't ask them to do that."

Hannah said nothing more, and Suzanne could see wheels turning in her head. "Hannah, please tell me what you're thinking."

"I will tell you when I have a plan."

Unfortunately, they had arrived at the gym, ending the discussion.

Chapter 14

The following days passed quickly. As promised, Hannah, Jackie, and Michelle walked with Suzanne as much as they could. Jessica helped as much as her schedule allowed. The two of them mostly walked to morning and evening meals together. Jessica's schedule differed from Suzanne's in the daytime. It was easy for Hannah because they had so many classes together. Hannah even talked to Alex, which made Suzanne grumble in frustration. She didn't want Alex to worry about her. However, Alex was happy to walk with her as often as he could. Suzanne didn't regret any moment they spent together. The extra time deepened the love she felt for him. The angry pictures shared by Stephen were dismissed from her mind as she knew how kind, caring, and compassionate Alex really was. On one of their walks together, he stopped to help another girl, who dropped her backpack and everything fell out of it. Alex chased after a paper being blown in the wind. The observation proved he was a good and loving man.

The next week, Suzanne and Alex found themselves wrapped up in an abduction of Michelle by that crazy girl, Vicki. Suzanne thought it was strange after just seeing her in the counseling center. Apparently, Michelle became absorbed in a sticky situation. A random guy stopped by Alex's and Michael's apartment, but Michael was out at the moment.

As soon as Michael returned, he called Hannah and Jackie with questions. Hannah and Jackie confirmed Michelle was involved in a situation with Vicki and another girl, Brandi. Michael discovered Danny was also being held hostage in the apartment with Michelle. Alex called the police before Michael returned, and the officer was Jake, someone they already knew from Hannah's kidnapping. Jake told them they needed more information before doing anything. They returned a call to the police, and Michael explained his findings.

Jackie, Hannah, and Michelle's brother, Jeff, arrived. Along with the police, it felt like chaos in the apartment.

Once the police rescued Michelle and Danny, who had been shot in the shoulder, Suzanne rode with the others to the hospital.

A few days later, Danny was home recovering. Their group took turns helping with meals for him and Michelle. They took part in another group session with Angela and Mark. Everything happening postponed Suzanne's plan to meet with Angela again. Suzanne worried about missing study time, but helping her friend was important as well.

That weekend, her parents came for a surprise visit. Alex traveled home to see his mom, so he could not join them. In a way, Suzanne was relieved because she remembered how overprotective her dad was the last time. Even though she tried pushing down her fears of Alex's anger, the thoughts lingered in the back of her mind while spending time with her mom and dad.

Thankfully, Jessica came to dinner. It added a pleasant distraction. Her parents adored Jessica. Earlier in the semester, Jessica visited their home. Her looks of awe at the enormity of their home showed Suzanne how well off her parents were. However, her parents were accepting of Jessica being there, and her roommate relaxed and enjoyed the time with Suzanne's family.

Two more weeks flew by. Suzanne and Alex dedicated as much time as they could together. Thanksgiving was only a week away, and Alex requested Suzanne set aside Saturday evening for a date with him. "Let's dress up," he requested. Suzanne was happy to agree.

***

Saturday evening finally arrived. Suzanne felt as if the week had crept by because she was ready for it to be there. She didn't plan it, but the night before, she found a gorgeous red dress. Hannah went shopping with her, and she convinced Suzanne to try the dress on. It was made of satin, and the dress fit her perfectly.

Alex's mouth dropped when he spotted her.

Suzanne's hair was partially pulled back to the crown of her head, and she fastened it with a barrette decorated with sequins. Her curls spilled down her back, stopping at her waistline. Her bangs were styled to perfection with a lot of hairspray. Suzanne applied a sparkling eye shadow, and the dark blending of colors made her eyes glow even more than normal.

Alex slowly stepped toward her. He put his hands on her shoulders and slid them down her arms to clasp both hands. "You look beautiful." He squeezed her hands as he leaned in for a gentle kiss.

"Thank you. You are so handsome."

"Would you two like a picture together?" A girl Suzanne recognized but didn't know was sitting behind the lobby desk. She pulled out a camera. "I can make copies and share them with you." The girl pointed to Suzanne.

"Yes," Alex said, as his eyes continued to drink Suzanne in.

The girl walked toward them, and she put them in a demure pose together before she counted. The camera flashed twice.

"Thank you," Suzanne said.

"Tell me your room number and I will get these pictures developed for you."

"Thank you." Suzanne gave the girl her name and room number.

"Please make a copy for me," Alex said with shining eyes.

Alex tucked her under his arm. When he got into the car after helping Suzanne into her seat, he pulled her toward him. His hands braced her neck. His fingers traced light circles around her jaw and neck. Alex kissed her, continuing to stroke her neck with his fingers. "You're so beautiful," he repeated.. Suzanne was thinking the same as she clasped his broad shoulders. Finally, Alex said, "We don't need to waste how we look, so let's go to dinner."

Suzanne chuckled at his frustrated tone as she reached up to caress his cheek with admiring eyes. "You look so wonderful, too."

Alex turned on some soft music, and he clasped her hand in his after starting the car and pulling out.

Alex didn't allow Suzanne to walk too far apart from him. Suzanne loved his possessiveness when they went out together. She cuddled against Alex's side. When Suzanne gazed up at him with trusting eyes, Alex touched her lips gently before helping her into the booth. He slid in beside her. Alex kissed her softly once more before studying their shared menu. "Order what you want," Alex said softly as he kissed the side of her hair.

Suzanne gazed up at him again, and he groaned, capturing her lips a second time. Alex leaned close and whispered, "I'm having a very hard time keeping my hands off of you."

Suzanne blushed, but she cuddled closer against him. "Me too," she whispered.

***

When Alex arrived at her dorm, he nearly lost his mind upon seeing Suzanne and how lovely she was. He was dressed in a sports jacket, red shirt and brown slacks. Suzanne looked devastating, and Alex's pulse increased. The moment his lips touched Suzanne's in his car, Alex was so tempted to skip dinner and go back to his place. He could see the same desire in Suzanne's eyes. It was amazing after just a few weeks how he was learning Suzanne's thought process.

Once they arrived at the restaurant, Suzanne clung to Alex's hand. When he pulled her close after opening her door, she snuggled up against his side. Alex loved it. He tightened his hold on her as they passed over tables. The host led them to a lovely table with a view of the water. It didn't take long for the two of them to decide because Suzanne ordered the same meal as the last time they were there.

Alex cherished the time just for the two of them. The following week would be chaotic with exams, and they would return for three weeks before the semester ended. The food tasted wonderful, just like last time. Suzanne leaned against Alex as they ate their meal, and his arm remained wrapped around her. Suzanne asked if it was difficult because he ate with only one hand. Alex gazed at her. "I'm not moving my arm from you, so I will be fine." The look in Suzanne's eyes made Alex want to rush through dinner.

Even though it was the week before Thanksgiving, the place was decorated for Christmas. Soft Christmas music was playing in the background, and couples were on the dance floor. As soon as they finished dessert, Alex held out his hand in invitation. Suzanne laid her head against Alex's chest. His arms wrapped around her, holding her close. Alex rested his chin on the top of her head, and he closed his eyes. The soft sigh exiting Suzanne's lips made him tighten his hold on her.

The song soon changed to an upbeat one, so Alex and Suzanne went to sit back down. They were not familiar with ballroom dancing moves and were not comfortable with the faster song. Instead, they ordered coffee, sipping it slowly while holding hands. They continued talking softly with each other. Suzanne commented that knew she wouldn't forget this wonderful evening and Alex's treatment of her.

Two hours later, Alex drove back to his apartment, and he helped Suzanne out of the car. He took her bag from her hand and hung it on his shoulders. Alex ushered her inside, and Suzanne gasped at the red roses waiting for her on the table.

"Alex, they're beautiful. Thank you so much."

Alex kissed the top of Suzanne's head. "You're welcome."

Suzanne took another moment to admire the roses, leaning down to smell their flowery scent. She turned in Alex's arms to kiss him. Alex extended the kiss for several seconds, moaning softly. Suzanne leaned against him, allowing him to envelop her in his embrace.

Alex pulled back, took Suzanne's hand, and led her into his bedroom. He shut the door softly. The two of them reached for each other, pressing their lips tightly together until Alex urged Suzanne to open her mouth. She did, and his tongue invaded. Suzanne gasped with pleasure as she gripped his upper arms.

Alex paused and stared into her eyes. "I love you, Suzanne."

"Alex, I love you too." Alex pulled Suzanne down on the bed beside him as he continued kissing her, deepening it with passion and desire. Suzanne leaned into his kiss, pressing herself against him. His fingers found their way to the back of her dress. Alex pulled on the zipper, lowering it slowly until one shoulder fell off. Alex leaned down to kiss Suzanne's bare shoulder while he finished unzipping her.

Suzanne was unbuttoning his shirt and sliding it off of his shoulders. The two of them paused their kisses to push the rest of their clothes onto the floor. Alex held up a hand for Suzanne to wait as he lifted her into his arms. He kissed her deeply, placing her on his bed.

Since Michael and Hannah were not there for the weekend, the two of them didn't hurry. Both of them took their time exploring each other, learning more about how to please each other.

When Alex leaned down to pull her nipple into his mouth, Suzanne inhaled sharply. "Alex!"

He continued playing and lapping it with his tongue before moving to her other breast. Suzanne gripped him in her hand before leaning down to lick his shaft. Alex allowed her to play with him for a few seconds before he pulled her up his body, flipping them over with her underneath. Alex quickly rolled on a condom.

Suzanne's mouth dropped open as he nudged against her entrance. Her eyes were half open with desire as he moved himself up and down her sex. Alex watched the pleasure on her face. "That's it," he whispered. "I want you ready for me."

Suzanne's eyes opened as she moaned. "I'm already there. You don't have to worry."

Alex continued teasing her warmth as he moved himself up and down, feeling her getting wetter by the second. Finally, he pushed himself inside as they groaned at the same time.

Alex moved, picking up speed as their moans became louder. Suzanne's head thrashed back and forth as she continued to whisper his name. Even though it was hard, Alex made himself wait. Once he observed the beginning of Suzanne's climax, his own orgasm overcame him. Alex collapsed on top of her, burying his nose in her collarbone.

After a few moments, he lifted off of Suzanne. He moved to pull her into his arms as they lay there, catching their breath.

Suzanne moved her head until she was gazing up at him. "I love you, Alex."

Alex kissed her softly. "Baby, I love you so much."

Chapter 15

The week of Thanksgiving passed slowly through Suzanne's mind. She missed her friends and Alex. She spent time with one of her cousins. They were close to her in age, but she would be ready for the time to return to school. Her heart skipped because Alex was on his way to visit her.

Alex called her half an hour ago. It would take him an hour to drive from his hometown to hers. Suzanne glanced at the clock and noticed thirty minutes had passed. "Not much longer," she whispered. Her mom turned into a crazy woman cleaning the house. Suzanne reminded her it was Alex, not one of their friends.

"The house needs to be just right," her mother said. Her mother bought a roast, potatoes, and carrots to make in the slow cooker. Suzanne suggested it because she remembered how much Alex liked it when pot roast was on the menu in the dining room at school. They still had dessert from Thanksgiving - an apple pie and a pecan pie.

Suzanne's father asked her quite a few questions about Alex that morning at breakfast. When Suzanne mentioned that his mother was a single parent, her dad said, "Hmmm..."

"What does that mean?" Suzanne asked, sitting up straighter in her chair.

"Please be nice to him," Suzanne said.

"I'm always nice," her father said.

Suzanne mumbled, "Guys were always scared of you." She moved to sit in front of the television to pass the time until he got there. Their living room sat toward the front of their house, so Suzanne watched when Alex pulled into their driveway.

Suzanne rushed out to the driveway as he exited the car. They both moved at the same time into a tight embrace. Suzanne breathed him in as she leaned back for Alex to kiss her gently. He didn't deepen the kiss. Suzanne knew it was because her parents were inside the house. Once they stepped back, Alex reached into his backseat to shoulder his overnight bag. Suzanne tugged his hand, and he followed her in the front door.

Her mom rushed forward. "Hello Alex." She shook his outstretched hand, and she pulled him into a gentle hug. "It's wonderful to see you again!"

"Thank you for having me, Mrs. Marks," Alex said with a smile. He turned, and his face grew serious as he noticed Suzanne's father approaching.

"It's nice to see you again, Alex," her father said. Suzanne noted the slight frown on Alex's face before he relaxed his face into a grin. Her father held out his hand, and Alex shook it firmly.

"Thank you, sir. I appreciate you letting me come and visit your home," Alex said politely.

"I'm going to show Alex to his room," Suzanne said as she quickly pulled him to follow behind her.

Alex chuckled. "You didn't give me much time to speak with your parents."

"Trust me, it's a good thing," Suzanne said as she led the way upstairs. Her heart was beating overtime with the excitement of Alex finally being here.

Suzanne opened the door to a vast bedroom. "This is where you will be staying."

"Wow!" Alex said, gazing around. Alex seemed overwhelmed by the size of the room.

"You have a bathroom through that door." She pointed to the door on the right of the room. Alex walked in. His mouth dropped open *at* the size of the bathroom and the huge walk-in shower. A feeling washed through Suzanne. She blushed and grimaced at the lush surroundings. It was something she hadn't considered before. Her father was a lawyer, and Suzanne never understood the wealth of her family until this moment with Alex.

After Alex explored his surroundings, he smiled at Suzanne. Alex tugged her into a gentle embrace. Suzanne leaned into his kiss, closing her eyes as love for him filled every part of her being. "I missed you," Alex whispered.

"I've missed you more than you can imagine," Suzanne said, but she pulled away because she heard the footsteps of her mother coming up the stairs.

Alex stepped back a respectful distance from Suzanne, and he placed his bag on a chair beside the television set.

"Alex, I hope you are finding everything suitable," Suzanne's mother said as she walked into the room. Suzanne rolled her eyes because she knew her mother came up to interrupt anything they might be doing.

"Yes, ma'am," Alex answered with his amiable smile. "You have a lovely home."

"Thank you. Why don't you both come downstairs and have a snack?" Suzanne rolled her eyes again at her mother's reference that the two of them not be alone upstairs. Her mother's passive-aggressive comments annoyed Suzanne.

"We'll be there in a moment, Mom. Alex needs to unpack."

***

Alex felt as if someone had punched him in the stomach. He knew Suzanne's dad was a lawyer, but he didn't expect them to live in this mansion. Michael shared about Hannah's family home, but this was much larger. Consternation filled him from the vast difference between their two families. His mother was a lovely person, but Alex didn't know if it was a good idea for any of them to meet each other. The house he grew up in was tiny compared to this one. Alex felt thankful that Pastor Brian had taught him how to shake a man's hand when he first entered the youth program at church.

A gate stood at the end of their driveway, but thankfully it was open. Alex felt as if he drove two miles up the driveway until the large home came into view. It was truly exquisite! He had half expected a butler to open the front door.

Alex hid his uncomfortable feelings as he smiled at Suzanne. He unzipped his duffel bag and placed his belongings inside the large walk-in closet. His small amount of clothing didn't even make a dent in its size.

"If you're hungry, we can go down and have the snack my mother mentioned," Suzanne said. Alex wondered if she noticed how quiet he was.

However, he turned with his gentle grin and said, "Sure. Lead the way."

As they walked down the winding staircase in the back of the house, Suzanne's home had two staircases, a sick feeling filled Alex. How on earth could he even think of giving Suzanne anything like this if they were to become more serious and get married? Suzanne was speaking to him as they walked into an enormous kitchen with updated countertops and appliances. Alex mumbled something in reply, and he hoped he had responded appropriately to what Suzanne had said.

When Suzanne offered him some leftover dessert from their Thanksgiving meal, he nodded his head. "That sounds nice."

Suzanne said, "Help yourself to anything you want to drink in the refrigerator."

Alex opened the large refrigerator door, and he noticed every kind of beverage under the sun. He quickly chose a bottle of apple juice. He pulled down two glasses and poured some for Suzanne. His movements were automatic as he poured an ample amount into each glass.

Suzanne smiled, and she kissed his cheek when he handed the glass to her. "Thank you," she said.

Alex felt as if he were having an out-of-body experience. It was as if he were looking over his own shoulder. Suzanne said something. Alex shook his head as he looked at her. "What?"

"Are you okay?" Suzanne frowned in concern.

"Just a little tired," Alex mumbled.

"Would you like to take a nap?" Suzanne asked.

Alex shook his head. "Please show me around your hometown."

Suzanne smiled as she grasped Alex's hand. "I'm so excited you are here!"

The rest of the weekend flew by as Suzanne drove Alex around the town where she grew up. Alex met both sets of grandparents, who also doted on Suzanne just as her parents. Suzanne's father commented several times about Alex not having a father in the picture, and Alex got the idea that he wasn't too happy the two of them were together. Her father's attitude didn't help ease Alex's fears of what the two of them were actually doing.

Finally, Sunday afternoon arrived. Alex and Suzanne prepared to drive back for the final three weeks of the semester.

Several times, Suzanne mentioned how quiet he was. He tried to appear relaxed and at ease, but more and more doubts filled his mind. He followed Suzanne to her dorm. She wanted him to stop there and tell her goodbye before driving back to his apartment.

Uncertainty was in Suzanne's gaze as she stepped out of her car. She tried to smile, but it was not a solid grin. "Thank you for coming and visiting my home."

"I had fun," Alex said. "Tell your parents I said *thank you.*"

Suzanne stepped closer, but she observed Alex's hesitation, causing her to step back. "Will I see you tomorrow morning?"

"Sure," Alex said, and he pulled Suzanne into a hug. He knew he needed to pretend not to be upset. Alex just never knew if he could ever work and provide for her like her dad did. He gently kissed her soft lips, whispering he would call her.

Chapter 16

Two days passed, and Suzanne only saw Alex at meals. He didn't offer to walk her to class, nor did he ask to spend time with her outside of their time in the dining hall. Suzanne pondered the time Alex spent with her family. Her brow puckered as she wondered what was going on. Did her dad speak to Alex and scare him off? He was so closed off from her that he barely spoke to her. Deep down, Suzanne feared he wanted to break up with her.

Suzanne went to the bathroom to prepare to take a shower when she heard the phone ring.

Jessica shouted, "Suzanne, it's for you! It's Alex."

Suzanne walked as if in slow motion to the phone. She had a bad feeling about the conversation because of the lack of time spent with Alex. "Hello."

"Suzanne," Alex said. He didn't call her 'baby' or use his loving voice when he spoke her name. "Can we go out and talk tomorrow night?"

Suzanne paused. "What do you want to talk about?"

"Nothing much," Alex said. Suzanne could tell he was avoiding her question. "I want to talk about how we are doing."

Suzanne twisted the telephone cord around her fingers as she gazed at the slippers on her feet. "I guess so."

"How about we go to the diner down the road?" Alex asked.

Suzanne understood it would not be good from the way Alex sounded on the phone. "Okay, what time? I have to study at the library tomorrow afternoon."

"How about six-thirty? I can come and pick you up."

Suzanne's stomach was telling her this wouldn't be good. "I will meet you there. It will be easier for me to leave the library after studying."

"Alright," Alex said. "Good night, Suzanne." His voice deepened slightly. It was the only warmth she had heard in his voice since his visit to her home.

Suzanne mumbled something, and she hung up the phone. Tears sprang to her eyes because she knew he was going to break up with her. What on earth did her dad say? He must have frightened Alex at some point. She had a session scheduled with Angela later this week, but Suzanne wished it were tomorrow.

Thankfully, Tuesday flew by quickly. Suzanne had a final study session and projects to polish up before turning them in. She didn't bother dressing up for Alex because, deep down, she suspected this dinner would not turn out as she wanted.

***

Suzanne drove into the parking lot of the diner. She noticed Alex's car as she stepped out. The host led her to the table in the back, and Suzanne knew beyond any doubt that this was the end of her and Alex.

Alex stood politely as she slid into the booth opposite him. If things were good between them, Alex would sit beside her.

"Thanks for coming," Alex said

Suzanne remained quiet as she stared at him. Finally, she said, "What's going on, Alex?"

Alex looked down at the table. Before he said anything, the server stepped up and took their order. Suzanne wondered why she even bothered, but she went through the motions of ordering a hot chocolate.

"Suzanne," Alex began. "I know I've been acting strangely ever since we came back from your home." He looked at her.

Suzanne could see an apology in his eyes. She closed her menu and looked straight at him. "Just say it, Alex."

"What are you talking about?" Suzanne could tell that Alex was delaying the inevitable.

Still looking directly into his eyes, she said, "You don't want to see me anymore, do you?"

Alex attempted to touch her hand, but Suzanne snatched it away. "It's not you, Suzanne. It's me."

Suzanne rolled her eyes. "Did my father say anything to make you change your mind about us?"

Alex hesitated. "He did, but that's not why I want us to take a break."

"What did he say?" Suzanne demanded.

Alex cleared his throat. "He made a couple of comments about not having a dad and being raised by a single parent."

Suzanne's eyes filled with tears. "I'm sorry. I can talk to him and try to work this out."

"Ba.." Alex began. Suzanne realized he was going to call her, *baby*. "Suzanne. You and I are so different, and our backgrounds are opposite from one another. I don't know that I'm the guy to give you everything you want."

Suzanne crossed her arms. "What do you think I need that you can't provide?"

Alex paused. "Suzanne, you come from a different place than I do. I will not be in a job that makes a ton of money. I hope to do okay so that I can help my mom, but I don't know that I can ever gain wealth like your family."

Anger filled Suzanne's eyes. "Why do you think that would even matter to me? If you really knew me, you would understand that I don't care about any of that."

"I know you say that, but I fear you would eventually resent me!" Alex's voice grew in volume, and several people looked their way.

Suzanne's eyes were filled with fire, and her nostrils flared. "If you think you can judge me like that, then we probably shouldn't be together. I'm not a selfish person, Alex."

"I never said that you were!" Alex tried to continue, but Suzanne held up her hand.

"That's exactly what you are doing. Let me make this easy for you. You and I are finished. I expect you to leave me alone from now on. Do you hear me, Alex?"

"Suzanne..." Alex tried to interject, but Suzanne was already standing outside of the booth. The server appeared with two beverages and a dessert for Alex, but Suzanne ignored him.

"Goodbye, Alex." Suzanne shouldered her purse as she stalked out of the restaurant without bothering to see what Alex was doing. She heard him call her name, but she ignored it. As she cranked her car, tears streamed down her face. Suzanne thought she had found love, but she couldn't have been more wrong!

***

Alex should have been relieved, but he felt like someone punched him in the stomach when Suzanne left. He thought they could have a mature conversation, and Alex could tell her his thoughts and feelings. Alex never meant to make her so angry. The way she looked at him drove guilt through every part of his being. Alex thought he was doing the right thing, so why did he feel so bereft when she walked away from him?

He moved the food around his plate, signaled the server, and asked them to box it up. Once Alex paid the bill, he drove back to his apartment. When he pulled into the driveway, he was relieved to see Michael's car was gone. Alex needed some time to think without questions from his roommate. His stomach churned, and he regretted eating what he did from his meal. Alex shoved the container into the refrigerator, and he moved to his bedroom. As he went through the motions of showering and changing clothes, he wondered if he had just made a huge mistake breaking up with Suzanne.

After stepping out of the shower, Alex shoved his fingers into his wet hair and groaned in misery. The idea of not seeing Suzanne anymore filled him with aching. She was the sunshine in his daily routine. But the fear of not being able to measure up was more than he could ponder. After seeing how Suzanne grew up, Alex believed there was no way he could be a man who made a lot of money. Even though every bone in his body ached from his decision, he felt like he had made the correct one. Suzanne was better off without him. The thought of her dating someone else filled his head. Alex hung his head while bracing both hands against the wall.

Alex knew the weeks of Christmas break would be rough now that Suzanne would not be coming to see him. He planned to work during the month-long January term, but his mom insisted he sign up for it. She told Alex she saved to pay for it separately from his spring tuition.

Not wanting to disappoint her, he agreed. Alex decided he would look for a part-time job to supplement what she spent on him to attend this extra term.

Alex felt more mixed up than ever. Alex remembered how much Michael enjoyed seeing Mark, he wondered if he should schedule another appointment with him. It had been on his mind to meet with him again, but time got away from him. As the thought left his head, he heard a key in the door.

Michael strolled through, and he stopped when he noticed his roommate. "Alex, are you okay? You look like hell."

Alex smirked. "Thanks for the buildup, man."

"Seriously, are you okay?" Michael's brow dipped in concern.

Alex blew out a breath, knowing what his friend's response would be. "I broke up with Suzanne."

"Are you okay? Why? What happened?"

Alex exhaled a second time. "You remember I went to visit her after Thanksgiving break, right?" Michael nodded, and Alex continued. He shook his head. "Her parents are loaded. She grew up in a mansion."

"So?" Michael asked. "Hannah's parents have money, too, but we're not letting that stop us."

Alex shook his head for the second time. "This is more than you've ever talked about with Hannah. Her house has a gate, and you drive up this huge, winding driveway before you even get near the house. I've never seen a house so big before."

"Alex," Michael said. "Why are you letting that bother you? It's clear that Suzanne loves you for more than money."

Alex sat on the couch and gazed at the floor. "Her dad commented twice about where I grew up and not having a dad. It's clear that he doesn't think I'm good enough for her." Alex's eyes were filled with bleakness. "I can't help but wonder if he's right. I will never make money like that." Alex stood and began pacing across the room.

Michael stood beside him, and when Alex glanced up, his roommate spoke. "You're scared, man. That's all this is. So what if you won't make as much money as her dad? I told you that Suzanne doesn't love you for that reason. Alex, she adores you." This time, Michael shook his head. "Don't mess up like I did." Michael broke things off with Hannah because he was afraid that getting too serious would impede his life's goals. Alex had been the one to tell him he was being an idiot.

Alex gazed at his best friend. "I think I screwed things up. She was so angry when she left the diner. I'm not sure she will even talk to me again."

Michael picked up the cordless phone and handed it to Alex. "There's only one way to find out."

Alex took it and dialed Suzanne's room. It went straight to the answering machine, so he hung up and gripped his head in his hands. "I'm so stupid," he moaned.

***

His plan was coming along. Stephen had worked and saved for them. Suzanne would finally be his! She just spent Thanksgiving at home with her family, so they wouldn't miss her too badly. And that loser, Alex, just broke up with her. Stephen couldn't wait to be the one to help pick up the pieces. He almost ran from his car to her when he witnessed the tears on her face. Stephen realized he needed to wait. The next step was to get her to meet him at his mother's house. He didn't want to, but he had a sedative prescribed to his mother that he could use if Suzanne refused to go with him to their new home.

Stephen picked up the phone and dialed her number.

Her roommate, Jessica, answered with a terse, "Hello."

"Uhh...is Suzanne there?" Stephen asked.

"Who is this?" Jessica asked.

Stephen clenched his hand into a fist, angry at her reluctance to hand the phone to Suzanne. "This is Stephen Matthews, a friend of hers from class."

Jessica paused, as if she were debating on giving the phone to Suzanne. "Hold on a minute." She must have put the receiver to her chest so Stephen wouldn't hear her conversation with Suzanne.

"Hello." Stephen's eyes closed in pleasure at the sound of Suzanne's melodic voice.

"Hi Suzanne. This is Stephen."

"Oh, hi, Stephen." Shock laced the tone of her voice, and irritation raced through him. He could hear the rawness in her voice, and Stephen knew she had been crying.

"I know we are almost finished with the semester and our work is complete, but I wondered if you would come to my house. Actually, it's my mom's, but I live with her."

Again, Suzanne was silent. "Why, Stephen?"

Anger coursed through him, but he steadied his voice. "I've missed spending time with you and just wanted to hang out as friends."

Silence. Finally, Suzanne said, "Stephen, there is so much to do right now. I'm not sure there is time just to hang out."

"Please, Suzanne? Just for an hour tomorrow night? I'm sorry to do this, but I really need a friend to talk to right now." Stephen understood he was playing on Suzanne's weakness and that she wouldn't refuse him now.

"Okay, give me your address. What time?" Suzanne asked. Then she continued, "I also need your phone number in case something comes up."

"Thank you, Suzanne. How about seven? We could both use a break by then," Stephen frowned at her words, stating something might come up. Not wanting to sound weird, he gave his street address, telling her how to get to his mom's house. Then he told her his phone number.

"See you tomorrow, Stephen," Suzanne said before she hung up the phone.

Chapter 17

The next morning, Suzanne woke up feeling as if she had come down with the flu. Her eyes hurt from crying so hard, and nausea filled her. When she had come back into her room, Jessica had been there, and Suzanne spewed out what Alex had done. And then there was the strange phone call from Stephen.

Jessica fumed and growled about what a jerk Alex had been, but she allowed Suzanne to cry on her shoulder.

"Hey, friend," Jessica said beside her. She held a cup of orange juice.

"No thanks," Suzanne mumbled. "I can't eat or drink anything."

Jessica sat beside her on the bed, continuing to hold out the cup. "Put something in your stomach. You have eaten nothing since lunch yesterday. I know what Alex did sucks, but I don't need you wasting away. By the way, there are some messages from him on the answering machine."

Jessica turned off the ringer on the phone, but she kept the answering machine connected in case their families called or there was an emergency. Suzanne was grateful to have such a wonderful friend.

Suzanne took the offered cup, took a sip, and realized that her stomach churned because of its being empty. She sipped it slowly as Jessica handed her a banana and a muffin. Suzanne was thankful it was

Wednesday because her class didn't start until ten. "Where did you get the juice and food?" Her voice sounded hoarse from crying so hard.

"You needed the rest, so I went to breakfast and brought it back for you."

Suzanne smiled at her friend. "Thank you. What would I do without you?"

Jessica looked at her. "Hannah asked about you and why you skipped breakfast."

"Oh no, did you tell her? It's so humiliating!"

"I told her, but she wasn't upset with you or feeling sorry for you. She fumed at Alex for hurting you. Michelle and Jackie wanted to confront him and chew him out, but I stopped them. I asked them to give you space this morning, but they will probably call or come check on you."

Tears filled Suzanne's eyes. She wondered if she would lose her new friends because she and Alex broke up. "I can't go back to meals with them for a while."

Jessica placed her hand over Suzanne's. "I understand your thinking there, but you can't let him control your friendships. He was an idiot to break up with you, but you have to stand up for yourself and show him he can't ruin the rest of your life."

Suzanne didn't say anything. "Not today, though. I will go back tomorrow."

Jessica nodded her head. "Okay, but you and I are going out to dinner tonight. It will help you get your mind off of all this." Just as she said it, there was a knock at the door. When Jessica opened it, Suzanne's eyes filled with tears again as she saw Hannah, Jackie, and Michelle standing there.

"I told y'all not this morning," Jessica admonished.

"It's okay," Suzanne said. "They can come in."

Hannah rushed toward her. "Oh, Suzanne. I'm so sorry!"

Suzanne couldn't reply, from the emotions welling inside of her from seeing these wonderful friends.

"I gave Alex a piece of my mind," Michelle said. "He's a total jerk for doing this to you!"

The four girls surrounded Suzanne with a hug. She looked at them with watery eyes. "Thank you so much for being here."

Hannah's eyes were filled with gentleness. "I know Alex is Michael's best friend, but I can't even look at him right now. I can't believe he hurt you like this!"

Tears rolled down Suzanne's cheeks. "What hurts the most is that he thought all I care about is money. I never stopped to think about my parents being wealthy and having a large house. Alex made it sound as if I'm a rich snob."

"Of course you're not that way," Michelle said. "He's a moron for thinking that about you. Anyone can see how loving and genuine you are."

"Look at how kind you are with Stephen," Hannah said.

Suzanne rubbed her head. "That reminds me. Stephen wants to meet with me."

"What are you talking about?" Hannah's voice sharpened.

"He called, and he invited me to come to his house so we could talk. He needs me to listen." Suzanne said.

Hannah was quiet. Finally she said, "You said no, right?"

"Why would I do that?" Suzanne asked.

"Suzanne! You can't go to his house." Hannah argued.

"Why not?" Suzanne asked.

Hannah shook her head. "You know I don't trust him. Why did he just call you up out of the blue? Especially since he's been keeping his distance from you lately."

Suzanne kept the irritation out of her voice. "I think you're overreacting. I'm sure everything will be fine."

Because of Hannah's concern, Michelle said, "Tell me you will not go to his house."

Suzanne stayed quiet.

Hannah said, "Please, Suzanne. Don't go to meet him. Call him and tell him you can't come."

Michelle, Jackie and Jessica also joined in the pleading for Suzanne not to go.

"Okay, okay," Suzanne held up her hands. "I'll call him right now." She picked up the phone to dial Stephen's number.

Suzanne found the sheet of paper in her desk with Stephen's address and phone number. It rang several times, and Suzanne wondered if she would need to leave a message on the answering machine.

"Hello," Stephen's voice sounded angry.

Suzanne swallowed. "Hi Stephen, this is Suzanne."

"Suzanne," Stephen's voice warmed a bit. "What can I do for you?"

"Stephen, I need to cancel coming over tomorrow night." Suzanne's mind scrambled for a reason. She didn't have anywhere to go other than the library. "My parents are calling me to talk about our Christmas holidays. It's a big thing involving my grandparents and everything. I'm so sorry. Hopefully, we can do it again sometime." Suzanne's gut twisted from the lie she had just told.

There was a pause. "I'm sorry to hear this, Suzanne. I bought some snacks and everything. It's kind of last minute for you to cancel."

Suzanne frowned at the anger in Stephen's voice. Also, it was the day before. What was wrong with canceling at this point? "I'm really sorry, Stephen. My mom will be upset if I'm not here to talk to her."

Stephen didn't speak. "I'm sorry too, Suzanne," Stephen said. But his voice sounded rather ominous.

"Thanks for understanding, Stephen," Suzanne said. "See you in class."

*****

The next day, Alex called Suzanne's number again. This time, her roommate, Jessica, answered. After asking to speak with Suzanne, Jessica said, "If you think she's going to talk to you after what you did to her, you're crazier than I thought! Just leave her alone!"

Alex winced when she slammed the phone down. He growled in frustration. Suzanne must have heard his messages of wanting to talk to her, but her roommate was a brick wall and he wouldn't be able to get through.

Mealtimes were miserable as he watched Hannah and Michael. Michelle and Danny had also recently connected, and he felt terrible for being envious. Even after the trauma Michelle and Danny went through, they were in a loving place. Suzanne sat at their table, but she always placed herself at the other end of the table, and she refused to acknowledge him or even look at him. With all of her friends surrounding her with support, Alex didn't stand a chance of trying to talk to her.

Yesterday morning, Hannah, Michelle and Jackie cornered him in the student center. They yelled at him for what he had done. It wasn't any worse than the things he said to himself, so he let them rant and rave before he hung his head and walked away.

Thankful he remembered Suzanne's schedule, Alex planned to wait for her outside of her class for the day.

Alex perched on the stone wall beside the building where Suzanne had her class. Relief filled him when he saw her walk out of class behind the rest of the class.

"Suzanne," he yelled as he jogged toward her before she could dart away. When she glanced at him, he felt as if she had slapped him.

"What do you want, Alex?" She tapped her foot impatiently. If Alex weren't so miserable, he would have found it adorable. Suzanne was still so beautiful to him with her long hair falling down her back. His heart broke at seeing how tired she was.

Alex held out his hand. "Can I help carry your bag?"

Suzanne continued to glare at him, and she didn't hand it over. "I don't think so."

Alex looked down at his feet. "Look, Suzanne. I'm sorry about how things ended. Do you think we can go somewhere and talk?"

Reassurance washed over Alex when he saw longing and desire in Suzanne's eyes. She rapidly blinked it away. "I'm not sure I want to talk to you right now."

"Damn it, Suzanne. I'm so sorry I hurt you." Alex pleaded with her. "I realize I messed up. Please, can we find a time to talk about it?"

"Fine," Suzanne said. "But I don't have time today. I have a gigantic project that needs to be completed before tomorrow."

"What about tomorrow night?" Alex asked.

"Don't you have basketball practice?" Suzanne asked.

"We have tomorrow night off," Alex said.

"Sure, tomorrow night." Suzanne said. "What time?"

Alex attempted a smile. "Can I come pick you up at six?"

Suzanne shook her head in refusal. "I will meet you."

Alex nodded his head. "Okay. Why don't we go to the Mexican restaurant? They have booths at the back of the restaurant."

"Okay," Suzanne said. "I need to go now."

"Bye, ba.., er, Suzanne," the desire to call her *baby* nearly made him push too fast. He saw the look in Suzanne's eyes when he almost used that term of endearment. Alex understood he needed to go slow to regain her trust. That she agreed to meet him for dinner filled him with hope he could fix what he broke.

As he walked away, he glanced to the left and spied Stephen Matthews sitting in a car down the street. Alex squinted when he noticed Stephen watching someone. He turned Stephen's line of sight, and his heart dropped when he saw Stephen's gaze fixed on Suzanne. He was watching her intensely. Alex knew the two of them had become friends. He also recalled Hannah had concerns regarding him, and all of them walked with Suzanne. Would Stephen try to make a move on Suzanne? Alex knew the guy had a crush on her. The way he watched her filled him with unease, but he quickly pushed it away. Christmas break was just a few days away. Surely Suzanne would be safe until she traveled home. However, the sense of unease didn't let up as he watched Stephen start his car. As Stephen began driving, he noticed Alex. The smirk on his face filled Alex with dread. He agreed with Hannah that Stephen was up to no good regarding Suzanne.

Alex developed a friendship with a deputy in the police department because of the emergency with Hannah. The two of them went fishing together after Hannah's abduction. With the situations he and his friends were caught up in, Jake was someone he could ask for a favor. Alex walked back to his apartment to make the call. Hopefully, Jake could do a background check on Stephen. As he dialed, Alex was thankful for another chance with Suzanne the next night. Even though they were not together, Alex hoped he could warn her away from Stephen.

***

How dare she cancel on him? Stephen slammed the phone down with a growl of frustration. After everything he had done to make sure she would be taken care of, Suzanne called and told him she couldn't meet him on Friday.

Anger continued to course through Stephen at the rejection. As he sat and continued to think about their situation, certainty filled him. Suzanne was his. Whether she wanted to come with him, she didn't have a choice. The time had come for Stephen to make a tough decision.

Suzanne would be upset with him at first, but he would make her see that she was making a mistake. She was supposed to be with him. Once Suzanne saw how much Stephen loved her, she would come to love him, too.

Stephen sat in the chair beside the phone, hearing his mother snoring down the hall. His hands fisted in his lap as a new idea formed.

It wouldn't be too difficult to get to Suzanne. Stephen planned, smiling as he realized how much better it would work out.

The next day, he sat and watched her walk out of the class he didn't attend with her. That dirtbag Alex was also sitting and waiting for her. Rage filled Stephen, and he wanted to smash the guy's face in for hurting her. Alex looked in his direction, recognizing him. Stephen became nervous when Alex studied him for several moments. As soon as he stood and walked toward Suzanne, Stephen started his car and drove to the parking lot of another building on campus. Unable to help himself, Stephen smirked at Alex in triumph over finally winning Suzanne. The suspicion in Alex's eyes made him avert his eyes quickly.

Stephen knew Suzanne's schedule. She would go to the library on Friday, so he would wait for her there and follow her inside, pretending to study.

Today was not the actual day for her to become his. Stephen realized her friends would surround her and would miss her when she was gone. Hannah, Jackie and Michelle probably had plans on Friday night with their significant others. Stephen would wait until he could get to Suzanne without her idiot friends around her.

***

Friday arrived, and Suzanne usually had a date with Alex. However, that had changed. She knew Hannah and Michelle both had plans with their guys. Jackie was going out with a girl she liked, Jennifer. Jessica had gone to a movie with some other friends from her classes.

Suzanne was at a loss about what to do with her time. She didn't want to sit around her room by herself. Jessica invited her to join them, but Suzanne didn't know the other girls. They were friends from her business class. Still heartbroken, Suzanne declined, knowing her negative attitude would only bring Jessica down. She was extremely thankful to her roommate, along with her friends. They had been so supportive, but Suzanne understood she couldn't spend every waking minute with them.

Suzanne listlessly packed her backpack. She would go to the library to get in some extra studying for a few hours. Her friends were still worried about her concerning Stephen, but she canceled going to see him just as Hannah requested. Suzanne doubted Stephen would be anywhere on the campus that evening. She believed it was perfectly safe to walk across the campus. Her mind completely forgot her agreement to meet Alex at the Mexican restaurant to talk. Suzanne needed to focus on her studies as well. She had been distracted after what had happened between her and Alex.

Just as she thought, the walk to the library was safe and nobody was even around to be a bother to her. She sat at a table, pulled out her study materials and spent the next two hours reviewing. Exams would start on Monday, and Suzanne realized she would have plenty of extra study time with Alex out of her life. As her mind turned to Alex, she gasped, looking at her watch. She completely lost track of time. As much as she loved Alex, Suzanne forgot about their plan to meet for dinner. Maybe she pushed it away because of her lack of desire to even see Alex. Suzanne shoved everything into her backpack and raced outside. As she was dashing out the front of the library, suddenly a dark figure came out from the side of the building. Suzanne turned to look when she felt a sting on the side of her neck. She collapsed into oblivion.

***

Finally! His plan worked, and there wasn't anyone around to witness it. As Suzanne fell, Stephen lifted her into his arms. Unable to stop himself, he thrust his nose into her hair, smelling her floral scent. After all of his planning and waiting, Suzanne Marks was now his! Stephen didn't give her much of the sedative, just enough to get her to their new place.

Stephen cradled her gently and walked her to his car. For her safely, he placed her into the trunk of his car for the drive to the house on the edge of town. Stephen moved her to where he could place restraints on her wrists and ankles. He hated the idea of damaging her perfect skin, but it was for her own good. Slight paranoia filled him at the thought of her friends and roommate, eventually wondering where Suzanne was. Stephen shook his head at himself. The small home outside of town was completely obscured. There wasn't any chance that Suzanne's friends could track them down.

It took fifteen minutes to drive the back roads to their new place, their new home together. He knew the sedative he had gained from his mom would last another thirty minutes. How lucky he was that his mother had a stash of illegal liquid sleep medicine? Stephen had no idea how she had gained it, but he didn't care. He injected a small dose into Suzanne so as not to hurt her. Stephen knew it was the only way she would come with him.

Stephen drove his car down the long dirt path to the small building, and he ran to unlock the padlock on the door. He opened the trunk and gently lifted Suzanne out. Stephen gazed down at her body, so thankful that they could be together from this point on. He walked into the one-bedroom dwelling. He laid her down on the bed and knelt beside her, brushing the hair back from her face. Stephen didn't remove the restraints. He understood she would be frightened when she woke up, and he wanted time to explain before releasing her hands and feet.

***

Alex was fuming inside. He slammed his money onto the table and stalked out of the restaurant. Suzanne stood him up! Alex knew he hurt her, but her not showing up to talk to him was rude and inexcusable. Alex walked to his car and slammed the door, starting the engine. Even though she was angry at him, Suzanne owed him an explanation. He pounded the steering wheel as he drove to her dorm. Thankfully, there weren't many people around as he barreled through the front door to the phone in the lobby. Alex dialed Suzanne's number. It rang nine times before he hung up, frowning. Hopefully, she was at the library, or maybe she was sleeping. It would explain why she didn't show up at the restaurant. Alex drove his hands through his hair, thinking about what he should do.

He walked to the desk where the resident assistant on duty for the evening was sitting. "Excuse me."

The girl glanced up and said, "Can I help you?"

"I tried calling Suzanne Marks' room, and she didn't answer. She was supposed to meet me for dinner tonight, and she never showed up. Would you mind checking to see if she's in her room?"

"Did you call her room?" The girl asked.

"Yes, I just said that, and it went straight to her answering machine. I was wondering if she possibly fell asleep."

The girl studied Alex momentarily. "I guess I can walk to her room and check."

"Thank you," Alex said, telling himself to calm down. "I'm Alex, by the way."

"Rachel," the girl said. Her eyes crinkled with humor. "I recognize you from waiting many times in the lobby."

Alex chuckled. "Thank you for checking on Suzanne."

Rachel grabbed the keys on the wall beside the desk. "I will be right back."

Alex nodded. He walked over to the window. As he did, his mind drifted to the way Stephen Matthews had been watching Suzanne yesterday. A niggling sensation was at the back of Alex's mind. He walked to the phone in the dorm lobby. Alex dialed the number of his friend, Jake, at the police department. Jake didn't answer. He wasn't there when he called the day before either. Another officer took down his number and told him they would relay the message. After working things out with Suzanne, Alex would convince her to come with him to his apartment so she would be safe.

"Excuse me, Alex." Rachel stood there awkwardly. "Suzanne isn't in her room."

"Really? Okay, sorry I disturbed you, Rachel. Thanks for checking. She probably went to the library." Alex smiled at Rachel as he turned and walked out of the dorm. A sour taste was in his mouth as a slight feeling of dread filled him. He ran to his car. Alex drove to the library instead of walking. Suzanne might need him to pick her up if Stephen was there harassing her. Alex ran inside the library. He looked at the tables situated near the stacks. Then he jogged to the study rooms, glancing inside all of them. Because it was a Friday evening, they were all empty. The dread built with momentum, and Alex's stomach started rolling. He never believed in having a sixth sense until Hannah's abduction with Rhonda. The situation with Danny and Michelle also told him not to dismiss his anxiety.

Alex walked to the circulation desk. "Excuse me," he said to the woman sitting at the desk. The lady glanced up. "Have you seen anyone here recently? I'm looking for a girl with long brown hair. She's about five, four.

The lady stood as she said, "Yes, she was in here about an hour ago. She was sitting over at those tables." The lady pointed to the tables near the stacks, but they were empty. "She left. I'm assuming she walked back to her dorm."

Alex felt a weight in his chest as chills rushed over him. "Thank you." He walked outside and stood wondering what to do. Alex looked to his left, and he noticed a backpack on the ground. His heart stopped as he walked over to it. Alex knew it was Suzanne's. If her backpack was on the ground, where was she?

Chapter 18

Suzanne felt a wave of nausea as she opened her eyes. She tried turning over, but her hands and feet were tied together. Suzanne jerked in an effort to release her feet and hands as tears sprang to her eyes. Where was she? What happened? She looked around. Suzanne was in a small, crude room. It was made of wood paneling and it had a wood floor. She noticed a small window on the opposite wall.

She must have made a noise, because the door opened. When Stephen walked inside, Suzanne cried and sprung back in fear. "Stephen, where am I? What's going on?"

"You're finally here with me, where you belong," Stephen had a strange look in his eyes. He walked over and sat on the bed. When he reached out to touch Suzanne's face, she shrunk back. Anger filled his eyes, and he grabbed her arm roughly. "Don't fight this, Suzanne. This is where you belong."

Suzanne refused to show that Stephen's hand was bruising her wrist. She made herself relax. Suzanne asked, "Where are we?"

"We're home. This is where you and I are going to live together." Stephen murmured as his hand began stroking her wrist. Suzanne kept herself from showing revulsion at his touch and the way he was gazing at her.

"What do you mean? Stephen, you and I can't stay here. I have family and friends. They will miss me if I stay here." Suzanne kept her voice level and with no trace of the fear racing through her bones.

Stephen's eyes changed as he reached out to touch Suzanne's cheek. She forced herself to hold still while holding her breath. More than anything, she wanted to slap his hand away. Stephen said, "You are home. You and I are going to make a wonderful home together."

Bile rose in the back of Suzanne's throat as she thought about Hannah's continued warnings regarding Stephen. Her friend was right and now Suzanne wouldn't be able to talk to her about it again. Suzanne swallowed. "Stephen, that sounds lovely. But my mom and dad will be worried sick about me."

"I understand," Stephen said. "You will call them tomorrow and tell them you're with me now. That way, they will know where you are."

"What about my friends?" Suzanne asked as her tone rose to a squeak.

Stephen's eyes became hard. "If they're your genuine friends, then they will leave you alone. You deserve to be happy, Suzanne."

"I need a restroom, Stephen. Can you please untie me?"

"Okay, but don't run away. Soon you will see this is where you belong." Stephen cut the ties on her arms and legs. Suzanne was shaky as she rose and walked to the bathroom, locking the door. She ran to the toilet and retched.

Suzanne slid down the door frame as shakes overcame her. *What am I going to do? Why didn't I listen to Hannah?* Tears leaked out as she thought about not seeing Alex again. She felt terrible that he thought she had stood him up instead of meeting him tonight to talk. Now she wouldn't be able to say she was sorry. Suzanne braced her head in her hands as she thought of how she might escape. She did not know where she was, but it dawned on her she must have dropped her backpack. Someone should have found it by now, and they would at least try to find Jessica to give it back to her. Hopefully, Jessica would realize she was missing. She jumped when she heard pounding on the door.

"Suzanne, you need to finish and come out now."

"I'm almost finished." Suzanne flushed the toilet and ran water to sound like she was washing her hands. She splashed water on her face and rinsed out her mouth. Suzanne used the towel to wipe the extra drips before opening the door.

***

Alex clenched his fists, and he felt faint when he arrived at his apartment. Where on earth was Suzanne? He didn't know how to get in touch with Stephen. Alex shoved Suzanne's backpack onto a chair as he picked up the phone in the kitchen. He dialed the number of the police station again. "Can I please speak with Officer Jake Toms?"

"Just a moment and I will connect you to his extension."

"Thank you." Alex nervously tapped his fingers on his leg as he waited.

"Hello,"

"Jake, thank goodness you're there! There's a situation. My girlfriend, Suzanne, has been abducted. She was at the library studying, and I found her backpack on the ground outside of the library." Alex knew he was babbling and rambling. His voice sounded breathless as adrenaline shot through him.

"Whoa, Alex, slow down and take a breath," Jake said. "In fact, take three deep breaths."

Alex breathed deeply, following Jake's instructions.

Jake said, "Okay, tell me slowly what happened."

Alex explained his fears and how he had searched for Suzanne and couldn't find her anywhere.

"Is there any chance she could have taken off, maybe to her parents' house?" Jake asked.

"Why would she leave her backpack on the sidewalk if she did that? Come on, Jake. I need your help on this." Alex sensed an increase in his heart rate, and he felt short of breath.

"Okay, I will locate Stephen Matthew's number. I will also send someone over there to see if he's there."

"Thanks, Jake."

"I'll swing by your place in thirty minutes," Jake said.

Alex dropped into the nearest chair after hanging up the phone. He lowered his head between his knees because he felt faint. After a few seconds of sitting like that, he called Suzanne's room to see if Jessica had made it back. As he stood to reach for the phone again, the key turned in the lock. Michael and Hannah walked in with surprised expressions.

"Hey, man. I thought you would be with Suzanne right now," Michael said.

"Thank god you're back!" Alex's voice was shaking.

"Alex, what's wrong?" Hannah's eyes widened with fear when she saw tears in his eyes. "Alex, please talk to us."

"Suzanne didn't make it to supper, so I went to her dorm, and she wasn't there. I drove to the library to look for her. Her backpack was outside on the sidewalk. I think Stephen Matthews took her." Alex collapsed in the chair as he began sobbing.

Hannah raced to the phone, and she dialed Suzanne's room. Jessica must have answered. "Jessica, do you know where Suzanne is?

Have you seen her?" Hannah listened and then she said, "Alex found Suzanne's backpack on the sidewalk outside of the library. He thinks Stephen took her. Okay, see you soon." Hannah hung up and turned toward Michael and Alex. "Jessica is on her way over. Have you called the police?"

Alex nodded. "Jake Toms is calling Stephen's home and sending someone over there. He's coming here in a few minutes." As soon as Alex finished, there was a knock on the door. Michael opened it and Jake was standing there.

Alex rushed toward him. "Tell me what's happening. Please tell me you found Suzanne."

Jake's face looked grim. "Stephen wasn't home. An officer searched his room, and Stephen's room was a shrine to Suzanne. There were pictures of her all over the walls. We found a woman's shirt, which must belong to her. Alex, I think you're right. It's clear that he was stalking her."

"I knew it," Hannah moaned as she was also overcome by tears. Michael pulled her against him, whispering soothing words. She looked at Jake. "I warned Suzanne that something wasn't right with him. Suzanne thought he was a normal student."

"After some investigating, it appears Stephen was only attending classes to be near Suzanne," Jake said. "The boy barely graduated from high school, and his mother knew nothing about his attending any classes."

Alex felt his heart drop with the words. Hannah cried into Michael's chest.

***

Suzanne walked out of the bathroom, and Stephen had a tray with some food on it. A glass of water was also on the tray. "I brought you some food. It's some of your favorites," he said.

Suzanne noticed fried chicken, mashed potatoes, and green beans on the tray. She closed her eyes in agony as she realized Stephen had learned so many things about her, including her favorite foods. Hannah's instincts were correct in that something was wrong with their friendship.

The thought of putting anything in her stomach at the moment brought on more nausea. But Suzanne smiled and said, "Thank you, Stephen." She sat on the bed as Stephen walked the tray over to her.

"I think you will be comfortable here, Suzanne. I will do all I can to meet your needs," Stephen said.

Suzanne picked up a biscuit and chewed off a small piece. She took a sip of water before she spoke. "Stephen, you can't keep me here. I believe you think you have feelings for me, but everyone is going to worry. People are probably already looking for me."

Before Suzanne realized it, Stephen slapped her face. Tears sprang to her eyes, but she blinked them away. "You belong here with me, Suzanne. I'm sorry I had to do that, but it's time for you to accept it. I'm always going to be looking out for your best interests. As long as you do as I say, it will be a wonderful home for you."

The little food that Suzanne swallowed came rushing up, and she raced to the bathroom. Suzanne leaned over the toilet and threw up a second time. She realized Stephen wouldn't let her go. She was officially his prisoner. It was going to be up to her to figure out how to escape.

As she walked out, Stephen still sat on the bed. "Come lie down, darling. You need rest. The sedative I gave you needs to wear off. Come and I will tuck you in." Stephen was saying the words in a singsong voice. Suzanne pretended to play along.

"Thank you, Stephen." She walked to the bed and lay down. Stephen pulled a blanket over Suzanne. It was pink, her favorite color. She noticed that many other items in the room were the same color. When Stephen covered her up, his hand stroked her face and neck. Suzanne closed her eyes and pushed down more nausea. As she opened them, Stephen's face was close to hers. He leaned down and kissed her cheek.

"Your skin is so soft. Sleep, my love. In two days, you and I are getting married. I have your dress and everything. Then we will be together forever." Stephen walked to the door. "I'm going out to run some errands, but I will be back later. Everything you need is inside your closet and bathroom." As he closed the door, Suzanne heard a click.

"No.." she murmured as she shoved the blanket off of her and ran to the door. Suzanne rattled the knob, but Stephen locked her inside the room. He was planning to keep her prisoner in this horrible place. Suzanne covered her eyes, and she collapsed on the floor in tears.

***

Alex's eyes darkened. "What are you going to do to find her? What can I do?"

"You're going to stay here and remain calm," Jake said.

Alex shook his head in refusal, clenching his jaw. "No. I can't sit here and do nothing. It's making me crazy."

Jake was quiet as he stared at Alex. "Let's sit down and think for a moment."

After everyone moved into the living room, Jake said, "Stephen's mother didn't know where he was. As I explained, she didn't know of his enrolling in classes at the university. His mother told us he'd been working a lot of hours, but she had no idea where he stashed any of his money. Stephen's mom didn't look in great shape to talk to us about anything because she was hungover from booze and drugs."

Alex closed his eyes in agony. He ran his hand down his face. "What can we do? How are we going to find Suzanne?" In Alex's mind, he regretted his decision to break things off with Suzanne. If they were still together, she would have been with him this evening. Stephen wouldn't have been able to get her.

"I have an agent going to Stephen's work to ask questions to see if it might give us an idea of where he might have taken her." Jake said. "Another officer is questioning people in the human resources office to see if they can get any more information."

Tears sprang to his eyes as he moaned, "What is he doing to her? I can't stand the thought of her being hurt."

Hannah was beside Alex, sobbing. "There's got to be something we can do to help. Please tell us."

As soon as she said the words, the phone rang. Michael was beside it, so he picked it up and said, "Hello." He handed it to Jake. "It's for you."

"I hope it's an update," Jake said as he grabbed the phone. He listened to the other officer share what he had found. Jake's face looked grim when he hung up. "Officer Perry questioned the other employees where Stephen worked, but they knew little. One of them talked about how Stephen was saving his money. He mentioned a surprise for his girlfriend. Another guy talked about Stephen mentioning a place outside of town. I'm going back to see if his mom has any idea where it might be."

"Can I come with you?" Alex asked. "I will stay quiet and let you ask the questions. I need to do something, man."

Jake paused. "Okay, but not a word out of you, got it?" Alex nodded, and he ran to his bedroom to grab his wallet. As he did, the phone rang again. Alex said, "I'll get it," and he walked toward the portable phone in the living room.

"Alex!" Suzanne's voice came across the line.

"Suzanne, baby. Are you okay? Where are you?" Alex was yelling as frantically as he felt. Hannah, Jessica, Michael, and Jake joined him in the living room.

"Oh my god, Suzanne!" Hannah cried. "Please tell me she's okay."

"I don't know where I am," Suzanne sobbed. "Stephen grabbed me outside the library. Alex, he drugged me and brought me somewhere. I don't know where."

"Honey, it's okay," Alex said in a soothing tone. "I'm putting you on speaker so the others can hear you. We're all worried. How are you able to call? Where is he?"

"He went out." Suzanne's cries increased. "I'm locked in a room. It has similar clothing and items I use every day. The room is decorated in all my favorite colors. Alex, he's learned everything about me."

"Suzanne, I'm here. Keep talking, baby. How are you able to call me?" Alex said.

"I used a bobby pin in the bathroom to pick the lock to the door of the room where he put me. Thankfully, he stocked the bathroom with toiletries and items I use every day." Suzanne took a shaky breath. "I can't stay out here long because he's coming back."

Alex's voice lowered. "Suzanne, did he hurt you?"

Suzanne was silent for a moment. "No. But he says we're getting married in two days." Her cries became silent, but everyone could hear her across the phone line. Even Michael had tears in his eyes. Jessica and Hannah were crying, with their faces in their hands.

"Over my dead body," Alex said. "Suzanne, my friend Jake, is here. He's with the police department. I'm going to let him ask you some questions. Okay?"

Alex could hear her trying to breathe through her sobs. "Okay."

"Suzanne, this is Jake. Is there a window where you are? Are you able to look out?"

"Umm... there's a couple of them, but they're up really high. Everything in this place is made of wood, the walls and the floors."

"Suzanne, that's good. Is there any way you can get to a window to look outside?" Alex heard something dragging across the floor.

"I'm getting up on a chair to see out," Suzanne said.

"Suzanne, baby, be careful," Alex said. He realized the moment she got out of this situation that he would never let her go again.

"Okay, I'm looking out. All I see are trees. This shack is at the bottom of a hill. Oh, my, he's coming back. I need to get off and get back in the bedroom."

"Suzanne, don't go yet," Alex said, but she had already hung up the phone. He plowed his hands through his hair.

"Let's go question Stephen's mom again. I will also call the station to see if they can tap the call Suzanne just made. She was on the line for a while, so maybe there's a way to look back into the call history. We also should notify her parents." Jake walked outside to his patrol car. He spoke into his radio, probably asking for the tap on the wires of their phone line.

Alex looked at Jessica. "Do you have Suzanne's parents' phone number? If you wouldn't mind, can you call them?"

Jessica nodded. Her eyes shone with the fear they all felt. "I'll call them right now."

Hannah looked at Alex. "We will stay here in case Suzanne calls again. Alex, please be careful."

"I'll be fine," Alex said. "It's Suzanne we need to worry about." He followed Jake out to his squad car and got into the passenger side.

***

Suzanne barely got herself locked back into her bedroom again before Stephen walked back in. She was shaking all over from the fear of his finding out she picked the lock to her room. As she sat on the bed, waiting for him to come into her room, Suzanne studied the window above her. It was small, but she might squeeze through it. The next time Stephen left, she would try.

The doorknob jiggled, and Stephen walked in. "Hello, my darling. Did you miss me? I brought your wedding dress for you, along with your dinner."

Suzanne made herself smile. "Thank you, Stephen."

Stephen laid a garment bag on the chair beside the bed. He said, "Let me put your food on a plate, and I will be back." A lone tear leaked out of her eye. "Don't cry, darling. You never need to cry again. I will always be here to care for you." Stephen stroked a finger down her cheek in a worshipful manner.

Suzanne let out a breath when he walked out, and a strangled cry also escaped. She shivered at his finger on her face. Her eyes gazed at the garment back and she saw lace peeking out of the top. Suzanne covered her mouth and was short of breath at the thought of him buying it for her. Stephen was going to force her to marry him and then he would do whatever he wanted with her. "Please, no," she whispered to herself.

Right now, she would play along because if she argued, he might hit her again.

Stephen carried two plates into the room. Suzanne went through the motions, pretending to eat tiny bites. When she tried to stand, Stephen grabbed her arm roughly, saying, "You must learn to sit with me until I'm finished. If we're going to be husband and wife, you need to learn your role. Okay, my darling?"

Suzanne pushed bile down her throat. "Why do you want to marry me, Stephen? We don't know each other very well."

Stephen's eyes appeared glassy. Suzanne wondered if he had been drinking. "I understand you, my love. You should thank me for being your guardian angel all these months."

"Stephen, are you okay?" Suzanne asked. "Your eyes don't look good right now." Not expecting it, Stephen reared back and landed the back of his hand across her face. Suzanne tasted blood, but she refused to cry.

"Never question me like that again. You must learn not to ask questions about how I look. Now, I need you to take these dishes into the kitchen and wash them."

Suzanne didn't say a word as she stacked their plates to walk into the tiny kitchen. Not knowing where to find things, she looked in some cabinets. After looking under the sink, she found dishwashing liquid. When she finished washing the few dishes, she turned and saw Stephen watching her.

"Oh my love, we are finally together. I promise you will be happy with me." Stephen held out his arms. Suzanne wanted to cringe, but she made herself walk across the floor on what felt like wooden legs. Stephen stroked the hair out of her face before pulling her into his arms. Suzanne feared she might throw up again as she awkwardly patted his shoulder. She wasn't sure how long he wanted her to stand there as he held her. Suzanne was terrified of being hit again, so she waited miserably until Stephen finally pulled away.

"Now, my love, you can read or watch something on television." Stephen gestured to the small television set on the other side of the small room. A sagging couch and chair sat in front of it. "There are magazines you like, along with books."

"Thank you." Suzanne moved to sit on the chair when Stephen grabbed her arm roughly.

"You will sit on the couch," he said. "I will sit in the chair every night."

Suzanne sat down gingerly on the couch. As she sat, Suzanne formed a plan of escape. There was no way she could endure being Stephen's hostage anymore. She turned to Stephen. "Can I make you a cup of tea?"

Stephen smiled at her. "Yes, my love. That would be nice."

Suzanne got the kettle on the stove and filled it with water. Stephen was surfing through channels on the television, so she rummaged through cabinets. She wanted it to look like she was trying to locate tea bags. Her eyes landed on a medicine bottle. Suzanne read the label and noticed the warning about causing drowsiness. Thankfully, Stephen was intently watching something on the television. Suzanne grabbed the bottle and shook out four pills. Stephen glanced her way, so she pushed them into the pocket of her blue jeans. She found the tea bags and pulled one out. Then she looked until she found a teacup.

"The water needs a minute to boil. I'm going to the restroom, and I will be right back."

Stephen looked like he wanted to object. "Stephen, let me go to the bathroom." Suzanne was terrified of saying because she was afraid of him hitting her again.

Stephen studied her, and then he nodded. "Yes, my love."

Suzanne locked the bathroom door. She rummaged through the cabinets. She was looking for something to crush the pills so that she could slip them into Stephen's tea. In the last drawer, Suzanne noticed a pair of scissors. She went through the motion of flushing the toilet to sound like she was truly using the restroom. Then, she used the scissors to grind the pills into powder. Suzanne dusted the powder into a cup by the sink. Somehow Stephen knew she used one when she brushed her teeth. When she opened the door, Stephen looked her way. "I accidentally knocked my cup into the trash can, so I'm going to wash it."

Stephen nodded and turned back to the program he was watching. Suzanne made a motion of looking like she was washing the cup, and she snatched the mug. She quickly dusted the powder into the bottom of the mug just as the kettle whistled. Suzanne dunked a tea bag into the hot water. "Do you want some cream or sugar?"

Stephen smiled at her. "No, black is fine."

Suzanne smiled at him as she walked the mug to him. "Here you go." She sat on the couch and pretended to watch the show. Suzanne prayed the medicine would work quickly.

***

Jake parked outside Stephen's house. Alex realized Stephen didn't have a great home life. It was obvious to see that his mom didn't care about where they lived. The outside was worn and shoddy, with a sagging porch. A wooden swing hung from one rung.

Jake knocked on the door, and they waited several minutes before a woman answered the door. She was sagging just like the house, and she looked as if she had seen better days. The lady rolled her eyes. "I've already answered all of your questions." She moved to shut the door as Jake propped it open with one foot.

"I'm sorry to bother you again, Ms. Matthews. We have a few more questions for you. If we can just have five more minutes."

The woman rolled her eyes again as she stepped back for them to stand in the entryway. Jake questioned her about a cabin outside of town. Thankfully, she was familiar with the small place on the outside of town. She named a road, and Jake wrote it down in his notebook.

Alex glanced around him at the roach-infested surroundings, and he would never regret how he grew up ever again. He and his mom might not have a lot of money, but his home was a castle compared to this dump.

"So now what? Are we going to look?" Alex asked as they got back into the police car.

Jake shook his head. "I'm taking you back before calling in for backup."

"Jake, I kept my promise," Alex said. "I didn't get involved. Please let me go with you. Suzanne isn't familiar with you, but she knows me."

Jake studied Alex with indecision in his eyes. He groaned. "Fine. But if we find anything, you're staying in the car, got it?"

"Absolutely," Alex agreed.

Chapter 19

Suzanne fixed her eyes on the television, pretending she was deep into the show when her eyes kept drifting to Stephen. Whenever he glanced in her direction, Suzanne smiled as if she were mesmerized and in love. Suzanne watched as drowsiness set in and he leaned back in the recliner. It was amazing how much he fought sleep, though. His eyes didn't close for another forty-five minutes. Suzanne was still sitting on the couch when sleep finally overcame Stephen, even to the point of his snoring.

With a racing pulse and clenched jaw, Suzanne walked quietly into her room. She popped her head out and was thankful Stephen hadn't moved. Suzanne wanted to climb out her bedroom window, but the thought of Stephen waking up and catching her was inconceivable. Therefore, she gently carried the chair by the bed into the bathroom.

Suzanne shut and locked the bathroom door. She turned on the shower to make it sound like she was taking a shower. Suzanne pushed the linen basket in front of the door in her attempt to escape, just in case Stephen woke up. Suzanne pushed down the terror racing through her as her breaths increased. *Don't be overcome with anxiety now,* Suzanne told herself. She climbed up onto the chair and pushed on the windowpane above the sink. It didn't budge. "Don't give up," she whispered to herself.

Suzanne reached up and pushed with all her might. To her surprise, the window moved slightly. It was wedged with dust and grime, but Suzanne was determined to pry it open. She knew it was her only way out of this situation. Alex's face came to her mind, and Suzanne knew she still loved him. Even though he hurt her, she would convince him that she didn't care about money. If she could somehow survive this.

Suzanne took a deep breath. Then she noticed the plunger on the floor by the toilet. She hopped down, picked it up. Suzanne used the wooden end to push the window further open. Suzanne took another deep breath, and she continued to push until she was certain she might squeeze herself through.

Suzanne stepped onto the ledge of the sink in order to pull herself up to the window. It took some maneuvering, but she pulled her lower torso through the window. As she sat on the ledge, she looked at the high drop below. Her breathing became shallower as she gulped. "Better to be injured than to be trapped here forever," she whispered to herself.

Suzanne pushed herself out and hung onto the windowsill as long as she could. She closed her eyes and took another deep breath. "Let go," she whispered to herself. "You will be okay."

Suzanne released her hold on the ledge as she dropped. She held her breath as she tumbled down through some branches in a tree. As she did, she felt the sharp edges scratch against her torso. Suzanne knew it broke the skin because her shirt was pushed up as she fell. She made a hard landing on her right side. Suzanne blocked her head by raising her arms. As she landed, a sharp pain ripped through her right ankle. The pain radiated up her leg.

Suzanne brought a hand up to her mouth, and several tears leaked out. She bit down on a finger to keep from crying out. The pain was excruciating. Slowly, she stood, wincing in pain. Suzanne glanced around. She didn't know which way to go. Suzanne realized the woods would be the best way for her to shield herself. She didn't allow herself to dwell on the thought of wild animals. Suzanne climbed up the hill as fast as she could hobble. Once at the top of the hill, she ran as fast as her ankle would allow her. Silent cries were escaping as she pushed down the pain and fear. She tripped on a root protruding from the ground, but she made herself bite her finger again as she fell hard on her knees. After wincing and taking another deep breath, Suzanne forced herself to her feet. She couldn't let the pain overwhelm her, or she might never get away.

Suzanne prayed that the woods would lead her to civilization. At the back of her mind, she feared Stephen had woken and discovered she was gone. She knew he would hunt for her until he found her again.

***

Jake drove toward Stagecoach Road. The worker at Stephen's work and his mother both named it as the road to their property on the outskirts of town. There was history behind the word, but neither of them cared to find out. Jake wasn't certain where to turn off, so he drove at a snail's pace as they searched.

Jake used his radio to alert all other officers at the station of their search for Stephen and Suzanne. They stopped at a gas station, and Alex called the apartment. Michael informed him that Suzanne's parents were on the way. He also stated that her dad used his leverage as an attorney to file a missing person's report. Suzanne had been missing for twelve hours, and most police departments didn't allow it that soon after. Alex was thankful that Suzanne's parents were on the way.

Michael said there had been no word from Suzanne since the phone call several hours ago.

Alex felt his heart sink as he hung up the pay phone. While he called his friends, Jake questioned the attendant working, asking about properties in the general vicinity of where they were.

"Good news," Jake said when Alex joined him. "This guy said Stephen had come into the gas station three hours ago. He got gas and stocked up on some other supplies. I showed him the picture of Stephen we got from his room, and he recognized his face. He also talked about a dirt road two miles from here. The man mentioned a small shack located back in the woods."

Hope filled Alex's heart. "Let's go," he said.

Jake placed a hand on Alex's arm. "Hold on a minute. You definitely need to stay in the car if we find it. Do you understand?"

"I promise as long as we get Suzanne out of there," Alex said. "My primary concern is to make sure she is safe."

As they got back into the police car, Jake started the engine to pull out. They were silent as he drove the two miles. Jake slowed the car. "This looks like it might be where we need to turn." He made a slow turn on the dirt road.

Alex shot up in his seat. "Jake, look." His finger was pointing to a lone figure a large distance away. The person was limping. As they grew closer, Alex began sobbing, "It's her, man. It's Suzanne." He wanted to tell Jake to press on the gas to get to her quicker, but he refrained. When Jake stopped the car, Alex flung open the door. "Suzanne," he yelled.

Suzanne froze. She cried out when she recognized Alex, and he raced toward her. Suzanne hobbled, her mouth turned down in a grimace, because of her ankle. The minute Suzanne was in Alex's arms, she broke down into heart-wrenching sobs. Alex picked her up and cradled her tightly in his arms. He cried along with Suzanne. "Thank God you're okay," Alex murmured as he rubbed her hair, her back and her shoulders. Tears flowed from both of them as he tightened his hold, hoping he wasn't choking her. Alex was terrified that this was a dream and she would disappear.

When she finally pulled back, Alex's heart dropped from seeing the bruise on one side of her face. He was gentle as he pushed the hair off her forehead. "Suzanne, baby. Did Stephen do this to you?"

Unable to speak, Suzanne nodded. She was taking rapid, shallow breaths, and Suzanne was shaking all over. With a soothing voice, Alex asked nothing else. He sat on the passenger seat of the police car with her perched on his lap. Alex continued the gentle massage of her back and her hair. The movements had a calming effect, and her breathing evened out.

Suzanne jerked up, swabbing a hand across her face. "He won't stop looking for me, Alex. Stephen won't let me go." Alex's heart broke as she wrapped her arms around herself, shivering uncontrollably.

"The hell he won't," Alex growled. "He's not touching you ever again." He cradled her face in his hands, pushing her hair behind her ears. Tenderly, he asked, "How did you get away?"

Suzanne was rocking back and forth, moaning. "I found some sleeping pills, and I crushed them up in his tea that I made for him." Tears rolled down her face as she relived the moments of captivity. "I thought he wouldn't ever fall asleep. And then when I was climbing out the window, I was terrified he would catch me and lock me up again." Suzanne's words came out in a rush as she was short of breath again. Alex tightened his hold on her, pulling her against his chest as tears rolled down his cheeks again. He cradled her like a baby, but his heart couldn't take the blank look in her eyes.

"Shh..." Alex whispered, and he rocked her in his arms to calm her down.

Jake spoke up. "Suzanne, I know this has been an awful situation, but I need to know where Stephen is. Can you tell me the direction of the cabin where he held you?"

Suzanne pointed to her left, the direction she walked from. "I'm not sure. It took me a little while to find this road. The cabin is down a very large hill." As she described what she could remember, two other police cars approached with sirens blaring.

Jake approached his colleagues and told them what Suzanne had relayed. He looked at Alex. "An ambulance is almost here. I'm leaving Officer Geary to stay with you while we search."

Alex nodded, completely content to hold Suzanne. Her head was pillowed on his shoulder, and her breathing was calmer. They heard the siren of the ambulance in the background.

Suddenly, Stephen burst through the woods. With wild eyes, he glanced around. Upon seeing Suzanne, he made a beeline for her. "Suzanne, how dare you escape from me? You will pay for this!"

Suzanne's eyes filled with tears, and she cried out. She curled into a fetal position on Alex's lap. The panic attack returned as she shivered in Alex's arms. "I told you he would come after me."

Alex sensed a rage he'd never experienced. "Take care of him now before I do!" Alex yelled, causing Suzanne to startle. He chided himself, gathering Suzanne closely against him a second time. Alex whispered, "I'm sorry, baby."

Officer Geary called for the others as he aimed his gun at Stephen. "Don't come any closer to her." The others came running, also with their weapons trained on Stephen.

"Suzanne, darling. You are supposed to be with me. I love you!" Stephen continued yelling as the officers pulled his arms behind his back. Once the handcuffs were on him, they forced him into the back of another police car while reading his rights. Throughout, Stephen continued yelling about his love for Suzanne.

Suzanne was whimpering, shaking, and crying. Alex tightened his arms around her. "Suzanne, baby. They've got him. He can't hurt you anymore." The paramedics approached, but Alex refused to let Suzanne go until she was calmer.

"We have oxygen that will help," the medic said with kind eyes.

Alex gently placed Suzanne on the gurney, but he kept her hand in his.

Once the medics moved in to examine her, Alex stood with his eyes on her, refusing to move back.

***

The paramedics set Suzanne's ankle as best as they could until she could get an x-ray at the hospital. Her cries of pain were hoarse because of her weeping earlier. Silent tears trailed down her cheeks when the medic apologetically inserted a needle for an IV. Alex had to force his hands to his sides so he wouldn't shove the paramedic working on her. "Help her, she's in pain!" Alex yelled. More than anything, he wanted to hold Suzanne and comfort her. As soon as her ankle was secure, he knelt beside her. Alex murmured calming words as he leaned down to kiss her brow.

"We're ready to load her into the ambulance," the paramedic said, glancing at Alex with widened eyes. She looked uncertain about what he might do. Alex realized she had noticed his anger. Alex took a few deep breaths and nodded as Suzanne squeezed his hand.

"I'm sorry for yelling at you," Alex said. "This has been the scariest night of my life."

The medic touched his shoulder. "I understand, and we will take good care of her."

Suzanne whimpered, "You're coming too. Right? Please don't leave me."

Alex's eyes filled with tears as he leaned down to kiss her softly. "There's no way I'm leaving you now. I'll be right by your side."

The two of them gazed into each other's eyes, even as Suzanne was lifted into the ambulance. Alex climbed in beside her, holding her hand and stroking her forehead. The pain medicine was taking effect. Suzanne soon relaxed and drifted off to sleep. Alex kept her hand in his as she slept.

Once they got to the hospital, Alex watched the emergency room nurse wheel Suzanne back for an x-ray. Suzanne had woken up, but her eyes were unfocused. Alex continued holding and massaging her hand. Once Suzanne was out of sight, he asked at the reception desk for a phone. After being directed down the hall, Alex called his apartment. He updated Michael, Hannah and Jessica. Hannah told him Jackie and Michelle were also there with Danny and Jennifer. She also told Alex that she and Michael would wait for Suzanne's parents so that they could accompany them to the hospital.

Ten minutes later, Jessica, Michelle, Danny, Jackie, and Jennifer came into the emergency room. Each of them gave Alex a comforting hug. He updated them on Suzanne's status. As he was talking, the same nurse wheeled Suzanne out to a small cubicle of the trauma room. Suzanne was still sleeping from the pain medicine.

Alex rushed toward them. "How is she?"

"Her ankle is broken, so now we are waiting for a doctor to come and place a splint around it. She will need to go to his office to get an official cast placed on the ankle." The nurse had kind eyes.

"Thank you," Alex said.

"Are her parents here?"

"Not yet," Alex said, "but they are on the way. I will wait with her until then."

Michelle placed a hand on Alex's arm and she held out a water bottle. "We will wait in the lobby and bring them back when they arrive."

"Thanks, Michelle," Alex said, taking the water. He unscrewed the cap and took several drinks. The cold water felt good on his throat.

Alex didn't realize it, but as he leaned a chair against the wall, he must have dozed off. A shuffling noise outside the curtain alerted him. Michelle pushed the curtain back and said, "Here they are."

"Oh my word," Suzanne's mom pushed forward, tears streaming down her face. "My baby girl!"

Suzanne's dad stood staring at Suzanne. Then he looked at Alex. "I understand you were a part of the search for Suzanne. Is that correct?"

Alex shook his outstretched hand. "Yes sir."

"Oh, Alex, thank you for helping to find her," Suzanne's mom sobbed. She tugged Alex into a hug, and he was squashed against her.

"You're quite welcome, ma'am," he said when he stepped out of her embrace. "I would do anything for your daughter."

Suzanne's dad studied Alex. "I was wrong about you, son. You've proven that you can care for Suzanne. For that, I want to apologize."

Alex's heart lifted upon seeing the sincerity in Mr. Mark's eyes. Her mother was already beside Suzanne again. As she squeezed her daughter's hand, Suzanne's eyes opened.

"Mom," she croaked. Her voice was hoarse from so much crying. "What are you doing here?"

"Jessica called us, and I'm so glad she did." Suzanne's eyes filled again as both of her parents leaned down to kiss each cheek.

"I love both of you so much," Suzanne said.

"Sweetheart, we love you," Suzanne's dad said with tears in his eyes.

Alex moved to step out when Suzanne said, "No. Alex, please don't leave."

Her parents stepped back, smiling at him. Mrs. Marks touched his cheek softly. "You are welcome to stay as long as you like."

Warmth spread through Alex's body as he smiled and moved to hold Suzanne's hand. "Thank you."

***

Later that night, Suzanne was released from the hospital, and her parents drove her home to help care for her. Her dad would call the university in the morning to get her excused from classes for the rest of the week. She would return during the week of final exams. Alex volunteered to help drive her around so that she could get from building to building for her classes. All of her friends also said they would help any way they could.

Before they left, Suzanne's parents thanked Alex again. Suzanne's mother invited him to visit their home. "Please come and stay with us this weekend. You can visit with her. I know it will cheer her up."

Alex smiled and accepted a hug from her. "I would like that. My last class ends at noon on Friday, so I will come that afternoon."

True to his word, Alex left at twelve thirty on Friday to travel to Suzanne's home. He had spoken with her on the phone several times, but neither of them mentioned their relationship. Alex hoped for some alone time with her because he wanted to talk to her about reconnecting.

He tapped the steering wheel impatiently as he drove. Thankfully, her home was only an hour away. This time, when he pulled up to the gate and pressed the button, Alex wasn't as overwhelmed. The house was still huge, but he was determined not to let it impede his love for Suzanne.

Once Alex parked in the circular driveway, he grabbed his overnight bag and walked to the front door. Suzanne's mom immediately hugged him upon answering the door. "I'm so glad you were able to come. Suzanne is bored out of her mind!"

Alex laughed as he stepped inside. "Thank you for inviting me. And I'm sure she doesn't like just lying around." Alex had a view of the family room, and his heart jumped when he saw Suzanne on the sofa with her legs outstretched in front of her. When she smiled, Alex thought his heart might stop.

Suzanne held out her hand. "Hi."

Alex placed his bag beside the door, and he walked to join Suzanne in the chair beside her. "Hey, beautiful," he whispered, taking her outstretched hand. Alex relished seeing the blush on Suzanne's face. It gave him hope that they still had a chance.

Suzanne's mom entered the family room. "I have some things to complete in the kitchen, so I will let the two of you visit." She walked out the other door and into the kitchen.

As soon as she stepped away, Alex raised her hand to his lips and kissed it softly. "How are you?"

"I'm doing okay, but I have to wear this cast for six weeks," Suzanne grimaced as she removed the blanket to show a bright pink cast.

Alex sat on the chair. "I'm so sorry that this happened to you, Suzanne. If we were still together, Stephen wouldn't have been able to get to you." His voice cracked, and his eyes closed. Alex rubbed a hand over his face.

Suzanne pulled her hand out of his to touch his arm. "Alex, look at me." Alex's eyes were troubled as he gazed at Suzanne. "This is not your fault. Stephen was obsessed with me. Hannah kept telling me that something didn't feel right, and I didn't listen to her. It's as much my fault as anyone else's. And I think he would have found a way even if we were still together. He might have harmed you."

"There's no way you are at fault in any of this," Alex whispered, grasping Suzanne's face in his hands. He gazed intently into her eyes, praying she believed his words. "I would much rather be the one injured than you."

Suzanne leaned toward him, and she shocked him when she kissed his cheek. As much as Alex wanted to lengthen the kiss, he pulled back and intertwined their fingers instead.

Suzanne's eyes filled with tears. "It was horrible. I will be honest about that, but I would not have wanted him to hurt you. He was able to get drugs to use on me, so who knows if he would have gotten a gun?"

"Mentally, how are you really?" Alex asked. Suzanne attempted to move her legs so he could sit beside her. Alex stopped her with his hand. He lifted her feet, moved beside her on the couch, and placed them on his lap.

Suzanne sighed. "I'm kind of messed up. Honestly, I've never been so helpless as when I was trapped in that cabin with Stephen. I was terrified of not being able to get out." Suzanne's breathing quickened as tears rolled down her face.

Alex said, "Slow down and breathe. You don't have to talk about it if it's too much."

"No, I want to tell you," Suzanne said as she took three deep breaths. Alex was rubbing his hand over her good leg, attempting to soothe her. After a long pause, Suzanne whispered, "Stephen told me we were going to get married. He even picked out a dress for me."

"Oh my god," Alex covered his eyes with his other hand while squeezing her leg.

"The three times Stephen hit me, he said it was for my own good. He told me I would eventually come to love him." Suzanne's voice choked as she said the last words. Her face was streaked with tears. "I keep seeing him in my dreams. He's coming toward me with the syringe he used on me at the library." The emergency room doctor ran tests and discovered Suzanne's bloodstream had traces of a popular sedative.

"Baby, I am so sorry." Tears leaked from Alex's eyes as he shifted her to embrace her, careful of the leg with the cast on it. Alex wrapped her tightly in his arms. Suzanne cried for several minutes.

As she pulled back, Alex found a tissue box. He pulled a couple out and handed them to Suzanne.

"Thank you," Suzanne whispered as she wiped her face. "I'm glad you're here. I love my parents, but I'm not comfortable sharing the details with them. My mom wants me to get professional help, but I told her I would make an appointment with Angela when I return to school."

"We'll both make appointments," Alex said. "I need to talk to Mark. Then I can drive you to and from the counseling center."

Suzanne leaned her head against Alex's shoulder, and he kissed the top of her head. His arms tightened around her because it felt wonderful to hold her close. Suzanne snuggled closer to Alex, wrapping her arms around his waist.

"I also want to apologize," Alex said. "I wanted some time alone to talk to you. Suzanne, I was wrong to put a stop to our relationship. I don't know what I was thinking, but it was the biggest mistake of my life."

Suzanne leaned back to look him in the eye. "It hurt so badly when you told me you couldn't provide for me like my parents."

"I know," Alex said. He glanced down at her hand in his. "I have a weakness for overreacting, and it causes me to become angry. Sometimes I feel like I'm not as good as others around me. It's why I need to keep seeing Mark and talking to him."

Suzanne was quiet, but she continued to lean against him as he talked. "What does this mean?"

Alex tilted her head so that he could look deeply into her eyes. "I love you more than life, Suzanne Marks. The thought of losing you made me insane. I want you to give me another chance, sweetheart."

"Oh, Alex. I love you, too. I didn't know what to do when you broke up with me." Alex kissed away the new tears rolling down Suzanne's cheeks.

"Do you forgive me?" Alex asked.

"Yes, as long as you promise to trust me. I love you for who you are. I don't need you to be anything else," Suzanne said with a yearning look in her eyes.

Alex used his free hand to tilt her chin upward. He leaned in to kiss her softly. Suzanne's eyes filled with panic. Alex pulled back and kissed her forehead instead.

"I'm sorry," Suzanne whispered, shaking all over.

"Suzanne, you've been through so much. It's fine." Alex said, as his heart broke from the terror in her eyes.

"Do you want to watch a movie?" Suzanne asked.

"As long as I'm with you, I don't care what we do." Alex kissed the top of her head, pulling her against him. He was thankful when she allowed him to hold her close. Alex accepted that her becoming comfortable with intimate gestures would take time. He vowed to take things slowly with her.

Chapter 20

On Saturday evening, Suzanne's parents had plans with friends of theirs for the evening. Alex got their approval, but he wanted to take Suzanne out of the house for dinner. Suzanne's mother quickly agreed, and Suzanne realized she needed a break from being her nurse. Guilt filled Suzanne. At some point, she needed to thank her mother. Alex promised to help Suzanne walk with the crutches into and out of the restaurant. He also promised to come straight home afterward.

Suzanne was elated about a date night with Alex. However, her fear of Alex kissing her was overwhelming, and intense guilt filled her. Stephen's abduction must have done a number on her mental state. Suzanne was fine if Alex held her. Deep down, she was terrified of scaring Alex away with her panic attacks. Suzanne was eager to meet with Angela to get help with why she had reacted in that way.

Before Suzanne's parents left, her mom helped her in and out of the shower. Suzanne didn't have as much energy to get ready, so her movements were slow. Her mom also blew dry her hair, and it hung in natural waves around her shoulders. Suzanne applied a small amount of makeup to conceal the fading bruises. Her mom assisted her in putting on a skirt and blouse. Because the holidays were near, Suzanne chose a red blouse and a black skirt.

Alex's eyes shone when she hobbled into the living room. His eyes were filled with adoration as he hugged her. "You are beautiful."

"I'm sorry it's not how I normally get ready. Everything has been harder with the crutches." Suzanne gazed down.

Alex touched her chin to raise her eyes to his. He placed her hand over his racing heart. "Trust me when I say you are just as lovely as you always have been."

Suzanne slowly smiled up at him, and she let out a huge breath. "Thank you. You look pretty wonderful as well."

Suzanne's mom smiled at the two of them. Her heart skipped at how her parents had grown to accept Alex in her life. Again, Suzanne would find time to talk to her mom.

"You kids have fun," her mother said as she moved back up the stairs. Suzanne's dad was taking her mother out for a much-needed break.

Alex moved Suzanne's crutches and leaned them against the couch. Suzanne looked at him with a puzzled expression. "What are you doing?" she asked. Before she could say her next words, Alex lifted her into his arms.

"I'm helping you to the car," Alex said with a sharp gaze.

"You don't have to carry me," Suzanne said.

Alex's eyes glinted playfully. "Why wouldn't I jump at an opportunity to hold you close?"

Suzanne chuckled softly as she laid her head on his shoulder. Alex walked out to his car, and he placed her gently on the passenger seat. When he shut her door, Alex jogged inside for the crutches. After laying them on the back seat, they were on the way.

When Alex pulled into the parking lot, Suzanne gasped, "I love this place! How did you know?"

"I might have had a little help from your dad," Alex said. He parked and walked around to Suzanne's side. Alex pulled the crutches out of the back seat, and he lifted Suzanne out before gently placing her on her good leg. Suzanne felt like a princess with his gentle treatment of her.

Alex placed his arm around her waist, and he walked slowly inside with Suzanne. Suzanne paused; tears were shining in her eyes. Alex was about to ask when she whispered, "Thank you for being so wonderful."

Alex leaned down to kiss Suzanne's nose. "My pleasure." Her heart leapt with joy when she didn't withdraw away from it.

"Are you sure this isn't too expensive?" Suzanne asked.

Alex kissed her head. "I've got it covered."

Suzanne felt as if her life was returning to normal when Alex slid into the booth beside her and wrapped his arm around her while studying the menu. Alex apologized and said he still loved her, but Suzanne's heart plummeted at the idea of him breaking it a second time. She wouldn't survive it. Even though she wanted to enjoy it, insecurity and fear overwhelmed her thoughts. Her mouth pursed as she wondered if that was why she was afraid for Alex to kiss her.

***

Alex and Suzanne enjoyed a lovely dinner, and he drove them back to Suzanne's home. The evening before, Alex asked Suzanne's dad for suggestions of a nice place where he could take Suzanne for dinner. Her dad called and made a reservation for them at the lovely Italian restaurant. Alex sat and explained his feelings about Suzanne. Her father reacted in the typical way that an overprotective father would.

Alex understood he cared only about Suzanne's well-being. Once Alex spoke his mind, Suzanne's dad shook his hand and thanked him for his honesty.

"I hate to ask you this, but will you help me change clothes?" Suzanne's eyes looked worried.

"Absolutely, baby. And you can trust me to do only that." Other than the attempted kiss on his first day there, Alex only held Suzanne's hand. Tonight was the first time he had placed his arm around her shoulders. Elation filled him when she leaned against his side. Alex recognized that Suzanne's guardedness was likely a response to the trauma with Stephen, coupled with Alex ending their relationship. He was also sensing that she was holding back emotionally from him. Alex realized he needed to earn her trust back after hurting her so badly.

After both of them changed clothes, Alex insisted on carrying Suzanne to the living room. He saw the exhaustion on her face. Alex walked back to his car and brought her crutches into the living room. He asked Suzanne to make a choice of a movie. Once Alex set it up, he moved behind Suzanne on the couch. Alex pulled her back against his chest, and he placed the lap blanket over her legs. He could sense Suzanne's contentment when she leaned back into his arms. Alex kissed her cheek and pressed *play* on the remote control. Again, his heart found peace when she welcomed his arms around her.

At one point, Suzanne asked, "Are you hungry or need something to drink?"

"I can get us something," Alex said against her ear, causing Suzanne to shiver. He wondered if it was a good shiver or a bad one. "What would you like?"

"There are a variety of sodas in the refrigerator, and my mom has a box of popcorn in the pantry." Suzanne reached for her crutches as Alex tried to protest. "I need to move around some so that my leg doesn't ache."

Alex helped her stand, and they plodded into the kitchen. He seized the opportunity to ask, "Suzanne, can I ask you a question?"

Suzanne was perched on the stools on the other side of the bar where Alex was pouring their drinks. "Sure."

"Do you trust me?" Alex put the soda can on the counter and watched Suzanne. "What I mean is, have I caused you to feel uncertain about where we stand in this relationship?"

Suzanne was quiet, and she was looking at her hands. Alex was patient and waited until she was ready to share. He unwrapped the bag of popcorn, and placed it in the microwave. "Where are the bowls?" Alex asked. Suzanne pointed to the cupboard above his head.

"Alex, I want to trust you. More than anything, I wish I could trust this is real. I guess I'm afraid you might get cold feet again. I don't think I can stand getting hurt a second time." Suzanne stared behind Alex.

The microwave beeped. Alex pulled out the bag of popcorn and he ripped it open. He poured equal amounts into each bowl. He placed the drinks and bowls on the tray he found. "Can you get your crutches?"

"Yes, I'm fine." Suzanne pulled the crutches under her armpits and hobbled back into the living room.

This time they were sitting side by side so that neither of them would spill their snack. Alex took Suzanne's bowl, and he placed it on the coffee table. Then, Alex took both of Suzanne's hands in his, and he faced her. His eyes shone with sincerity. "Suzanne, I'm so sorry that I've caused you to doubt my intentions. I want you to know that I will be patient and wait for you. But I will not stop telling you I love you or spending time with you. Please tell me that's okay."

Suzanne's eyes were bright with tears. She nodded her head, unable to speak.

"I'm going to attend as many counseling sessions as it takes to work on myself. And I'm going to prove to you I will not hurt you intentionally ever again."

Suzanne blew out a breath. "Okay," her voice was shaky as she answered. "I'm sorry that I'm struggling with this."

"Baby, you have nothing to be sorry about." Alex lifted one of her hands and kissed it. "You've been through an awful situation. And I understand I am partly to blame for your lack of trust as well."

Suzanne gazed at Alex. "Can we take things a little slower? I just don't feel comfortable becoming as intimate as we were."

"I will not push you. We will take it as slow as you need. I'm not going anywhere." Alex shook his head as he spoke. He lowered his gaze to catch Suzanne's. "Are you comfortable if I kiss you right now?"

"I think so." A tear spilled over as Suzanne nodded while dashing it away. Alex's thumb caught the rest of it as he stroked her cheek. He leaned gently toward Suzanne and captured her lips in a brief kiss. Alex didn't think Suzanne knew it, but she made a whimpering noise and his heart burst at the sound. He pulled back and whispered, "I love you, Suzanne Marks."

Another tear escaped. "I love you, too, Alex."

"Let's finish the movie," Alex said, grabbing the remote while handing Suzanne her popcorn and drink.

***

Sunday was a lazy day. Suzanne's parents stayed home from church to give her another morning to sleep in and rest. They decided Alex could drive Suzanne back to school that afternoon so that she could take her final exams for the week. Alex took a moment to speak to Suzanne's mother in the kitchen while Suzanne was still sleeping. Suzanne's dad was out for a run in the neighborhood. Alex shared his intentions toward Suzanne, just as he had done with her father.

Dana Marks looked at Alex. "Thank you for sharing that with me. I realize we were wrong about you." She leaned forward and grasped Alex's hands in hers. "I appreciate your telling me."

Alex smiled at her. "I promise to do only what is best regarding Suzanne and her future. If she doesn't feel the same toward me and it means letting her go, then I will."

Suzanne's mom's eyes teared up. They were also filled with respect toward Alex. "Deep down, Suzanne doesn't want you to let her go. What I see in her eyes is permanent. It's the same way I look at her dad."

"Thank you, Mrs. Marks," Alex said.

"Alex, you've earned the right to call me Dana." Dana squeezed Alex's hands.

Alex smiled again, but he didn't comment.

Later that afternoon, Alex and Suzanne packed for their trip back to the university. After a tearful goodbye from Suzanne's mom, Alex began the drive back to school.

"Thank you for coming to visit me," Suzanne said as she gazed out the window.

"Wild horses couldn't have kept me away," Alex said, glancing at her. He entwined their fingers together, driving with the other hand. "Suzanne, look at me."

When Suzanne gazed at him, Alex said, "I think you are worried that I won't love you if we don't kiss."

Suzanne bit her lip before saying, "I feel like I'm broken right now. You had nothing to do with Stephen, so I don't know why kissing you is so scary to me."

"Baby, I've told you I think my hurting you, combined with Stephen's kidnapping, did a number on your heart," Alex said.

"What if I never get better? Alex, I don't want you to waste time on me if we can't ever be intimate." Suzanne tried to pull her hand away, but Alex wouldn't release it.

He was quiet for a few moments. "Suzanne, my feelings for you are so much more than kissing and sex. I don't want to live without you in my life anymore. It might be good for us to get to know each other without the intimate moments. I mean, yeah, I like them. What guy doesn't? What I'm trying to say is that I can live without that, but I don't want to live without you."

Quiet sobs were escaping Suzanne's mouth. "Alex, I don't want to live without you, either." Suzanne knew she didn't deserve someone as wonderful as Alex. She wondered if this was how someone understood beyond any doubt they had met their lifelong partner. Suzanne always pondered the connection between her parents. Suzanne was brought back to the present when Alex lifted her hand to his lips and kissed it softly.

When Alex pulled into a parking spot outside Suzanne's dorm, he told her to wait until he could come around and help her out. Alex helped carry her bag into the lobby as Suzanne maneuvered with the crutches. They stepped up to the desk where the resident assistant had her head buried in a textbook.

"Excuse me," Suzanne said. The girl looked up. "Can I call my roommate to come out and help me? As you can see, I can't carry my bag into my room with these crutches."

The girl hopped up. "I can take it down there for you."

"Thank you," Suzanne said. She turned toward Alex.

Alex gave her hand a squeeze. "I will call you later," he whispered in Suzanne's ear only. "I love you."

"I love you, too." Suzanne whispered.

***

The next day, Alex arrived to pick Suzanne up. Both of them had scheduled counseling sessions. She was watching out the window, so she hurried out to his car when he arrived. Suzanne was learning how to move more quickly on the crutches.

"Slow down, baby," Alex leapt out of the car and ran up the steps to help her.

Suzanne waved his hand away. "I have to learn how to do things by myself on these things."

"Okay, okay," Alex said. "I will just walk beside you."

When he parked across from the counseling center, Suzanne refused to wait for him. "My, you're a firecracker today," Alex said, chuckling.

"Thank you for all your help," Suzanne said. "I want to learn how to be independent, even on crutches."

Alex said, "I can respect that. Can I at least hold the door open for you?"

A smile lurked on Suzanne's face as she said, "Yes, Mr. smarty pants." They paused before breaking into laughter together.

As they stepped into the center, Angela was standing behind the desk. "Suzanne," she said as she walked toward Suzanne. Careful of her crutches, Angela pulled Suzanne into a side hug. "I'm so sorry to hear this happened to you. Hello, Alex. Mark is almost finished with his session."

"Thank you," Suzanne smiled. "I'm doing better." Alex waved and sat on the couch.

"Let's go back to my office," Angela said. Angela was patient in allowing Suzanne to lead the way, maneuvering down the hallway. "You seem to move pretty swiftly on those crutches!"

Suzanne dropped onto the couch, and she sighed. "I have to learn how to manage these things on my own. I can't rely on Alex and my friends for every moment of every day."

Angela picked up her notepad. "Let's talk about what happened to you."

Suzanne nodded, and her throat tightened. She knew this was coming. Suzanne blew out a breath. "Okay." She shared her developing friendship with Stephen. Suzanne talked about Hannah's sense that something was wrong with Stephen. Then, she went into detail about the kidnapping. Tears were streaming down her face as she talked about what had happened in the cabin.

Angela listened. She didn't speak, letting Suzanne share the details. Angela picked up the tissue box, passing it to Suzanne. Suzanne reached for one with shaking hands.

Once Suzanne was finished, Angela said, "Let's talk about Hannah's feelings concerning Stephen. You talked about it, but you quickly changed the subject. Why was that?"

Suzanne looked at her hands as she twiddled her fingers. "Hannah kept telling me that something wasn't right with Stephen." Suzanne burst into tears and covered her face with her hands. "I didn't believe her. I kept saying everything was fine. It's my fault that he kidnapped me. I should have listened to her!" Suzanne was wailing by the time she finished the sentence.

"Suzanne, look at me." Angela touched her arm. When Suzanne raised her gaze, Angela said, "You did not cause Stephen to kidnap you. It wasn't your fault. I need you to understand that this is misplaced guilt."

Suzanne watched Angela, but she said nothing. "I should've listened to Hannah. With all she's been through, I should have realized that her instincts were correct."

Angela said, "Suzanne, you made a decision. You have a wonderful, loving heart. Don't dissuade that. Should you learn to become more aware of the world? Probably. But you couldn't have stopped Stephen's obsession with you." Angela remained silent. "Tell me about the pictures Stephen shared again."

Suzanne stared behind Angela. "He brought pictures of Alex playing basketball in high school. Stephen said someone gave them to him because he was friends with me. He was concerned that we were dating and Alex had anger issues."

Angela nodded as she jotted notes. She looked up and said, "I want you to learn to observe other people. If you take time to watch people and truly hear what they say and do, I believe you can develop your own intuition. Stephen was someone you thought you could trust. But when you had that gut feeling and told him to stay out of your relationship, it was your body and mind connecting. We need to get you to trust that more deeply."

Suzanne's eyebrows dipped, and she rubbed her chin thoughtfully. "How should I do that?"

Angela said, "You still have the journal from your first session, correct?" Suzanne nodded. Angela continued, "Sit outside in the middle of the campus and watch people. Write what you observe. When you bring it back, we can talk about what you wrote."

Suzanne's eyes clouded. "I don't want to look like I'm staring because people might fear that I'm a stalker."

Angela nodded. "Watch for a few seconds, but let your eyes move around. You don't want them to stay with just one person. Then jot down what you thought about. Next week when you come, we will role-play. I will find several scenarios, and we will talk about what your body and mind are telling you about them"

Suzanne nodded again. "That sounds good. I want to learn how to be independent and trust myself."

Angela smiled. "I know you do. I believe in you, Suzanne. We will also take time to reflect on past events in your life and identify any patterns you see."

"My biggest pattern is my overprotective parents," Suzanne muttered, and Angela smiled again.

"It may get to a point where you need to communicate with your parents concerning this matter. Maybe they could even join you for one of these sessions." Angela said.

"I don't know if I'm comfortable sharing what I share with you." Suzanne clenched her hands as she stated those words.

"That is perfectly normal, Suzanne. You and I can meet first. Then they could join us after your session." Angela paused. "How were they with Alex concerning this?"

Suzanne paused for a moment. Angela remained quiet. It was one thing Suzanne loved about her. Angela gave her space to process her thoughts. Suzanne also loved that she didn't repeat questions.

"In answer to your question about them and Alex, they totally trust him now. Alex went to great lengths to help find me, and I believe that scored some major points with both of them." Suzanne gazed at the wall, not blinking for a few seconds.

Angela leaned forward. "Let's stop there for today. With all you've been through, I think we should take your sessions one step at a time."

Suzanne stood, and this time she initiated the hug. "Thank you so much. You've already helped so much."

"You are very welcome," Angela said.

Chapter 21

Mark walked another client out to the lobby. When Alex stood, Mark walked to him and stretched out his hand. After greeting each other, Mark said, "Let's go back to my office." Mark gestured for Alex to lead the way.

Alex's legs felt like lead. It had been several weeks since his last meeting with Mark. He realized he had forgotten the spiral notebook. Guilt filled him at the realization of not completing the assignment.

Mark said, "Have a seat," as he shut his door. After he picked up his pen and notepad, Mark said, "How have you been?"

Alex didn't mean for the words to gush out. "Look, I forgot the notebook. I wrote a little in it after the last time, but I haven't done it since. I'm really sorry."

"Alex, these sessions are not graded. I will not chastise you for not completing your homework. I understand that life gets in the way. From what happened with Suzanne, you have a good excuse." Mark's eyes were kind.

Alex blew out a breath. "Yeah, and I was so stupid to break up with her a couple of days before that."

Mark propped a leg on the other. "Tell me about that."

"I visited Suzanne's home. She lives in an enormous house. Her dad is a lawyer. It's obvious he makes a ton of money. I've been nowhere near wealthy, and I don't think I will ever have that much money in my life with an accounting degree."

Mark nodded. "How did you react when you saw the house?"

"I assumed I couldn't be good enough for Suzanne. She's grown up with so much, and I'm afraid of disappointing her." Alex said.

"Has Suzanne ever mentioned wanting to live in a large house?" Mark asked.

"No," Alex said.

"Has she talked about wanting to settle down with someone who makes a lot of money?" Mark asked again.

"No," Alex repeated.

Mark paused for a millisecond. "What made you think she might feel that way?"

"I know, I know," Alex moaned. "I was so stupid to have assumed what she might want. It hurt her so badly. She's afraid to trust me now."

"Alex, I could tell you that Suzanne has a right to feel that way," Mark said, "but that will not help you to overcome this. I don't want to drag you down even further. I asked these questions so that you could think through the decision you made."

Alex sat listening. "How do I win back Suzanne's trust?"

"First, we need to work on you. I'm going to say something that will probably sting and make you want to put yourself down," Mark said.

"Okay..." Alex said.

Mark leaned forward in his chair. "Alex, you have an inferiority complex. We talked about your history the last time you were here. I took some time to review it and look at it before today. I believe it stems from your father's abandoning you and your mom. You have a great heart, but trying to put pressure on your shoulders to help your mom increases your feelings of failure." Mark paused, letting his words sink in.

Alex was looking down at his feet, and he said nothing.

"Alex, you are not responsible for your mother," Mark said.

Alex quickly shifted his gaze back to Mark. "She needs my help."

"Alex, your mother is the parent. She is an adult. Her job was to take care of you and your siblings. I'm sure she is thankful to have a son with compassion and a willingness to help her out. But I imagine she doesn't expect you to carry such a heavy burden. I think you have placed that on yourself." Mark paused again.

Tears flooded Alex's eyes. "It was so hard to watch her struggle to make ends meet. Sometimes, she went without breakfast or lunch to make sure I had food to eat. My mom didn't shop for herself or spend money on things she wanted. I wanted to help lift her burden." Alex allowed himself to cry softly with his chin on his chest.

Mark placed a hand on Alex's arm. "Like I said before, Alex, you have a wonderful, giving heart. I admire the love you have for your mother. And I think you need to release some of the pressure you've placed on yourself concerning her. I imagine if you shared these thoughts with her, she would agree. Your mother sounds like a reasonable person."

Alex's eyes were red-rimmed when he looked back at Mark. "How do I get over this inferiority complex?"

Mark smiled. "One way to face it is by writing in your journal, but don't beat yourself up if you don't do it all the time."

Alex smiled back at him. "Okay, is that all?"

Mark reached down to the bottom shelf of his side table. "I want you to listen to this cassette tape. It is about cognitive-behavioral therapy, or what counselors call CBT. This will teach you what it is and how to recognize when you have negative thoughts."

"Okay," Alex took the tape.

"Alex, you won't like this, but I want you to write when you recognize a negative thought about yourself. What makes you think this way? What caused it? I believe that will be the first step in learning to overcome your fear of not measuring up."

Alex's eyes burned with purpose. "I am going to do that because I promised Suzanne I would work on myself."

Mark stood. "Good, but do this for yourself as much as for her." When Mark opened the door, the two of them walked back into the lobby. Suzanne was sitting on the couch, waiting. She had a textbook open, so Alex assumed she was trying to study.

Alex set up his next session with Mark. He walked to Suzanne and pulled her gently to her feet. Alex wrapped her in his arms. "Hey, baby. How did it go for you?"

Suzanne's eyes were filled with peace. "It went really well."

"Mine did, too. I would like to tell you about it. I'm here if you want to talk about yours, but I don't want to put any pressure on you." Alex smiled into Suzanne's eyes.

"I'd like that," Suzanne said.

"Do you have time to get something to eat tonight?" Alex pushed a strand of hair behind Suzanne's ear.

"Yeah, as long as I can study for a while before that," Suzanne said.

Alex took her hand, entwining their fingers together. "I need to study, too. How about if I come for you at six?"

Suzanne nodded her head, and Alex squeezed her hand.

***

Suzanne freshened up a bit, as best as she could with crutches. Her phone rang. She hobbled over to answer it. Jessica was at the library. Alex told her he was in the lobby. Suzanne strapped her backpack across her back. It was the only way she could carry personal items and still use the crutches.

Alex drove them to the Mexican restaurant they were supposed to eat at a few days ago. "Can I ask you to wait for me because I want to be a gentleman?" His smile was teasing.

Suzanne giggled. "Yes, I will wait."

Once they were at a table, Alex slid onto Suzanne's side of the booth. He ordered chips, salsa, and cheese dip after both of them placed their drink orders.

"I want you to share with you about how Mark helped identify what's going on with me," Alex said, as he placed his arm on the back of the booth behind Suzanne.

Suzanne's eyes were curious. "Okay."

Alex looked down at the table. "I have an *inferiority complex*. Mark wants me to learn about cognitive-behavioral therapy. He gave me a tape, and I listened to part of it. It's great."

The server brought their drinks and appetizers.

Suzanne placed her hand on Alex's. "I understand that's probably difficult to talk about. I appreciate your sharing it with me."

Alex squeezed her hand while his arm was still around her. As he spoke again, Suzanne interrupted. "Angela told me some things about myself as well. I actually want to ask for your help. She wants me to learn to trust my intuition so that I can learn to sense when something isn't right. I should have listened to Hannah concerning Stephen, but I didn't."

Alex was listening avidly. "I will help you however you need."

Suzanne hesitated. "Will you sit with me on a bench in the middle of the campus tomorrow afternoon? I am supposed to watch and observe people. Then, I have to write about it. I don't want to look like a stalker, so I want you to sit with me. You can study or do anything else you need." Suzanne's mouth was pursed and her fingers tightened into a fist.

"Suzanne, look at me." When Suzanne gazed up at him, Alex said, "I am here for you. Whatever you might ask me, I will try to do it. I'm learning that I might mess up or not do it perfectly, but I will try my best to meet all of your needs."

Suzanne's gaze turned warm. She leaned in and started a kiss, shocking herself. When she leaned back, Suzanne could tell Alex was also surprised. "I love you, Alex."

Alex cradled her face. "I love you more than I can express. Can I kiss you deeper? I don't want to make you uncomfortable."

"I won't know unless I try it," Suzanne said.

Alex caressed Suzanne's cheek. "Please tell me if it is too much. When Suzanne nodded, he leaned in to kiss her again. Alex increased the pressure, tilting his head for a deeper kiss. Sparks flew through him. It was the same sensation he had when they first kissed. A few seconds later, Alex pulled back. Alex studied Suzanne's face, then he smiled. "I think you liked that."

Suzanne was beaming. "It felt like our first kiss."

Alex leaned his forehead against Suzanne's. "I wonder what changed."

"We're talking to each other and sharing our hearts. I believe you are sincere in your intentions now." Suzanne said as she reached up to stroke Alex's cheek.

Alex groaned before he kissed her deeply once more. "I need to stop," he said. "I'm afraid I might do inappropriate things."

***

The week flew by quickly. Alex and Suzanne's friends helped her in getting around campus so she could attend her last classes or study at the library. Suzanne and Alex spent Monday afternoon sitting in the quad, which was the center of the campus. The two of them spent a few moments talking and kissing each other. Then, Alex pulled out a textbook while Suzanne completed her homework assignment to observe others and write about it.

After he finished reviewing, Alex talked to her about cognitive-behavioral therapy. He confided his fear of not being good enough, especially with his mom. Suzanne loved hearing him open up about his personal struggles. Their connection became stronger emotionally.

On Wednesday, Alex drove them back to the counseling center for another session with Mark and Angela. Alex and Suzanne requested a session with all four of them because of how they were growing in their relationship.

Mark and Angela were waiting for them. After a quick kiss on Suzanne's cheek, the two of them walked in opposite directions to the office.

Angela shut the door behind her. Suzanne sat down as she asked, "So how are you doing?"

Suzanne said, "I completed the assignment of observing other people." She handed Angela the notebook.

Angela read Suzanne's observations. "These are great, Suzanne. You gave solid observations of people around you. You talked about a couple nearby and how they were in the middle of a disagreement. I'm proud of how you expressed feelings of unease as they argued."

Suzanne beamed. "Thank you. I didn't stop to notice the thoughts I have when I observe people around me until this assignment."

"I want you to learn to be cognizant wherever you are. You are now learning to recognize it. I think you're ready for the next step. You may not be happy with me after this assignment, but I want us to role play a scenario. It will help you learn how to navigate situations when you are uncomfortable around unfamiliar people," Angela said.

Suzanne nodded, but she said nothing as her eyes widened.

Angela picked up a sheet of paper and handed it to Suzanne. She had another copy of it in her hand. "I want us to work on a scene similar to what you went through with Stephen. It is wonderful to have a trusting heart, but in this case, it became a dangerous situation."

"Okay," Suzanne whispered with uncertainty in her voice.

Angela looked at Suzanne. "Are you ready?" When Suzanne nodded, she continued. "We can create the setting in a familiar place. Why don't you decide what it should be?"

"How about at the student center?" Suzanne said. "It's where students mingle the most."

"Sure," Angela said. "You are in the student center with...who do you want with you?"

"Jessica, Hannah, Michelle and Jackie," Suzanne said.

"The five of you are sitting around talking and relaxing after a long day of classes," Angela adds to the setting of this pretend scene.

Angela coached Suzanne through two situations involving strangers. By the time she finished, Suzanne's eyes began to droop. More than anything, she wanted to lie down and sleep.

"You look exhausted," Angela said.

"I am," Suzanne said.

"And how has your thinking changed since your initial meeting with Stephen?" Angela asks.

Suzanne sighed. "I should have listened to my gut when he approached all of us at the restaurant. I pushed it down, telling myself that he just wanted to get to know me. When Hannah mentioned a strange feeling, it should have cemented my uncertainty."

"That's great, Suzanne. Your homework is to go back and rest. Don't forget to drink a lot of water," Angela touched her arm.

Suzanne nodded, too tired to respond. She sat on the couch to wait for Alex, laying her head back and closing her eyes.

***

Meanwhile, Alex and Mark were in the middle of their counseling session. Mark praised Alex for the journaling of his thoughts after listening to the cognitive-behavioral therapy tape Mark shared with him.

"Alex, this is great stuff. You are learning how to share thoughts we haven't covered yet," Mark said, handing the notebook back to Alex.

"I've always known about my anger issues. I struggled with sitting still in a classroom as a kid. When the teacher disciplined me, I didn't handle it well. It often caused more consequences because I became extremely mad." Alex said, surprising himself at sharing his childhood thoughts.

Mark nodded. "That's typical when facing negative behavior patterns. They lead to other negative thoughts and actions."

Alex shook his head. "I've got to get my anger under control. My relationship with Suzanne is too important."

"I want us to get to the root of why you struggle with anger. We've explored a minor part of it, but some of your mental struggles lead to reacting in this way." Mark said. "Let's explore what triggers your anger. That means thoughts, feelings, and how you developed coping skills in your situation."

Alex nodded, but he didn't respond.

Mark continued. "It's quite clear that your feelings of abandonment from your dad are a large part of what sets you off. I want you to consider other times as a child when you reacted negatively in anger. It sounds as if some of your classroom experiences were part of it as well. What caused you to do this in school?"

Alex stared off behind Mark. "I went to a school where some wealthy families attended. Our house was on the edge of the zone of some rich homes. I realize my mom chose that neighborhood so I could grow up in a safe environment as a child.""

"How did you feel next to the wealthier kids?" Mark asked.

"Some of them weren't bad, but there were also kids who felt totally entitled. They would treat their teachers horribly as well as kids like me," Alex said.

"And how did that make you feel?" Mark repeated.

Alex groaned. "I hated seeing how they had spoken to teachers. My mom would have grounded me for life if I spoke to an adult in that way."

Mark nodded. "Alex, you have a large capacity to empathize with others around you. You struggled with watching your mother have a hard time making ends meet. It's my understanding that you carried that misconception with you to school."

"Yes, I can see that now," Alex said.

"I think it's why you struggled with anger when you got in trouble with your teachers. You couldn't communicate with them. You hated to see them mistreated by some of your classmates. The anger came from being misunderstood." Mark said.

"This is unbelievable," Alex said. "I never realized that I was mad because I wanted to help my teachers."

Mark nodded. "That anger has built momentum throughout your life. Are there times when you blow your top and you wonder why you got so upset?"

Alex's eyes bulged. "Yes," he breathed, "all the time."

Mark said, "This is just the beginning, but I want you to learn to recognize when your brain senses a problem. Using breathing techniques and relaxation methods, you can learn to manage your anger."

"Okay," Alex said. "Let's start. I'm ready to learn how to work through all of this."

Mark held up his hand. "Slow down a bit. It's time to end this session because this is enough for today. Your homework is to write about your feelings every single day. Try to recall when you felt frustrated or angry. Go back and recognize where the negative thoughts intruded."

"Okay," Alex said, with a disappointed tone to his voice.

Mark chuckled. "Alex, I admire your tenacity. But this is going to be a lifelong struggle and process."

"Okay, you're right." Alex answered. "I just want to get better."

"You will," Mark said as he stood up, signaling the end to their session.

Alex set up his next appointment when they walked to the lobby. Suzanne was leaning against the couch. Alex frowned as he approached her. "Suzanne, baby, are you alright?" Alex asked.

Suzanne opened her eyes and smiled. "I'm fine. The session was good, just exhausting."

"Let me help you up," Alex said, holding out his hand. Suzanne took it and stood in front of him.

"I love you, Alex Fleming," Suzanne said.

Alex noticed Mark and Angela smiling in their direction, so he simply kissed Suzanne's cheek and said, "I love you, too. We will pick this up later."

Suzanne smiled up at him. "I can't wait."

Alex smiled into her eyes. "Mark and Angela are watching us."

Suzanne pulled away quickly as a flush came across her neck and face. Alex chuckled, but he kissed her forehead before he released her. "Do you want to plan a time for the four of us?"

"Yes," Suzanne said as they turned back to the desk. After making an appointment for a couple's session on Thursday, the two of them walked outside.

Alex said, "Do you want to plan a date this weekend?"

"Yes," Suzanne said.

Alex paused. "Are you ready for more intimacy, or would you rather wait?"

Suzanne leaned up and kissed Alex softly on the lips. "I think I'm ready for more. Can we see what happens and stop if I freeze up?"

"Baby, I will do whatever you need. I care more about you than doing that," Alex pressed his forehead against Suzanne's.

"Okay, then I think I'm ready to try," Suzanne said.

"I need to see what Michael is planning to do." Alex said. "But right now, you need to take a nap."

"I need to study," Suzanne said, frowning.

Alex frowned. "You've been studying nonstop. It won't hurt for you to rest a bit. You can come and sleep in my room so that I can monitor you."

Suzanne's scowl was adorable, but she didn't argue as Alex took her bag to help her to his car.

When she had fallen asleep in his bed, Alex watched her. Gently, he pushed the hair off of her face and kissed her forehead. Suzanne didn't move. Alex realized just how precious she was to him.

"I love you, Suzanne Marks," he whispered. Alex sat up and turned on his television, finding a basketball game to watch as Suzanne continued to sleep.

***

Thursday's session with Mark and Angela was a wonderful time of sharing. Alex and Suzanne became more secure in their relationship because of the open conversations. Alex shared the root of his anger from when he was a child. Suzanne talked about the role-play scenarios she practiced with Angela in order to become more aware of people.

Alex offered to drive Suzanne to her home on Saturday for Christmas break. Her parents were happy that he had offered. Alex would stay one night before traveling home to be with his mom. Suzanne was going to his house the week after Christmas to spend with him and his mother. Suzanne's heart skipped at how Alex was proving his sincerity in their relationship.

Suzanne was ecstatic when her last final was over. She had exceeded all of them, keeping her goal of straight A's. Tonight, she wanted to celebrate. And what better way to do it than to spend it with Alex? Suzanne wore the same dress she wore to the last dinner out at the beautiful restaurant on the lake. Alex made reservations for them to return to it. Jessica was also leaving the next day, so she volunteered to help Suzanne get ready since Suzanne was still limited in her mobility because of her crutches.

The two of them were happy to spend more time together before the long break. Jessica was not planning to attend the January session.

Suzanne was sitting in a chair while Jessica applied her makeup and curled her hair. Jessica was sharing about a couple of dates with a guy she really liked.

"I'm happy for you," Suzanne said.

"We've only been on two dates," Jessica said. "But he's coming to my house the week after Christmas."

Suzanne smiled. "I hope it works out for you."

Ten minutes later, Suzanne was ready. Jessica said, "You look fabulous, if I say so myself!"

Suzanne hugged her roommate. "Thank you. I appreciate you!"

"Have a fabulous time," Jessica said, wagging her eyebrows up and down. Suzanne laughed as the phone rang. She knew it was Alex. Her backpack was stuffed full since she was planning to stay the night. Michael and Hannah had already traveled to his house for a few days before Christmas.

Alex's eyes turned warm when he saw Suzanne. "You look beautiful," he said as he kissed her softly.

"Thank you. You look wonderful," Suzanne said.

Dinner was as delicious as the other times they had been to that restaurant. Alex and Suzanne ordered dessert and coffee, lingering at the table. Because of Suzanne's cast, they couldn't dance, but lovely Christmas music was playing. Alex stood and held out his hand to help Suzanne out of her seat. Once he helped her position her crutches, they walked to his car.

When Alex pulled up to his apartment, Suzanne felt flutters in her stomach. She was excited about staying the night with Alex. Their time spent sharing deepened her desire to be with him.

Alex unlocked his door, and he allowed Suzanne to move inside. "Are you comfortable going to my room, or would you rather stay in the living room?"

Suzanne looked at him. "Let's go to your room."

Alex's eyes turned smoky as he stepped back to let Suzanne move her crutches into his bedroom. Alex shut the door. He moved to take Suzanne's crutches from her. Then he leaned them against the desk on the other side of his bedroom. He lifted her into his arms, touching his lips to hers at the same time.

Suzanne melted into his kiss, and she didn't realize she had made a noise until Alex moaned. He pulled her tighter into his arms before forcing himself to move back. Alex placed Suzanne on the bed. He reached for the hem of her dress with a question in his eyes. Suzanne helped him raise it over her hips so that he could pull it off of her.

Alex's eyes glowed. "You are so beautiful," he whispered. He unbuttoned his own shirt and shoved it off onto the floor. Suzanne removed her pantyhose, and she moved back onto the bed in her bra and panties. Her heart was pounding as she gazed at him with what she hoped was an invitation.

Alex crawled toward her on the bed. When he reached her, Alex grasped the back of her head and pulled her mouth back to his.

Suzanne's hands were roving over Alex's chest and back. Alex's hand stopped over the cups of her bra, and he shoved them down, gazing at Suzanne's breasts. He made a gasping noise as his hand cupped her breast, squeezing it. His fingers rounded her nipple. Alex pulled it to a sharp peak as Suzanne moaned. She tried reaching behind her to unclasp her bra. Alex helped her open it, and he threw it on the floor with his shirt.

Suzanne whimpered as he kissed a trail down her neck to her breast. Alex pulled it into his mouth, and Suzanne moaned a second time.

Suzanne brazenly trailed her hand down Alex's chest, kissing it as she went. She stopped at the band of Alex's underwear. Her fingers whispered over his length. Alex gasped and moaned as Suzanne reached into his briefs and grasped him in her hand. As Alex groaned again, it was caught in a kiss as he touched his lips to Suzanne's again. Alex moved to where she was underneath him and he reached between her legs. Alex touched her outside of her panties. Suzanne reached to pull them off. Alex helped her. Once he removed his own, he leaned over her. Alex kissed Suzanne, deepening the kiss as their tongues touched and danced together.

Suzanne realized it wasn't their first time, but this time with Alex was just as intense as their first time together. Alex's fingers found their way between Suzanne's legs, causing her to gasp loudly. He trailed his fingers over her folds, slipping a finger inside of her. Suzanne said, "Oh my word."

Alex leaned down to pull a breast into his mouth as he continued stroking his finger in and out of her opening. Suzanne was thrashing her head from side to side. "I love watching you when I touch you," Alex whispered in her ear.

Suzanne stroked him a few times as he continued to touch her. Finally, Alex reached for a condom. After slipping it on, he positioned himself between Suzanne's legs. Suzanne's hands were urging him to slide in.

They both gasped with pleasure. As Alex increased his thrusts, the two of them continued to moan. As always, Alex brought Suzanne to climax first before allowing his own orgasm to overtake him.

Afterward, neither of them moved for a while. Alex moved to the side to dispose of the condom before he pulled Suzanne onto his chest. She lay there content, stroking her hand up and down his abdomen.

"I love you, Suzanne," Alex said, staring at the ceiling.

"Oh, Alex. I love you, too," Suzanne said.

"That was just as magical as our first time," Alex said, stroking his fingers through her long hair.

Suzanne leaned up to look into his eyes. "It felt like our first time together."

Alex gazed at her before sitting up. "I hope every time is that way."

"Me too," Suzanne said.

Alex stood, waving at Suzanne to remain where she was. "I talked to your dad about my feelings being permanent toward you."

"You did?" Suzanne asked, astonished.

"I did." Alex pulled a small, wrapped box out of his desk drawer. He walked it over to the bed and handed it to Suzanne.

"I need to get your gift," Suzanne moved to get up.

Alex said, "Open mine first."

Suzanne unwrapped the small box to see a jewelry box inside it. She gasped as she opened it.

"I understand we have a while to go, and we can certainly take our time," Alex said. "But I love you more than anything in this world. What I'm trying to say is, Suzanne Marks, will you marry me?"

Suzanne's eyes were shining with tears as she nodded. "Yes, yes, I will marry you."

Alex wrapped her in a bear hug on his bed, rocking her back and forth. Then he pulled back, opened the box and slid the ring onto her left hand.

"What about your mom?" Suzanne asked.

"I talked to her right after speaking with your dad, and she is completely supportive. She could see that we were the ones for each other," Alex said.

Suzanne gazed at him. "After everything, you and I are finally going to be together forever."

"Always and forever," Alex murmured as he kissed her gently while pushing her back onto the bed.

"What about your gift?" Suzanne asked.

"You are my gift," Alex whispered before he kissed her deeply.

Epilogue

December, 1991

Suzanne

Suzanne took a deep breath as she stared at herself in the mirror. After two long years, the day arrived. She was marrying Alex! Her heart skipped two beats as Suzanne pondered their years together.

It hadn't been easy, but the two of them committed to one another. Many months of counseling gave them the wisdom to work through the deep underlying issues in each other's lives. They were still a work in progress. Suzanne knew it would be a lifelong battle, but she was determined to work through it at Alex's side.

The door opened, and her mom stopped in the doorway. Her mom's hand flew to her mouth as tears filled her eyes and spilled over. "My baby! You look like an angel!"

"Thanks, Mom." Suzanne turned and embraced her mother. The relationship with her parents grew throughout these years as well. Their acceptance and love of Alex as a son had grown.

As they hugged tightly, another knock sounded at the door. When Suzanne opened the door, her dad stood there, looking extremely handsome in his tuxedo.

Suzanne's dad grasped her hands and stood back. "You are breathtaking, little girl."

"Thank you, Dad," Suzanne whispered as she moved into her father's arms.

The wedding coordinator opened the door. "It's time. Let's move you to the alcove of the church."

The three of them stepped out into the lovely December day. The sun sparkled. Suzanne believed the weather was keeping in step with her heart.

Music was playing as Suzanne and her parents stepped through the front doors of the church. Hannah, Jackie, Michelle, and Jessica were waiting. The five of them spent many hours that morning laughing and enjoying preparing for this epic day in Suzanne's life. These ladies became the best friends Suzanne ever knew.

Hannah couldn't stop herself from rushing to Suzanne for another hug. "I'm so happy for you," she whispered. Hannah and Michael had been married for six months. Danny and Michelle's wedding was the following spring.

Suzanne's eyes welled, but she refused to allow the tears to fall. "Thank you. I love you so much!" She looked at the other girls. "All of you."

The doors opened. Alex escorted his mom to her seat. Then Alex insisted he should walk Suzanne's mom down the aisle. Suzanne stood behind a pillar as she watched Alex extend his elbow to her mom. It was good she was getting a glimpse of Alex now. He was devastatingly handsome. Suzanne knew she would have been speechless upon seeing him after walking down the aisle. She might bumble her vows in the process of looking at him.

The music changed. Hannah and Suzanne's other friends joined the other groomsmen, Michael, Danny, and James. Brian, he asked them to stop calling him Pastor Brian, extended his elbow for Jessica. Suzanne struggled with choosing a maid of honor. Jessica was her oldest friend. After much deliberation, Suzanne asked her roommate to stand in for her.

Then it was just Suzanne and her dad. Her dad pulled at his collar. He cleared his throat. "Are you ready?"

"More than ready," Suzanne said, leaning up to kiss her dad's cheek. "Thank you, Dad."

Suzanne's nerves soon left her as she fixed her gaze on her handsome fiancé. Alex's eyes shone clear and steady as she began the slow walk down the aisle. Suzanne felt as if she were walking on a cloud. She wanted to remember this day, but she did not know how she got to the altar. Suzanne glanced at her father, knowing it was his steady arm that kept her moving.

The pastor of Suzanne's church was leading part of the service. Pastor Brian would lead the rest of it.

When the pastor spoke, asking who was giving her away, her father spoke firmly. Suzanne turned and grasped Alex's fingers, gazing up into his eyes.

Alex's eyes were dark. His eyes were filled with wonder as he looked at Suzanne. She knew he was overwhelmed by how she looked in her dress.

Alex squeezed her fingers, mouthing, "I love you."

Suzanne mouthed them back, and then Brian began the vows. The rest of the service became a blur. The two of them firmly promised to love and cherish one another.

Alex yanked Suzanne into his arms when Pastor Brian said, "You may kiss the bride." The audience laughed when he pulled her before Brian finished his sentence. They kissed deeply for a few seconds before pulling away.

"Finally," Alex murmured as he kissed Suzanne's forehead.

"Finally," she repeated.

Alex

Alex always believed Suzanne to be beautiful, but today surpassed his wildest dreams. She appeared as a vision in white. Alex realized he was marrying an angel. Overwhelmed, Alex found himself unable to remove his gaze from her face. He wasn't sure breath escaped him.

The pastor from Suzanne's church asked the traditional question of who gave the bride away. Once Suzanne's dad answered, Alex gently grasped her fingers in his own. He took a deep breath as tears shone in his eyes.

The pastor finished his part of the ceremony, and Pastor Brian began the vows. Alex gazed deeply into Suzanne's eyes, meaning every promise that he repeated. He continually squeezed Suzanne's fingers, overwhelmed at the thought of her becoming his wife.

Alex no longer suffered from fear. He knew beyond any doubt that Suzanne would be the love of his life.

The two of them placed the rings on each other's fingers, and Michael reached for the microphone to sing. Alex and Suzanne remained fixed on each other until his song ended.

Somehow, Alex remembered Brian pronouncing them man and wife. He yanked Suzanne against him as Brian said they could kiss. Brian laughed since Alex jumped the gun on that part.

"Finally," he whispered against Suzanne's forehead.

"Finally," Suzanne whispered back.

The two of them had finally found their happily ever after with one another

About the author

About the Author:

Liz Hamilton relocated with her husband to North Georgia, where they plan to retire. Having spent many years of her life growing up in Texas, she was able to use her experience of living there to help in writing this series of books. She has two children, Hannah and Caleb. She has two dogs, Walter and Chloe. Balancing a full time teaching position as a middle school reading intervention teacher, she was able to use her passion for writing to publish her first two books, and she hopes to make this a second career when she retires from education. Her other hobbies include reading, cooking, walking her dogs and traveling with her family.

Thanks

Thank you to my husband and best friend in life. Thank you to my two kids, Hannah and Caleb, for your support in my pursuing this as a dream. There were times I bounced ideas off of all of you and appreciated the feedback you were able to give me. Thank you to All Write Well for your mentorship through this overwhelming but exciting process. I appreciate your guidance throughout all of it. Thank you to Krystal Craiker for your support and feedback. Finally, thank you to all of my readers for supporting my dream.

Connect with me

www.ingramcontent.com/pod-product-compliance
Lightning Source LLC
Chambersburg PA
CBHW032356310726
48973CB00007B/2032